CHRISTIE'S

WINE COMPANION

CHRISTIE'S
WINE COMPANION

Edited by
PAMELA VANDYKE PRICE

With an Introduction by
MICHAEL BROADBENT

Webb & Bower

MICHAEL JOSEPH

First published in Great Britain 1989 by
Webb & Bower (Publishers) Limited
5 Cathedral Close, Exeter, Devon EX1 1EZ
in association with Michael Joseph Limited
27 Wright's Lane, London W8 5TZ
and Christie's Wine Publications
8 King Street, St James's
London SW1Y 8QT

Published in association with the Penguin Group
Penguin Books Ltd, Registered Offices: Harmondsworth, Middlesex
England
Viking Penguin Inc, 40 West 23rd Street, New York, NY 10010, US
Penguin Books Australia Ltd, Ringwood, Victoria, Australia
Penguin Books Canada Ltd, 2801 John Street, Markham, Ontario,
Canada L3R 1D4
Penguin Books (NZ) Ltd, 182–190 Wairau Road, Auckland 10, New Zealand

Designed by Ron Pickless

Production by Nick Facer/Rob Kendrew

Picture research by Anne-Marie Ehrlich

Text Copyright © 1989
Webb & Bower (Publishers) Ltd/Christie's Wine Publications

British Library Cataloguing in Publication Data

Christie's wine companion. – [New ed.]
1. Wines
I. Price, Pamela Vandyke, 1923–
641.2'2

ISBN 0–86350–308–X
Library of Congress 89–84314

Typeset in Great Britain by J&L Composition Ltd, Filey, North Yorkshire
Colour reproduction by Mandarin Offset

Printed and bound in Hong Kong

CONTENTS

INTRODUCTION

I do hope that the splendid vinous miscellany that follows gives you, the reader, as much pleasure as watching its growth gave me.

We have a new editor, a new broom, and it is exciting to witness the progress from fresh ideas to final stages. Of course, in Pamela Vandyke Price we have one of the most experienced wine writers and editors in the country: author of twenty-six books on wine, prolific wine columnist for more years than, tactfully, I will reveal; a former editor, and dare I say it the best, of *Wine & Food*. But above all, Pamela is a 'character' in an era which seems to have fewer and fewer, and she maintains an enthusiasm for wine, a zest, which reminds me of the continued flow of fine bubbles and effervescence of a great vintage Champagne. Needless to say, she is an old friend. I have admired the way that she came in from the outside, the first such to attend – and pass the examinations of — the courses of the Wine & Spirit Education Trust. But, as we all know, the best way to learn is to teach, and Pamela is one of the regular team of top lecturers on Christie's Wine Course.

Pamela's brief was simple. When Richard Webb, Delian Bower and I decided to invite Pamela to be editor, she was to have a completely free hand, just as I have had from the moment I joined Christie's in 1966, when, as now, from Chairman downwards, everyone in the company was keen on wine and gave enormous support — Christie's current Chairman, Lord Carrington, being no exception. Indeed, when we were first introduced, it was perfectly clear that his enthusiasm for wine was deep rooted. A good thing, for there are insidious pressures which, though ostensibly aimed at alcohol in general, are beginning to question attitudes to wine itself. Without alcohol, wine wouldn't be wine. But to tar with the same brush mindless boozing, lager louts and the minority of foolishly hard drinkers with those who appreciate the infinite variety, subtlety and sheer civilization of wine, is something we must not merely guard against, but counter-attack. In a sense, this is the underlying theme of the book: to demonstrate the wonderful influence of wine on the arts, upon crafts; to celebrate the patient husbandry of the growers and the care of the wine-makers but, above all, to stress the pure enjoyment to be found in wine.

So what's new, even news? The feature on the wonderful new window at Vintners' Hall — I hope that successive Masters will have all the glass as brilliantly engraved; the new mosaics recently excavated in Cyprus depicting the life of Dionysos and revealed, for the first time, in our *Companion*. And it is nice to know that we have in Sir Ewen Fergusson an Ambassador who, palate-wise, can more than hold his own with the French; mind you, it's the least I can expect from a fellow member of the Saintsbury Club!

Our hope is that the latest *Wine Companion* will please not only those who already love the subject but also those who seldom drink it. For over two centuries, Christie's have been auctioning wine, yet for us wine is always new and exciting. If some of our enthusiasm is conveyed, we shall be happy.

Michael Broadbent
Christie's

A PALATE IN THE RIGHT PLACE

His Excellency the British Ambassador in Paris talks to the Editor

Wistful criticisms are sometimes made about those in public life who, it is assumed, enjoy rare viands and rarer wines daily — or even twice a day. Why aren't VIPs more gastronomically inclined, people ask pettishly, surveying their sandwich and the glass of something or other 'Maison'?

Yet how many of the envious would sustain the tedium of the official dinner's apparently plastic *poulet*, the limp *poisson* in paperhangers' paste supposed to be 'sauce' and the beverages selected by caterers and banqueting managers to 'please' when the insipidity if not the downright nastiness of such should arouse the curse of Dionysos to accentuate the hangovers of those who made, sold and serve same?

Public people are seldom able to cultivate their palates.

Diplomacy does, however, accept that dining and wining are adjuncts to the establishment of cordial ententes; Talleyrand took the great Antoine Carême as his chef to the Congress of Vienna in 1815. Those who have read Laurence Durrell's sardonic studies of life among the 'dips' will, though, be aware of the perils of the 'national' fare at some postings and of ordeals by wine and spirit. Today's ambassadors may or may not, as Sir Henry Wotton wrote in 1604, be sent to 'lie abroad' for patriotic purposes — they are likely to have to tax their digestions.

The ambassador of any power appointed to Paris will be subjected to the cool appraisal of those who — with some justification — suppose themselves to be arbiters of wine and food. And the British Embassy here, scene of so many splendid, indeed historic parties — can one imagine an ascetic or a non-

Right
Menu card for the dinner given at the British Embassy in Paris to Their Royal Highnesses, the Prince and Princess of Wales, in 1988.

Left
Menu for the dinner given at the British Embassy for the United States' Ambassador to France, the Honourable Joe M Rodgers, in 1988.

drinker there? One cannot. Such a one might seriously endanger Franco-British relations. Fortunately, there's no need for apprehension. His Excellency, Sir Ewen Fergusson, KCMG, is very much a man of wine.

The Paris Embassy, in the rue du Faubourg Saint-Honoré, is a hidden house, shielded behind massive doors and high walls from the glitter of the chic boutiques and alluring old-established shops outside. It is a sunny autumn afternoon, the opalescent light making Paris seem to shimmer, when I cross the empty courtyard and mount the steps to the main entrance — even on my own, I feel I am taking part in an 'occasion': the shallow treads of the main staircase and the delicate wrought-iron balustrade would be the appropriate setting for someone with a sweeping train and diamonds winking back at the chandelier. The perspective of the gardens through the long windows is wistfully picturesque as a variety of differently coloured leaves flutter from the trees — a hint of English landscape in this, although indoors the splendour of the furnishings and furniture, the rich colourings of carpets and the formal décor throughout are distinctively French.

The Embassy was built in 1722 but first became renowned as a 'party place' when in 1803 Pauline, Princess Borghese, Napoleon's beautiful sister, bought it from the Duchesse de Charost. Ben the butler shows me through the rooms, high-ceilinged salons, made to be peopled by the important, the witty, the lovely, who seem to have left wisps of laughter and their own affection for the place in the air. The exquisite Pauline is said to have paraded naked through the rooms; there was the charming Ambassadress Lady Granville, squeezing herself into a fashionable shape and borrowing the Devonshire diamonds from her brother the Duke to cope with the hard stares of the French *elegantes* as she notes in her letters to her sister; the 'Iron Duke' stayed here; and one ambassador was Lord Lyons, who commented shrewdly 'If you're given Champagne for lunch there's a catch somewhere!'; another Ambassadress was the pre-Raphaelite beauty, Lady Lytton, who may have thought the Embassy somewhat small after her Indian years as Vicereine. Queen Victoria and Edward VII were visitors; Lady Diana, of the aquamarine eyes, was unable to tear herself away when Duff Cooper (the late Lord Norwich) ceased to be the Ambassador; and Nancy Mitford's account of the imaginary

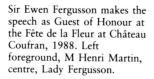

Sir Ewen Fergusson makes the speech as Guest of Honour at the Fête de la Fleur at Château Coufran, 1988. Left foreground, M Henri Martin, centre, Lady Fergusson.

Left
Menu cover created by Michael Broadbent for the Fête de la Fleur (celebration of the flowering of the vine) in 1988 at Château Coufran. Michael Broadbent presided and H E Sir Ewen Fergusson was guest of honour.

Below
Thomas Jefferson might have met characters like this *maître de chai* and even today there are small country wine stores in the Gironde that don't look very different, although the traditional Bordeaux *barriques* may not always be seen.

The Manor House at Groot Constantia at the Cape, South Africa, is now a national monument with a wine museum installed in the former cellar. Simon van der Stel built it in 1692 but the first vines were planted there prior to 1690 and Constantia wine became world renowned. Today the property is once again prospering and making fine wine.

Whitlands Vineyard, property of Brown Brothers of Milawa in
north-east Victoria, Australia. Described as 'an adventure in
cold climate viticulture' it is one of the newer vineyards that can
yield satisfactorily thanks to modern transport and detailed
knowledge on suiting vine varieties to soils and climates.

The Embassy dining-room, set for a formal dinner. The perspective of the table is magnificent — yet this picture does not show all the leaves in the long table!

departure of an imaginary Ambassadress in *Don't Tell Alfred* is one of those joyous set pieces of frothy prose that ought to have been true even if it wasn't. Later, there was the elegant Lady Gladwyn, who wrote *The Paris Embassy* (Collins, 1976) — and the lady who, as my late and dear friend Colonel Andrew Graham, at one time Comptroller of the Paris Household, remembered, was not wine minded and, at the end of a banquet, swept the ladies away from the table before any could so much as sip the superb Champagne poured as the final glass. A house such as this holds something of the personalities of those who have lived there — but today's Ambassador is completely a man of our times.

Sir Ewen Fergusson is tall, dark — and big, bigger than he seems at first sight. His elegance owes more to his bearing than to his tailor for he is, in the most admirable way, one of the British 'milords' who still move and walk as their ancestors did, confident, relaxed, with the difficult to define attribute that is the 'habit of command'. His pleasantly pitched voice and excellent articulation (welcome in this era of sloppy speech) match his compact, proportioned build — if he were a wine one might comment that he was 'well balanced'. For, although I tend to forget both his imposing presence and his importance because of the gentle charm of his welcome, I remind myself that he is a top sportsman. One of his Oxford contemporaries told me that 'he didn't really box, but when we had a match against Cambridge we needed a heavy weight, so we entered him and he won — he just stood there with his fist out and they all knocked themselves silly against it!'

We go into the Duff Cooper library, a high room, small enough to be — just —almost 'cosy', with a Latin inscription around the cornice which, translated, says 'So that readers might be numbered among his friends, Duff Cooper, Ambassador to France, made over this room to the friendly silence of books. Hail, friend, and read.' Although there are many scholarly seeming tomes in fine bindings on the shelves, it appeals to me more that, when Sir Ewen looks for a particular book on wine and doesn't find it, he says he supposes it must have been borrowed by butler Ben — which Ben later admits.

Sir Ewen cannot recall when wine was not a part of family life in his parents' house, for he was brought up in Australia, attending Geelong Grammar School — 'and my father would always let me taste the wines we drank — I specially remember Chateau Tahbilk'. At which I say 'Um' and look up from my notebook, because Tahbilk was the first fine Australian wine that I ever wrote about.

When Sir Ewen returned to England, he went to Rugby, and later to Oriel College, Oxford, where he read Modern History. He remembers a definite moment when, as a schoolboy still, wine began to be important: 'After some sort of gastric upset, I was convalescing in a house where we lived in Curzon Street and I read a review of André Simon's *A Wine Primer*, which became my bible. Once, when my father was home from Singapore, he took me to dinner at the Ritz and asked me to select the wine — I've always remembered that it was Château Margaux 1934.'

(And in 1988, the British Ambassador was the Guest of Honour at the Fête de la Fleur in the Médoc at Château Coufran . . . .)

Sir Ewen's tastes are not solely claret oriented, though. While he was studying at Tours he explored Loire wines, bringing six bottles of 1947 Bourgueil with him when he went up to Oxford. It was about this time that shippers and merchants began to try to attract the interest of the *jeunesse d'orée* of the universities, via wine societies and dining clubs: young Fergusson met Harry Waugh, who inculcated a love for fine white Burgundy, also the late Dr Otto Loeb; he started to try vintage port, notably Croft.

Then, during his period of national service in The King's Royal Rifle Corps, he spent some time in Germany, where Otto Loeb's instruction bore fruit: 'I love the fine Mosels in particular, but they're sometimes difficult to fit into the sort of life I live now — they're the wines to be drunk with friends, quite at leisure, a few of you sitting in front of the fire maybe, with an assortment of bottles — or possibly out in the garden. That's the sort of drinking I really enjoy, but you need the right people and the appropriate occasion.'

Just after his marriage in 1959 (Lady Fergusson, to whom I'm introduced when I'm leaving, is of enviable chic and slenderness, her sculptured features slightly evocative of an aristocratic Sophia Loren), Sir Ewen served as Second Secretary in Addis Ababa when 'it was that I discovered that I liked Sauternes'. Among bottles he happily remembers is the 1948 Château d'Yquem. He always tried to take at least some of the wine he owned with him when he was posted and he'd begun to lay down claret — 'Though my wife prefers Burgundy' — and he smiles as he thinks of vintages of Grace Dieu and the 1953 Grand Poujeaux — at which I join in the sigh of happy reminiscence. From 1967–1971 he was Head of the Industrial Section of the British Trade Development Office in New York — 'I took my 1955s with me' — when he started to get acquainted with California wines, Schramsberg, the products of Joe Heitz — 'but there were so many, so fascinating'. Then, from 1972, he became Head of Chancery in the UK Delegation to the European Community at Brussels — a city renowned for its restaurants, its gourmets and its percipient wine drinkers. That presented the opportunity to drink many more fine German wines (he bought about 300 bottles) and, also, to get to know the wines of Alsace; he recalls some superb red Burgundies, too, 1966 and 1964 Bonnes Mares in particular: 'We were lucky in being able to drink a lot while there!'

Wine doors opened even wider when in 1982 he was appointed HM

Ambassador to Pretoria/Cape Town, South Africa. Although His Excellency says he can't begin to like Pinotage (the grape variety and wine evolved at the Cape) he's enthusiastic about other wines he tried while there — 'I never had a bad bottle!' The estate wines of Meerlust, Kanonkop, Groot Constantia are only some of those that he — and now I, joining in — begin to name and we start saying 'Do you know — ' 'Have you tried — ' about so many friends, so many wines. Later, a Johannesburg friend says 'But I know *him*!' and tells me how Sir Ewen was invited by some of the top oenologists and estate owners to a tasting of twenty classed growth clarets — 'blind'. My informant spluttered 'Do you know, he identified sixteen of the twenty classed growth clarets of the 1966 vintage 'blind' — I didn't score anything like that!' And he remembers how, this pleasing achievement seeming of no account, H E lay on the grass outside the tasting room, gazing happily up at the sky, displaying what I term that certain British nonchalance that often baffles other people (by which we British mean 'foreigners' of course) but can be endearing because it is unintimidating.

Though of course the South Africans would have hardly disapproved of the appointment of someone who had played rugger both for Oxford University and also for Scotland.

The appointment to Paris was in June, 1987. Both Ambassador and butler admit that the cellars of the Embassy had been much depleted and were by no means in a state to satisfy either of them. It may surprise many to know that there are no government funds allocated to stock and replenish reserves of wine in such places. Today, temperature control has been installed and scrupulous cleanliness and order make the Paris Embassy impeccable below ground. Sir Ewen himself, outrunning the hour allowed for my interview, takes me to see: there was much personal involvement and work to get things as they should be. Special racks were constructed to accommodate the larger than bottle sized bottles of Château Latour, a wine often served both because of its associations with Britain via its owners and because H E likes it very much; Les Forts de Latour, such as the 1980, is often served here, sometimes as the 'mouthwash' wine that precedes the 'grand vin' at formal dinners.

Because His Excellency is a member of the Bontemps du Médoc et des Graves, there are the 1982 and 1983 vintages of the wine order's wine in the Paris cellars as well. (And I preen myself a little, because, although I am of course in a lower echelon of the Bontemps, I too have the right to the 'cent coups' or hundred bangs with the mallet in salutation when entering a *chai*.) There are bottles of the recently revived Rothschild property, Château La Cardonne — here another reminiscent smile and happy sigh between interviewee and interviewer — plus bottles of 1970 and 1980 Château Palmer — now we are both beginning to talk wine — and other clarets of the 1966, 1970 and 1976 vintages. The racks hold some young and youngish white Burgundies, also a little red — and some tawny port, for Sir Ewen shares with the shippers (and with me) a love of this delectable wine, often — my comment — a cause of astonishment to the French when they encounter it at its silky best.

Oh yes — and there is some English wine! For Sir Ewen, who opened the Embassy doors to entertain the entire Saintsbury Club recently, is as interested in the 'new' wines of today as the classics of yesteryear; he is not being merely diplomatic in stocking English wine in the Paris Embassy — he

Ben, the Embassy butler, preparing the clarets to be placed in cradles prior to being decanted in the impeccably set out and maintained cellars.

wants to know more about what these wines, as with those of the other New World countries, are and will be like.

Already I've had more than my requested hour and I begin to leave. Ben has conducted me through ballroom, throne room, dining-room, where the table has twenty-eight leaves that can be fitted to extend its length, so as to seat sixty guests. Though, as on the recent visit of Their Royal Highnesses, the Prince and Princess of Wales, small tables may be set in the dining-room so that more people can be included, amid a slightly less formal atmosphere.

No party is taking place in the Paris Embassy on this evening of my visit, although I am sure that, even if Sir Ewen and Lady Fergusson are having 'something on a tray' for their supper, the accompanying bottle will be worthy of the setting — and the palates of Their Excellencies. Throughout its history, the house has probably never been dominated by anyone with as great a sensitivity to and wide knowledge of wine as it is today.

PVP

A GENTLEMAN OF WINE: HARRY WALDO YOXALL OBE, MC, JP

by Patrick Matthews

Harry Yoxall was a man of many parts. He was head boy at St Paul's School in London and one of his proudest achievements was his scholarship to study classics at Balliol College, Oxford, famous for its classical traditions. During World War I he won a Military Cross and bar for bravery which, as he once stressed to someone who did not give the decoration its correct place in his honours, was specifically awarded to those who had earned it in action under fire. Then he began a distinguished career in publishing with Condé Nast Publications, being active in both the United States and Europe until his retirement in 1964.

Harry, a highly cultivated man who enjoyed playing golf until he was well advanced in years, also became a Justice of the Peace, a governor of the Star and Garter Home for disabled servicemen at Richmond, just outside London, and in later years was an active member of the Church of England, latterly attending Holy Trinity, Prince Consort Road in Kensington, where, at his wish, his funeral was held.

He was also a wit, a prolific writer on both wine and food, and a true amateur, in the best sense of the word, of wine. His book *The Wines of Burgundy* (Michael Joseph, with The International Wine & Food Society, 1968) won the Prix Littéraire of the Confrérie des Chevaliers du Tastevin, the Burgundy wine order; although he enjoyed many wines, Burgundy was his particular love and he ventured to study and appraise it with erudition and affection at a time when very little of worth existed in print about this complex wine. He kept himself up to date with what was happening in the world of wine during changes that might have depressed and been distasteful to someone of his generation. In 1976 he was one of the judges for the Glenfiddich Awards, the annual prizes started by the firm of William Grant in the early 1970s when wine writing was restricted in influence and style and, in 1982, Harry himself was voted 'Wine Writer of the Year' by the Glenfiddich judges. His style was always well-bred, poised and one writer of today aptly referred to him as 'the last of the gentlemanly wine writers', for Harry was not concerned with technicalities, nor seemed particularly interested in sampling young wines; he had enough friends among the top wine merchants of his time to get the best advice if he wanted to know what he should buy or lay down. The wine articles in the UK edition of *House & Garden* were, at the time he won the Glenfiddich Award, written under his own name, but previously he had used two pen names, his anonymity sometimes puzzling readers, who would write to the magazine to ask if they might contact the author—who was given out to be something of a recluse. Although the origin of these wine features was known to the entire staff, it is indicative of the respect in which Harry was held that neither they, nor any of those who, after

My lives at table

BY H W YOXALL

A personal record of adventures in eating and drinking

PART 1

Boyhood days in France to more martial times on the Western Front

[H W Yoxall was for many years Chairman of the Condé Nast Publications and is a leading authority on wine.]

Harry Yoxall, tall, lanky and a 'when in doubt' pipe smoker, was invariably impeccably dressed — attributes captured in this caricature.

working for him, went on to rise high in the publishing and writing worlds, ever gave the secret away.

In view of his high standing in the world in which he made his name, and his impressive appearance, it is also a tribute to Harry that he was a wise and generous friend to a wide circle of all ages, from his own grandchildren upwards. He could be both amusing and witty about his wine interests.

He was a comparatively late starter in the enjoyment of wine, for he came from a distinguished Wesleyan family of total abstainers. His grandmother used to stand outside public houses on Saturday nights trying to persuade ejected drunks to sign the pledge. The setting in which he grew up is told in his own words:

'Wine was not served at my family table. In fact my mother was an ardent teetotaller. My father didn't share her views, but he respected them at home. It wasn't till 1908, when I was twelve, that he judged me ready to assay the poisoned chalice. We were on holiday together in Touraine, and, as a change from visiting châteaux, we walked out one morning from Tours towards Vouvray. The hotel concierge had said there was a miller at Pont de Cisse who served meals. We arrived there on a brilliant summer noon, and found that indeed he did: he was serving a wedding breakfast for a rural company of some fifty villagers. My father excused us, and asked where else we could lunch. "But not at all," said my host: if Monsieur and his charming son (his epithet) could wait a little he would set us a *déjeuner à part*. We waited a little, in fact only twenty minutes, with the spectacle of the rustic fête to entertain us. It was like an episode from a film yet to be, from Jean Renoir or René Clair.

'Then came a perfect *omelette aux champignons*, a crispy-brown roast chicken with *frites* and a morning-gathered salad, cheese and a bowl of wild strawberries Chantilly. To crown it all my father ordered a bottle of Vouvray. I found this unknown potion delicious, so it was probably demi-sec, since youthful preference tends towards sweetness. Anyhow, seeds of the taste for wine were sown.'

In 1915 he joined the élite 60th King's Royal Rifles and his interest in drinking took another step forward. He relates:

'In the reserve, on a quiet night, I who had never touched alcohol till five years earlier would drink my half bottle of White Horse or Johnny Walker without turning a hair — so fit we were in that damp, cold, arduous existence.

'By bad luck I spent most of my active service in the beer area of Flanders rather than in the wine area of France. So when I was in rest, and could borrow a horse to ride to a base town, I affected Black Velvet, finding the local stout more palatable when mixed with cheap champagne from across the border. But there were repasts of a higher order. I have a note in our diary of our 1916 Christmas dinner, when we were in Divisional reserve, and we drank Krug '06, Graham '96 and Hine '75.'

In November 1917, after taking part in the heavy fighting on the Somme — for his part in which he was twice decorated — Harry was posted as an instructor to the British Military Mission in the United States. He wrote in his diary: 'To get away to anywhere from Passchendaele would have been a translation to heaven. But to go to the US, still hardly affected by the war, was a special apotheosis.' Characteristically, he found it tiresome to be called 'a British medalman' by the local newspapers.

After a brief spell again at Balliol, which, as an ex-serviceman, he found tiresome, Harry returned to the United States with his American bride, Josephine, whom he had married two years earlier. In 1921 he joined Condé Nast Publications in New York. Nast had a marvellous gift for collecting around him brilliant people, including Ernest Hemingway, Clare Luce, Dorothy Parker, Robert Benchley and Robert Sherwood among others; he recognized Harry Yoxall's many talents and it was then that his brilliant career began as a fashion publisher with that most famous of fashion magazines — *Vogue*.

When Harry and Josephine eventually came back to Europe it seemed proper to him to mark this return to an older civilization by a study of its oldest and most civilized and civilizing products. He found a restaurant in Soho where, for example, they served a pre-war Château Pontet Canet at 2s 9d (13½p) the half bottle — and his drinking career was at last launched on the right lines. At least twice a year he had to go to Paris on business and there château-bottled wines were available at similarly attractive prices — especially to anyone travelling on an expense account. As Harry says in *A Fashion of Life*, his own book (Heinemann, 1966):

'I don't propose to recount, much less try to describe, all the great bottles I've drunk. In fact I've only shared in a few of the historic pre-phylloxera vintages, and most of these were interesting rather than gratifying — ghosts of what they'd been, some noble ghosts, others rather pathetic. But I've relished two or three centenarian Madeiras; fine Madeira seems immortal. I've naturally tried the clarets of my birth-year, 1896.

'But I've been privileged to know all the post-World War I vintages. In many ways men of my generation have been unfortunate in their epoch; ten years of hot war, over twenty of cold, the great depression, several recessions and, since 1939, punitive taxation. But we had luck in one respect. Between the wars there was abundant sound wine at prices that now seem laughable or tragic, according to one's point of view. One could buy a case, in the early 1930s, for what one pays now for a single bottle of a fashionable year like 1959 or 1961.'

Harry Yoxall read George Saintsbury, Charles Walter Berry, Ian Maxwell Campbell, Maurice Healy and the other wine writers of his time, but the greatest educational influence on his wine life was that of André L Simon. He wasn't a founder member of the Wine & Food Society that André courageously started in 1933, but he joined next year, when talented chefs were delighted to organize special meals for members and when superb wines could be brought up from their cellars. He remembered a banquet in 1934 at the lovely Royal Pavilion in Brighton, in honour of the centenary of Carême, who had been *maître des cuisines* there to the Prince Regent (later George IV); the menu, with its many *relevés*, exactly reproduced a dinner that Carême had served; the wines, naturally, were only equivalents. But there were six of them, a generous quantity in those days. Forty years later Harry was particularly pleased to become the Chairman of what had by now become The International Wine & Food Society and many members still recall his frequent presiding at the 'Tastevin Dinner', featuring the wines of Burgundy, which was a regular event in the autumn programme of the IWFS.

I joined Harry's staff at the London office of Condé Nast Publications in 1937. It was at that moment that a friendship began that was to last for forty-seven years. How do I remember him? At first, like many others, I was slightly in awe of him — he could be very austere; but very soon his scholarly professionalism, his wit, kindness, understanding and patient encouragement of the young overcame this initial impression. Like many other men and women, I learned the trade under his guidance.

One of my special memories was when, as Managing Director, he gave bottles of wine to certain members of his staff at Christmas, with personal handwritten messages. One of mine read 'Cheval Blanc '49, a lovely full-blooded wine that you will like. I wish I could have given you a magnum. Thank you for all your good work this past year.' Another memory was his typical comment on the Paris haut couture fashion collections: 'Sexual excitement has to be whipped up too, with stories of plunging necklines and titillating revelations (the more absurd as the emaciated mannequins have so little to reveal).' Harry was a delicious flirt.

When World War II came in 1939 Harry went out and bought as much French wine as he could afford. He asked his local grocer if, by any chance, he had some French wine. The grocer replied that he had some with a funny name, Hort Bryan, but as it was rather old — it was labelled 1929 — he would let it go cheap at fifty bob to clear it, if Harry would care to take the whole case off his hands!

Memories of Harry's World War II drinking make intriguing reading: for instance, when one of his good friends, an American colonel, came back from the Normandy beachhead for a conference, Harry and Josephine decided to push the boat out for him.

'The day before the feast I went down to fetch two treasured bottles of Ch Pétrus '29, the best year (then) of the best Pomerol, kept for just such an occasion. My way back led to a straight flight of stone steps rising to the ground floor. I hadn't two wine cradles, so I was carrying a bottle solicitously in each hand, firmly held by the body to minimize agitation. When almost at the top I slipped, and cascaded down the entire flight. But though flayed myself — like Marsyas in arms and legs and chest — I still held the bottles aloft, intact and only slightly shaken, like the torches of learning and liberty that they indeed were.'

Obviously, Harry's stocks of wine, though diminished, were sufficient to celebrate the end of the war in some style. He wrote: 'I kept a sacred reserve of good vintages for V-Day — though my stock was slightly strained when there turned out to be two V-Days. For VE-Day we had eighteen to a buffet supper, including soldiers of five different armies, and I served six wines. Little business was possible at the office in the then excitement, and we had no servants; so I spent most of VE-Day polishing 108 wine glasses, and most of VE-Day plus one washing them up.'

The chairman's office in Bond Street the morning after an air raid on London — work continuing as usual in spite of the shattered windows and general debris everywhere, though the glass of water remains intact in one of those odd quirks of wartime bomb blasts.

It was just after the end of the war in Europe that Harry fell ill with a serious infection, was flown to the US and his life for a time hung in the balance. For three months he was fed by a tube passed down his throat, after which his already deep voice acquired the 'rich brown velvet' husky timbre as a result of the damage to his vocal cords. During this time he reflected profoundly on life, reading widely of philosophers and theologians and, eventually, wrote an 'apologia' of his own about his religious beliefs.

Back in Britain, he was elected to the Saintsbury Club, the most prestigious wine society in the UK, named after Professor Saintsbury, author of *Notes on a Cellar Book*; the Club has a small but very fine collection of wine donated by the members, which is lodged at Vintners' Hall in the City of London where, on the annual guest night of 'the Saintsbury' a dinner takes place in the great Hall itself; this is not only impressive and beautiful, but is near the site of the town house of Alderman Sir Henry Picard, Master of the Company who, in 1363, gave 'the feast of the five kings' — those of England, Scotland, France, Denmark and Cyprus — an event commemorated by a plaque on the wall. As Harry realistically commented: 'It's only fair to add that two of them were unwilling guests — prisoners of war, and another two were monarchs of very petty kingdoms.'

Harry Yoxall was once prompted to remark that his love of wine had caused him to drink more than 20,000 bottles, at which his collocutrix said: 'I didn't know that you were a heavy drinker.' 'But I'm not. That doesn't represent heavy drinking. Since 1924, when I took up the study of wine, it means approximately a bottle a day. Abstemious enough, surely.' He went on: 'Wine is God's second greatest secular gift to man. Nothing better promotes the sense of well-being. Drinking is a sociable exercise, releasing bonhomie and (with luck) wit. It increases the enjoyment of food, facilitates digestion,

and improves health. In comparison with other amusements it's not expensive. No money is better spent than on sound wine. Personal relationships usually let you down. But wine, intelligently used, never lets you down.'

Someone once described Harry as the last of that wonderful band of wine writers that included Denzil Batchelor, Edward Hyams, Morton Shand and André Simon among many others. They did not involve themselves with technical data and contemporary jargon. Each wrote in his own individual, elegant style. We can still admire the way they wrote, Harry especially, for he never allowed his enthusiasm for a wine to distort his opinions nor his descriptions.

Just after he died, someone who had been a very close friend of his wrote:

'How often Harry's friends sought his advice. His whole attention would be directed to the problem and his acute judgment tempered by a Christian forebearance of human foibles and frailty. He was prized as an after-dinner speaker, for in the same way that he had a total recall of the taste of wine enjoyed many years ago, so had he a distilled memory of apposite experiences that could illuminate an incident with wit and irony.

'What a remarkable range of knowledge and interests were his: it made him in a true sense a Renaissance man, for through him others enlarged their enjoyment of life. Paradoxically he admired the Edwardian era yet bought modern paintings, he loved both Proust and Simenon and appreciated old wine and youthful beauty. We are all the richer for having known him.'

The only sort of picture that Condé Nast were permitted to publish of 'F H Partington', the man behind many of their wine articles. When, later, Harry assumed another pseudonym and was asked what had happened to Mr Partington, he would chuckle 'I think he fell down the cellar steps and ended there.'

THE EPONYMOUS COMTE — CHAPTAL

by Christopher Fielden

Many of the men who have given their names to a significant word in a language have done so for comparatively irrelevant reasons. Though Lord Raglan may have wished that he was remembered more for his sleeves than for his incompetence as a general, the Earl of Sandwich might have preferred to be associated with his prowess at the gaming tables, rather than the snacks he ate there. The name of Jean-Antoine Chaptal, Comte de Chanteloup, however, is perpetuated by what is really no more than a footnote to a truly brilliant career.

Born in 1756, the son of indifferently off peasants from the Massif Central, he rose to be one of Napoleon's most outstanding ministers and then became a wealthy industrialist. By training a doctor, he was fortunate enough to receive an important inheritance from a wealthy uncle, a merchant in Montpellier in the south, and also to marry a wife who brought with her a considerable fortune.

His career from that time onwards seems to have moved ever upwards, though in a rather haphazard way. He became a professor of chemistry,

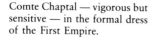

Comte Chaptal — vigorous but sensitive — in the formal dress of the First Empire.

established a chemicals factory in Montpellier, was appointed regional explosives inspector, became a member of the administration of the Hérault département and a director of the National Gunpowder Office. It seems somewhat illogical that he should then have been appointed, in November 1800, as Minister of the Interior to succeed Lucien Buonaparte; he was not one of the group close to Napoleon, those who had grown up with him, either in Corsica or in the army. For the most part it was these colleagues outstanding 'in aptitude and talent' who received preferment.

Under Napoleon the Ministry of the Interior was the most important office of all. It was responsible, according to authority Louis Bergeron, not only for the 'general administration' (such as the population, conscription, the National Guard), but also for the 'communal aspects: agriculture, living standards, commerce, industry, public assistance, prisons, academies of arts and sciences, public works, mines, highways, education, archives and statistics.' Chaptal had a team of no more than three hundred civil servants to help him in these multifarious tasks. It should, too, be remembered that for much of his time in office France was at war, so that the day-to-day pressures on those dealing with the running of the country were greatly increased.

Chaptal resigned in July 1804 — and was subsequently appointed to another important position, Treasurer of the Senate. During the whole of this period, his chemical empire had continued growing; there was now a factory at Neuilly, then one at Nanterre and also at Fos, outside Marseilles. He came to establish one of the first great industrial French dynasties.

What has 'chaptalization' to do with all this?

The word is the term given to the process of the augmentation of the strength of a wine by the addition of sugar at the time of fermentation. The answer lies partly in one of the many books that Chaptal wrote, *L'Art de Faire le Vin*, which first appeared in 1802, the same year that France and Britain signed what was the short-lived Peace of Amiens. There was nothing new in adding sugar to fermenting must, although, as a widespread practice, it seems to have started during the last quarter of the eighteenth century. It is certain that the monks at Clos Vougeot, shortly before their sequestration (at the time of the French Revolution, when church property was taken by the state), were, in poor vintages, in the habit of adding loaf sugar to the fermenting vats. In the anonymous *Le Parfait Vigneron*, which was published in Turin in 1783, there are a number of suggestions as to how wine can be made more full-bodied in deficient vintages: these include the possibility of adding a number of sweetening agents, such as sugar, honey, grape-syrup, manna, cassia or molasses. The first documented use of sugar for this purpose was apparently made by a chemist called Marquet, in 1776.

Whilst the concept of adding sugar might have been suggested and indeed have been followed for some time, it was not actively promoted until after the end of the Napoleonic Wars and then for reasons that had little to do with the quality of the resulting wine — it was for reasons of commercial necessity.

France had been the centre of the European sugar trade for many years, being supplied by its colonies in the West Indies and in the Indian Ocean. The British naval blockade, however, effectively cut off the French commercial lines of communication and the price of sugar rose ten times and alternative sources of supply had to be found quickly. Comte Parmentier (1737–1813), who is probably better known for giving his name to anything in which a potato is involved gastronomically, suggested grape-syrup; Chaptal became the leading supporter of beet sugar.

In 1811 Napoleon took the decision to put considerable resources behind the development of the sugar-beet industry. The refining of beet sugar was nothing new; Olivier de Serres (1539–1619, another eponymous character, for his considerable works in agriculture gave his name to the French word for a greenhouse, *une serre*) had suggested the idea as long ago as 1595 and, by Chaptal's time, there were already two small refineries outside Paris. The process was, however, totally uneconomic. So 100,000 acres (4,046,900 hectares) of land were put on one side for the experiment in refining, a budget of one million francs being granted to the man put in charge, Benjamin Delessert. Baron Delessert (1773–1847), known as 'le roi du sucre', was another great industrialist and financier — also founder of savings banks.

It was in 1812 that Chaptal took Napoleon to visit the refinery at Passy; here Delessert presented him with the first loaf of sugar from the production line. (Sugar was then made in 'loaves' or blocks, special cutters in the form of tongs being used to break off the required quantity). This gift is said to have excited the Emperor so much that he took the ribbon of the Légion d'Honneur from around his own neck and placed it around that of Delessert.

Napoleon Bonaparte, as Emperor of France in coronation robes — maybe a trifle too ostentatious, but then, think of the robes of the Prince Regent, later George IV, of England. The laurel wreath, however, is an appropriate headgear for such a victorious general.

26

Antoine-Auguste Parmentier, just the sort of humorous, practical man who would have succeeded in deriving knowledge and learning something new, even when a prisoner of war.

So far, so good. The crunch came at the end of the war when vast quantities of cane sugar again became available on the French market. What to do with the surplus? This was a question that foreshadowed the various Common Market 'lakes' and 'mountains' of commodities in our own time. Alternative uses had to be found for the beet sugar. Chaptal's answer: 'Put it in the wine.'

Does chaptalization improve a wine? Right from the beginning, opinion on this matter has been split. In Champagne, for example, there was little doubt about the matter and, in the eyes of some, Chaptal was credited with having given the local growers the means of making great wines for the first time.

In Burgundy there was more widespread opposition. A winegrowers' conference in Dijon in 1845 (Chaptal had died in 1832) unanimously adopted the resolution that 'Sugaring denatures wines, taking away from them that which is most precious to them; that incomparable bouquet and delicacy that is their true mark.' In the following year, the local writer Comte de Vergnette-Lamotte descended rather more to personalities when he wrote 'Chaptal, who was born in the Midi [actually his birthplace was Nojaret, Lozère] and, as such, only rated wine by its alcoholic degree, considered alcohol as the principal preservative for wine and it is on such misguided principles that are based the sad elements of vinification that hold sway today.' The sneer about rating wine according to its strength refers to the Midi peasants' preferences, but it is both incorrect in fact and a misstatement personally — by a Burgundian.

Chaptalization is now a matter of routine in many of the northern vineyards of Europe. In the Mediterranean basin, in California and in Australia it is forbidden. In some other areas it is a practice that is adopted, as a matter of course, every vintage. This is sad. The idea itself is not a bad one; it is the abuse of that idea that causes the problems.

Somehow, I feel unhappy that the great career of Chaptal should be remembered only for the controversy over the sugaring of musts. What was once an economic expediency has now become an annual occurrence in many of the vineyard regions of the world. Chaptal achieved so much — and yet it is for a minor aspect of his life that he is remembered. True, he was the author of *L'Art de Faire le Vin* but he was also a co-author of *L'Art de Faire le Beurre et les Meilleurs Fromages*. I don't think, though, that his name lingers on in the dairy trade.

How can one tell a chaptalized wine? The fact is that, as far as the ordinary consumer is concerned, one can not. As far as the wine chemist is concerned, it is more easy, though it can require quite sophisticated apparatus. Here I am talking about wines that have been chaptalized to the minimum necessity. It is ot too difficult to recognize a wine that has been denatured by the wilful addition of too much sugar. (Although I have been told of someone in the southern hemisphere who claims that, as cane sugar is used there for any chaptalizing that is required and permitted, he can detect the use of beet sugar both on the nose and the palate when it is used in French wines. But I have reservations about this.)

The real problem with chaptalization is not its use, but its abuse. This was something that soon took place. In Burgundy, chaptalizing was originally used to make the bottom quality wines of poor vintages at least drinkable. As M-A Puvis, writing in 1848, said of the growers in Burgundy: 'Things have happened just as they normally do in such a case; at first, they begin with moderate sugaring, perhaps one kilo of sugar per hectolitre (2.2 lbs per 22 gallons), in lower quality wines; the wine was notably better and sold more easily, for it was softer and had more body. Then they doubled and tripled the dose; then, in the bad vintages, they wanted to give the same advantages to the first growths by heavily dosing them with sugar, but these doses finished by being more harmful than useful.' In the end some growers, rather than adding one kilo (2.2 lbs) of sugar to each hectolitre (22 gallons) of must, were adding as much as twenty, thirty and forty. One's imagination must be stretched to conceive what the resultant product must have tasted like.

One other disadvantage of chaptalization is that, in the wrong hands, it can be deliberately used to 'stretch' a wine. This appears to have been a particular problem in Bordeaux where, in 1930, the wine was only fetching a half of what it had brought in just four years earlier. The situation was so serious that the Chamber of Deputies in Paris set up a Commission of Inquiry under the chairmanship of Marcel Barthe. In an article in a local newspaper *L'Avenir du Médoc*, a writer listed seven steps that had to be taken to save the Bordeaux wine trade: the first was 'The suppression of chaptalization, which, under the pretence of being used to improve the alcoholic level of musts, is actually being used to increase the total quantity of wine being made.'

How widespread is chaptalization today? The answer is that in many regions it is taken as a matter of course in all vintages. Sadly, in addition to it often occurring in vintages when it is not necessary, there is also a tendency for it to be abused where it is permitted and for it to take place where it is not permitted.

Both on the Côte d'Or and in the Beaujolais wines are often spoilt by the addition of too much sugar. Anthony Hanson, in his book *Burgundy* (Faber & Faber, 1982, revised edition now in preparation) is particularly critical of some of the most famous producers for their excessive use of sugar. He writes 'the formula which appears to correspond to what consumers actually enjoy today is no longer that of 10.5° or 11° light carafe wine' and he cites Pierre-

Marie Doutrelant, who states, in *Les Bons Vins et les Autres* (Editions du Seuil, Paris, 1976) that:

'Sugar is the besetting sin of the Beaujolais. Take a Beaujolais Villages coming from a vine which yielded forty hectolitres (880 gallons) per hectare (three acres); it will have a natural alcoholic degree of 11°–11.5°, and one will round it off with an additional 1° by adding sugar. Perfect. No consumer will complain. The wine will be balanced and able to travel. On the other hand, take a Beaujolais produced at the rate of a hundred hectolitres (2200 gallons) per hectare (three acres) as was common between 1970 and 1974. It will naturally have 8°–9° of alcohol and sugaring will automatically bring it up to 12.5°. Even if the consumer does not notice, this wine will damage his health more than the other.'

But Hanson adds: 'I do not find myself indignant over chaptalization excesses in the Beaujolais to the extent that I am in the Côte d'Or' and he is definite about this — 'the time has come for chaptalization levels to be observed (musts may be increased by 2°, no more)'. To me, one of the charms of a Beaujolais is its freshness and fruit. Too often these are masked because the grower has sought to add an unnecessary extra degree or two of alcohol.

In the Midi, chaptalization is forbidden, but I have no doubt that there are many growers who practice it every year. I well remember visiting a hypermarket in Carcassonne at vintage time. Stacked on pallets were sacks of sugar, on sale 'for jam-making'....

It is difficult to be definite as to whether the rôle played by Jean-Antoine Chaptal in the history of wine-making is for the better or not. I suppose that, in an ideal world, we would like our wines to be made of the pure juice of the grape — and nothing else. In such a world, however, much of the wine would be undrinkable and the growers in Burgundy and Champagne, for example, might only make reasonable wines one year in three. Even purity has its price.

HOW MUCH WILL THEY DRINK — AND WHAT?

One of the preoccupying worries of host or hostess when planning a party is 'how much to allow' and this is more alarming when it concerns drink rather than food. The family can eat up the 'menavolens', a word that is not easily traced in dictionaries but which signifies leftovers or remnants; if food runs out few are likely to fall on their sword like the unfortunate Vatel when he thought the fish hadn't been delivered (although just as he expired it was). If drink is insufficient for guests' requirements, however, the 'cheer' that should enliven the function tends to subside. People leave early. Late arrivals face eked out hospitality.

These days it is always possible to order wines and spirits on a 'sale or return' basis, but a century or so ago such an arrangement mightn't exist, nor could the butler send some minion round the corner or down to the village to replenish the supplies. So it is of interest to read a slim book, published in 1887 by Chapman & Hall, entitled *Breakfasts, Luncheons and Ball Suppers*. The author was Major L, who was credited on the title page with having written *The Pytchley Book of Refined Cookery and Bills of Fare*. This author, like the better known Colonel Newnham-Davies, was a true man about town, but was also practical: he cites suppliers of equipment, condiments, wines. He was what we might now think of as a 'food snob', insisting that oysters should be sent to table on the 'bottom shell' (what we should term the flat surface) and 'generally in the country one sees them served in the top shells which is exceedingly provincial and absolutely wrong'. But he had a slyly humorous attitude to meals.

In the three sorts of breakfast he describes, there are those 'for Large Parties', 'for Ladies and Men of Sedentary Habits and Pursuits' (the guests of house parties who might, perhaps, be 'in trade') and 'Sportsmen and those of active habits'. He gives menus for five different sorts of luncheon: 'ordinary house', 'hunting', 'race', 'railways and travelling' and 'shooting'. These indicate the social round the acceptable bachelor might enjoy — and the occasions for which he, returning hospitality, might wish to cater, doubtless with the aid of his 'man' and regular staff. But, as will be noted, there are tactful, unobtrusive hints for the man — maybe with his little wife — now beginning to enter a politer world than the one to which they were previously accustomed.

Major L is practical about drinks. In the breakfast section he says that 'tea, coffee and cocoa' should be served at each breakfast. Those who recollect the abundant breakfast table at Plumstead Episcopi in Trollope's *Last Chronicle of Barset*, or the intimations of ample fare in Surtees' novels, may be surprised to see the mention of 'cocoa' in the late nineteenth century. It has an impoverished ring to those who often made do with it as a watery drink in

World War II. But it was an acceptable beverage as recently as the 1920s, for, in John Galsworthy's *Maid in Waiting*, begun in 1928 and finished in 1930, there is a house party before a shoot, when the heroine comes down to breakfast and is asked by the son of the house 'Coffee, cocoatina or ginger beer?' She asks for a kipper but is told there are none and another guest requests kedgeree, likewise to be disappointed: there are 'kidneys, bacon, scrambled eggs, haddock, ham, cold partridge pie'. It is somewhat surprising to find 'ginger beer' offered at such a time of the day, but, it should be remembered, orange juice or the grapefruit were neither easily obtainable nor cheap in the between wars depression.

In 1887 Major L remarks that, at breakfast, ladies 'are much wiser, much more abstemious and capable of practising much more self-denial in the feeding business than the male sex' and 'they rarely, too, eat meat for breakfast'. He refers ladies who 'would prefer a more substantial meal' to turn to the chapter that is for 'those of robust constitution' although he 'strongly recommends them to drink tea, coffee, or cocoa, and not claret or beer'. He mentions that he has heard that 'the late Sir Tatton Sykes frequently breakfasted on "apple tart" washed down by "home brewed ale". *Chacun à son goût.*' He doubts very much if it was 'frequently', if there 'is any truth in the legend at all'. With a subservient flourish to 'this most worthy and excellent of baronets' Major L excuses himself for not putting 'such a Bill of Fare' amongst his menus.

There are no drinks suggested for 'Ordinary house luncheons'; the Major regrets that this is 'the ladies' meal', explaining that breakfast isn't, and that dinner 'in many cases is only slightly patronized'. When we see the pictures of

A Picnic at Netley Abbey, Hampshire, in 1883, when 'Major L's' recommendations seem to have been followed — there's a bottle of Champagne in the foreground! The grown-up ladies protect their complexions against the sun, but the younger girls, still in short skirts and hair not yet 'up', can lounge and, minus the 'Grecian bend' corsetry above the bustles of the epoch, enjoy more food.

31

many of the turn of the century society beauties, with their often ample forms, laced into the *tailleurs* in which they might stroll out during the day and even accompany the men to the butts, or the sketches of the flowing tea gowns — with no corsets underneath — in which they could pass the hours between early afternoon and the first dressing bell, when people not in their own rooms might be alerted to return thither, it is not unreasonable to suppose that dinner appetites might certainly be small. Toying with the minute helpings throughout several courses, sipping a little from each of the wine glasses at the place settings — no apéritifs in those days! — the lady might be inhibited from enjoying a dinner.

When it comes to coping with hunting, racing, shooting and railway luncheons the Major (he must have been a bachelor!) is enthusiastic, speaking from experience. He describes a 'hunting case' which will hold various tins to contain pies, cold cutlets and, on another side, bread, cakes or plum pudding; he becomes the old boy who has been the guest at many convivial excursions:

'What is the best thing to put in one's flask? The Author says decidedly whisky and aerated water, of any sort the reader prefers. If whisky is not liked, substitute brandy, and if any gentleman objects to spirits and must have port wine, let him get some old wine from the "wood". It is an idiotic thing to take fine old bottled port; it gets so shaken up that before one has jogged a mile it is completely spoilt, and is wasted; if, however, any one thinks the Author's remark idiotic, pray let him take old bottled port; probably many don't know the difference.'

For race luncheons, there are menus given for 'large parties on Drags and in rooms of Stands', plus 'small parties in Carriages, where there is a difficulty in taking plates, etc'. Here, for menus intended to supply thirty or forty people, 'the Author thinks a few words on what quantity of wine should be taken might be useful'. This comment is inserted as being for the benefit of 'those who are not accustomed to provide such luncheons'. Major L was being both polite and helpful to such hopeful social climbers as the Pooters, who appeared in *Diary of a Nobody* by George and Weedon Grossmith (1894). The Pooters' son, Lupin, might have been one of the Major's readers, although his parents probably remained loyal to their purchases of 'Jackson Frères' Champagne.

'As a general rule, a pint of champagne per head is more than will be consumed; in fact, unless in very hot weather, a dozen of champagne is sufficient; and three bottles of brown sherry, and a bottle of orange brandy (the latter can be obtained, of very excellent make, of Mr Kippling, of Buckby Wharf, Daventry).' If anyone taking a party of thirty or forty people to a race meeting today took only a case of Champagne, regardless of other bottles, the guests would consider this a very meagre allowance. Indeed, the sherry and orange brandy seem somewhat superfluous — unless they were to be the perks of the driver.

When Major L gives suggestions for a December luncheon, he admits that 'the most difficult business in a small Luncheon is to produce the champagne properly iced, and the only way in which this can be done is to obtain one of Messrs Farrow & Jackson's icing cases, to hold two or three bottles.' His menu for this occasion includes 'Plum and gingerbread cakes', so he advises that there should be a mere 'one bottle of good old Brown Sherry or Madeira to wash down the cake' and this would make even a 'small party' to rate 'this sort of Luncheon quite good enough even for an epicure.'

The 'travelling luncheons' are accompanied by a pertinent remark:

'If a long journey has to be taken it is rather difficult to know how long it may last, how long one may be snowed up in a drift, or how long delayed by a break-down of the locomotive; and to add to other inconveniences it is worse than a nuisance to be starved.... A good lunch and a glass of champagne assist to while away the tediousness of the journey, oil the wheels of life, and improve the temper.'

Gentlemen travelling for pleasure or sport within the British Isles had to confront such trials; small wonder if, with the advice of Major L and the resources of 'The Stores' (The Army & Navy) accompanying them, with the requisite equipment, on excursions not merely to the outskirts of civilization but beyond, they adjusted themselves to the exigencies of the most unprepossessing confrontations.

Packed luncheon baskets, Major L knew, were available at railway stations, but his gourmet attitude makes him dubious as to the freshness of both the sandwiches and the chicken therein — and this was when at least the birds would have been free range. He is doubtful about them 'and in summer both are liable to be sprinkled with dust'. So — travellers are, if possible, to take their own provender. The Major is critical of the bad design of the luncheon baskets then available, saying they consisted mostly of 'a large tin

Travelling set, including bottlescrew, engraved beaker with self-righting 'tumbler' base made in 1701 by Charles; the knife, fork, spoon unscrew; nutmeg grater (for spicing drinks) and box for other seasonings fit into a block that slips inside the beaker. The whole being packed in a black fishskin carrying case. The sportsman and intrepid single travellers carried such sets of essentials until very recent times.

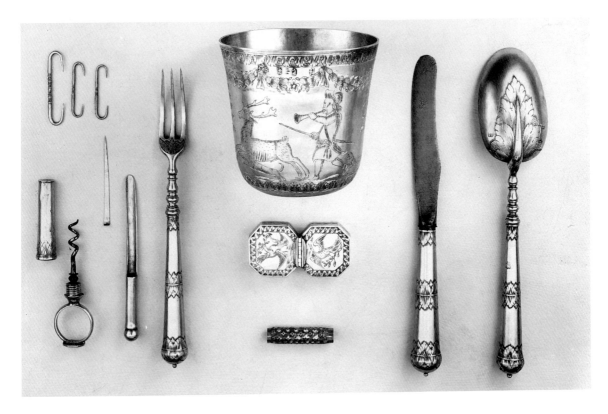

case with no divisions, one or two large bottles, which take up nearly all the room, and assist in spilling wine if decanted into them, three or four tumblers, and there you are – no room for what is really requisite.' The Major preens himself. He has designed a luncheon basket 'with the assistance of Messrs Farrow & Jackson' which, as well as holding various foods:

> '. . . is designed to hold two pint bottles, one for champagne or claret (those of Messrs Barton & Co, the well-known wine merchants of 59, St James's Street, SW, we strongly recommend) the other for sherry or Salutaris water. Instead of two tumblers and two small glasses, which take up so much room, it is fitted with two large and two small cups of transparent horn, fitting one inside the other, and taking up the room of one tumbler only; they are exceedingly light, clean, and nice.'

When the Major comes to shooting luncheons, he quotes lengthily from a correspondent in the magazine *World* (18.11.1885). It is possible that he was the author of this as well. Anyway, it says 'As for drink, whisky or claret is best; beer always interferes with walking, and sometimes with shooting; champagne should be inexorably banished. Just one glass of brown sherry is a sedative luxury, which may perhaps be condoned; then that precious half-pipe — and away once more.'

Although the Major may seem somewhat pontifical, his comments about Ball Suppers must endear him to us, a century away: 'I shall give only four Bills of Fare. Anyone who gives *more* than *four* balls in one year will probably be in a lunatic asylum before the next, so will not require more.' And there are no recommendations about drink!

Yet, said the *Naval and Military Gazette* when reviewing his *Pytchley Book*, 'The chapter devoted to wines, and how to bring them up to table, applied equally to cheaper as well as more costly vintages.'

Good old Major L!

PVP

THOMAS JEFFERSON IN FRANCE AND GERMANY

The great Thomas Jefferson's interest in the fine wines of Bordeaux is both well known and well documented. But, in his extensive travels in Europe — at a time, moreover, when conditions were hardly ideal for it was prior to the French Revolution, when a stranger risked being attacked on suspicion of being a 'spy' — the notes he made on other wines are of considerable interest. Jefferson was always practical and, in June 1788, wrote some notes of advice for a Mr Rutledge and a Mr Shippen:

'General Observations. — On arriving at a town, the first thing is to buy the plan of the town, and the book noting its curiosities. Walk round the ramparts when there are any, go to the top of a steeple to have a view of the town and its environs ....

'When one calls in the taverns for the *vin du pays*, they give what is natural and unadulterated and cheap: when *vin étrangère* is called for, it only gives a pretext for charging an extravagant price for an unwholesome

Rauchemaure on the Rhône

stuff, very often of their own brewery. The people you will naturally see the most of will be tavern keepers, *valets de place*, and postilions. These are the hackneyed rascals of every country. Of course they must never be considered when we calculate the national character.'

In March 1787, Jefferson travelled down the Rhône, commenting that 'Nature never formed a country of more savage aspect' and, when he surveyed the slopes of the Côte Rôtie he noted that:

'... those parts of the hills only which look to the sun at Mid-day or the earlier hours of the afternoon produce wines of the first quality .... The best red wine is produced at the upper end in the neighborhood of Ampuys; the best white next to Condrieux. They sell of the first quality and last vintage at 150 the Piece, equal to 12s the bottle. Transportation to Paris is 60 and the bottle at 20s. When old it costs 10s or 11 Louis the Piece. There is a quality which keeps well, bears transportation, and cannot be drunk under 4 years. Another must be drunk at a year old. They are equal in flavour and price .... The wine called Hermitage is made on the hills over the village of Tains ... the last hermit died in 1751.'

Then, as now, much depended on who grew and made the wine, some obviously being intended for short-term consumption. Jefferson observed that there were few châteaux in the Rhône region and that there were few farms either, these, being made of 'mud or round stone and mud', sound primitive; the inhabitants were mostly to be found in the villages and:

'They rarely eat meat, a single hog salted being the year's stock for a family. But they have plenty of cheese, eggs, potatoes and other vegetables, and walnut oil with their sallad. It is a trade here to gather dung along the road for their vines .... I have seen neither hares nor partridges since I left Paris, no wild fowl on any of the rivers.'

The reference to potatoes, however, is interesting because Parmentier (see p 25), after having seen what a useful food staple they could be while he was a prisoner in Germany, had been encouraging French farmers to plant them. Otherwise, only in Alsace did this crop get cultivated on a large scale, providing not only bulk but a useful source of Vitamin C for a peasantry who must have often suffered from malnutrition — even if they were able to get some Vitamin C from wine.

Further south, Jefferson found the countryside very beautiful and, apparently, the people slightly better nourished:

'On approaching Aix the valley which opens from thence towards the mouth of the Rhône and the sea is rich and beautiful: a perfect grove of olive trees, mixt among which is corn, lucerne and vines .... They drink what is called Piquette. This is made after the grapes are pressed, by pouring hot water on the pumice [pomace, or what we would call the cake or debris of the pressings].'

After going along what is now the Riviera, Jefferson crossed into Italy and

Thomas Jefferson as the great French sculptor Houdon portrayed him in 1789. Even if one did not know who the subject was, the personality is outstanding — a gentleman from Virginia, of whose people it was said 'Virginians must dance or die', an ideal minister in Paris.

arrived in Turin, then in Austrian hands. He commented on the arbour-like training of many of the vines and also tried a 'red wine of Nebiule .... It is about as sweet as the silky Madeira, as astringent on the palate as Bordeaux, and as brisk as Champagne. It is a pleasing wine.' Though he apparently found the various reds of Piedmont 'thick and strong' and a wine made at Noli was merely 'white and indifferent.'

What did make an impression on him a little later, when back again in France, was the sweet wine at Lunel:

'Lunel is famous for its *vin de muscat blanc*, thence called Lunel, or *vin Muscat de Lunel*. It is made from the *raison muscat*, without fermenting the grape in the hopper. When fermented, it makes a red Muscat, taking that tinge from the dissolution of the skin of the grape, which injures the quality. When a red Muscat is required, they prefer colouring it with a little Alicant wine. But the white is best .... It cannot be bought old, the demand being sufficient to take it all the first year.'

At that time, of course, the Muscats and other sweet wines were highly esteemed for drinking at various times, not merely with sweet dishes; the revival of interest in what are now known as *vins doux naturels* among the Muscats makes Jefferson's remark particularly pertinent. He went on to Frontignan after sampling the red and white Muscats at Montpellier, and observed the way in which the best Muscat de Frontignan was made:

'... it is then thick, must have a winter and the *fouet* to render it potable and brilliant. The *fouet* is like a chocolate mill, the handle of iron, the brush of stiff hair. In bottles this wine costs 24s the bottle &c included. It is potable the April after it is made, is best that year, and after 10 years begins to have a pitchy taste resembling it to Malaga. It is not permitted to ferment more than half a day, because it would not be so liquorish. The best colour, and its natural one, is the amber. By force of whipping it is made white but loses flavour. There are but 2 or three pieces a year, of red Muskat, made, there being but one vineyard of the red grape, which belongs to a baker called Pascal.'

The use of the *fouet*, or whisk, is, on a small scale, something equivalent to the 'rousing' of a cask by stirring up the contents; there were whisks in use to froth up chocolate; the way in which the colour of the 'amber' Muscat becomes white with whisking is the same sort of thing that happens when, for example, tomatoes are puréed in a liquidizer — they lose much of their brilliant colour.

Before he got back to Paris, Jefferson, after visiting the Bordeaux vineyards, passed through part of the Loire Valley at Anjou. Of this area he said: 'There is very good wine made on these hills; not equal, indeed, to the Bordeaux of best quality, but to that of good quality, and like it. It is a great article of exportation from Anjou and Touraine, and probably it is sold abroad under the name of Bordeaux.' He was realistic in appreciating that, in this time before controls on the provenance of a wine were in force, many inferior wines were marketed, especially for export, bearing famous and sought-after names.

In the spring of 1788 this continually curious and erudite statesman took a tour from Paris to Amsterdam and Strasburg, making copious notes in his journal. At Cologne he writes:

'Here the vines begin, and it is the most northern spot on the earth on which wine is made. Their first grapes come from Orleans, since then from Alsace, Champagne, &c. It is thirty-two years only since the first vines were sent from Cassel, near Mayence, to the Cape of Good Hope, of which the Cape wine is now made, and it is singular that the same vine should have furnished two wines as much opposed to each other in quality as in situation.'

Jefferson was not correct about this, because the first vintage from vines planted at the Cape had been made in February 1659. The provisioning of the ship *Leewin*, which arrived there in 1655, did include vines, but no record survives as to their provenance, although there was a shipment in 1656 that listed French vines on board. The wine that was ultimately made by Van Riebeeck three years later came from three vines, of which little is known save that one was Muscadel.

When travelling to Anderbach, Jefferson observed the heavily manured vines on the plains and commented that, by comparison with the hillside sites, 'the plains yield much wine, but bad. The good is furnished from the hills.' Going on to 'Coblentz', Jefferson commented in detail on many of the wines (today's reader may understand the places to which he refers if the often odd-looking names are pronounced out loud):

'The best Moselle wines are made about fifteen leagues from thence, in an excessively mountainous country. The first quality (without any comparison) is that made on the mountain of Brownberg, adjoining to the village of Dusmond; and the best crop if that of the Baron Breidbach Burresheim . . . . The last fine year was 1783 . . . Vialen is the second quality, ... 3 Crach-Bispost is the third . . . . I compared Crach of 1783 with Baron Burresheim's of the same year. The latter is quite clear of acid, stronger, and very sensibly the best. Selting . . . . 5 Kous-Berncastle, the fifth quality . . . . These wines must be five or six years old before they are quite ripe for drinking. One thousand plants yield a *foudre* of wine a year in the most plentiful vineyards. In other vineyards, it will take two thousand or two thousand and five hundred plants to yield a *foudre* . . . . The red wines of this country are very indifferent, and will not keep.'

Arriving in Frankfurt, Jefferson remarked: 'Among the poultry, I have seen no turkies in Germany till I arrived at this place. The stork, or crane, is very commonly tame here. It is a miserable, dirty, ill-looking bird.' When he crossed the Rhine by a bridge at 'Mayence', Jefferson finds wines of 'the very first quality' in the region between Rüdesheim to Hocheim; throughout, he puts down details of the soil and manuring of the vineyards and the production of the various owners and praises the wines of 'Johansberg' which 'used to be on a par with Hocheim and Rudesheim, but the place having come to the Bishop of Fulda, he improved its culture so as to render it stronger; and since the year 1775, it sells at double the price of the other two. It has none of

Rüdesheim on the Rhine

the acid of the Hocheim and other Rhenish wines.' And, of the wines of the area in general, he finds that they:

'begin to be drinkable at about five years old. The proprietors sell them old or young, according to the prices offered, and according to their own want of money. There is always a little difference between different casks, and therefore when you choose and buy a single cask, you pay three, four, five or six hundred florins for it. They are not at all acid, and to my taste much preferable to Hocheim, though but of the same price .... On the road between Maynce and Oppenheim are three cantons, which are also esteemed as yielding wines of the second quality. These are Laudenheim, Bodenheim, and Nierstein .... The hills between these villages are almost perpendicular, of a vermilion red, very poor and having as much rotten stone as earth.'

Then comes an interesting entry about various grapes:

'... for use in making white wine, (for I take no notice of the red wines, as being absolutely worthless.) 1 The Klemperien (sic), of which the inferior qualities of Rhenish wines are made, and is cultivated because of its hardness .... 2 The Rhysslin grape, which grows only from Hocheim down to Rudesheim. This is small and delicate, and therefore it succeeds only at this chosen spot. Even at Rudesheim it yields a fine wine only in the little spot called Hunder House ... the mass of good wines made at Rudesheim, below the village, being of the third kind of grape, which is called the Orleans grape.'

Jefferson had begun his tour on 3 March. By 16 April he got to Strasbourg and crossed the Rhine by a wooden bridge; he was to go on through Nancy, Toul, Ligny-en-Barrois and St Dizier before spending a few days in Champagne and returning to Paris on 23 April. The programme would be quite strenuous for a student of wine even today, but he also noted many different methods of agriculture, the animals and people he saw, as well as the state of the roads — with many beggars in Cleves and the state of the

highways 'only made by the carriages' over some stretches, with road taxes being heavy also in places.

His comment in 'Strasberg' is of an almost-forgotten wine:

'The *vin de paille* is produced in the neighborhood of Colmar .... It takes its name from the circumstance of spreading the grapes on straw, where they are preserved till spring, and then made into wine. The little juice then remaining in them makes a rich sweet wine, but the dearest in the world, without being the best by any means. They charge nine florins the bottle for it in the taverns of Strasberg. It is the caprice of wealth alone which continues so losing an operation. This wine is sought because dear, while the better wine of Frontignan is rarely seen at a good table because it is cheap.'

According to the excellent article by George Tener ('The Papers of Thomas Jefferson', Princeton University Press, Princeton, NJ, 1955) quoted in

Monticello, Jefferson's beloved home near Charlottesville, Virginia, is today a national monument. Here he laid out a vineyard and designed a capacious cellar. His hospitality was open-handed — sometimes twenty or fifty guests stayed for weeks or months at Monticello, his stocks of French wines being generously outpoured. After his death, Monticello and much of his property had to be sold to settle accrued debts, but his gracious way of life, augmented by his inventiveness and learning, make his achievements even as a country gentleman as memorable as that of his greatness as a statesman.

'Jefferson and Wine' of the Vinifera Wine Growers Association, 1976, the great man once remarked 'I would go to Hell for my country!' Even for a reasonably well-to-do traveller, the tours such as he made in 1787 and 1788 must have been taxing. There are no indications that he suffered aggravation from the officials or prejudice from the people he encountered, nor — maybe thanks to the wine he drank — did he seem to succumb to 'traveller's tummy' or even a cold in the head, although at the times of year when some of his tours took place the weather must often have been cold and wet.

There are scholarly suggestions that maybe he undertook these apparently unmotivated pleasant voyages not merely because he wished to explore the country and study different aspects of agriculture and, of course, wines, but so that he could investigate social conditions, being aware that there was much unrest in Europe, to see whether this was due to real hardship or some form of agitation. He does not give the names of people he met, except when citing owners of wine vines and other estates, yet a man of his importance must have been introduced to some of the more influential members of the various towns and cities where he stayed; was this tactfulness, or was he, in the event that his papers might be taken, trying to safeguard those who gave him information? He was, of course, no ordinary traveller, but the Englishman Arthur Young, who voyaged in France at the same period, had some very unpleasant encounters with officials and the police; local authorities, in remote places, cannot always interpret accredited documents, even those issued from the highest authorities.

Much remains to be written about this great and versatile man and, as his views and experiences in wine are brought before today's drinkers, it is irresistible to wish that he had written even more about the wines he bought when in Europe and those he drank back in his homeland. One's respect for his meticulous journal-keeping, when this must often have been done in some out of the way inn or tavern in conditions of discomfort if not actual squalor — for he couldn't always have been the guest of a comfortable 'contact' — enhance everything he says. He did the journey from Sens, in northern France, to Lyons in eleven days — 250 miles, says George Tener — and went from Cussy-les-Forges to Dijon in a day — fifty-three miles, which must have necessitated several changes of horse, not always first-rate mounts.

What a traveller! What an indefatigable seeker out of wine!

PVP

THEY CAME TO THE CAPE

It sounds like a quiz — what have the eldest daughter of the Earl of Balcarres, a Victorian novelist and the 'Iron Duke' in common? It is not certain what 'Mr Wellesley, ... on his way back to Bengal', as Lady Anne Barnard recorded, thought of Cape wines, but both she and Anthony Trollope enjoyed them and recorded their impressions. Admiral Lord Nelson, in fact, is said to have doubted the strategic value of the Cape of Good Hope but considered it was of importance as an 'immense tavern', where wine could be provided for the fleet. He was well aware of the necessity of drink being taken on board, both to inculcate a fighting spirit and, possibly without knowing why, to provide a useful additive to a diet deficient in fruit, vegetables and other foods, contributing vitamin C to counteract scurvy.

Lady Anne Lindsay's (her maiden name) charm and her delicately witty writing merit study. She wrote the touching ballad 'Auld Robin Gray' when only twenty-one but did not admit to the authorship until many years later. She was a sensitive, gentle-hearted person, crossed in love in her early life and not marrying until, when thirty-eight, she met Andrew Barnard, then twenty-six. They married in 1793 and a former suitor of hers offered the bridegroom the post of Colonial Secretary to the Cape of Good Hope. The couple, who were to become utterly devoted to each other, sailed in February 1797, landing in May. Lady Anne's account of the voyage includes the mention of a 'port vine', trees, cutlery and curtains in the baggage and once, when their vessel was menaced by a French ship, she admits to putting on a prudent two sets of underwear. She illustrated her letters and journals with deft drawings of everything she found of interest, including the 'salad garden' that the ship's captain grew on a frame, the shoots being germinated on flannel.

The Barnards had apartments in the Castle at Cape Town but the first dinner they gave, for the Governor, who had expressed a wish that they should entertain him, was a disaster. The meal was ruined — because the cook was drunk. Lady Anne's comment is typical: 'as I must often have laughed, or cried, I thought it best to do the first.' She had a shrewd sense of the ridiculous and what some might find a typically Scots outlook on the pretentious and incompetent. Writing from Stellenbosch, she remarks that 'At present there is one thing greatly against the improvements of the vine by any better modes than what are used — namely, that wine from the country is bought by the merchants in town at the market price without any reference to superiority or inferiority of quality.' As Anthony Trollope found towards the end of the century, there was little or no knowledge of how wine might be developed and improved by adequate cellaring, so no wonder the farmers retained what often proved to be excellent wine (after maturation) for their own use.

She is also very amusing about wine snobs who, then as now, tended to 'drink the labels' and only praised the 'known names'. She writes:

'I never saw the force of prejudice more apparent than in the way the Englishmen here turn up their foolish noses at the Cape wines *because* they are Cape wines. They will drink nothing but port, claret or medeira, pretending that the wines of the country give them bowel-ache! It may be so, if they drink three or four bottles at a time, and that very frequently, but Cape wines will not do so if used in moderation. Mr Barnard drinks nothing else himself, though we have every other good wine at table, champagne and burgundy excepted. I must tell you, as an illustration, of what happened with us one day after dinner. We had a little hock on board ship, two bottles of which remained over and we keep them for Lord Macartney when he is ill and wishes for a *bonne bouche*, as they happen to be very fine. After dinner I thought myself drinking up one of the bottles of this hock, and said to Mr Barnard "O fie! why do you give us this today — it is some of our fine hock." A certain lieutenant-colonel, who shall be nameless, on this filled his glass. "Lord bless me, what a fine wine this is!" said he; "I have not tasted a glass such as this since I came here." I then found, on asking, that it was Steine wine, a cheap Cape wine, which Mr Barnard had not liked, and had ordered for common use in the household. In a moment the colonel found fifty faults in it.'

But Lady Anne, although surprised, was not so foolish. It is possible that the wine, made from the Steen grape which is now recognized as the Chenin Blanc and which appears to have been early established in the Cape, had, after being

kept some months in the Barnard's cellar, improved out of all recognition.

The Barnards built a country cottage for themselves above Newlands Avenue and called it 'Paradise'. Here a garden was planted and then a small vineyard; already Anne had visited some of the established vineyards and took a lively interest in them, as well as in the wine itself. In 1798 she went, on a wagon, to Meerlust, still arguably the most beautiful of the Cape estates (until many others come to mind!) and was entertained to luncheon: 'The wine was very good, and the vegetables so too, butter the best I have tasted here.' (More than a century and a half later the dairy herd at Meerlust is still in production.) She went to the great estate of Constantia, where the owner, Hendrik Cloete, admitted he didn't like the British but had to accept that their advent encouraged prosperity. In 1796 an English officer, Robert Percival, had noted how famous the Constantia wine had become and how very difficult it was — without bribing the estate's slaves — to get any to take away, or even to be allowed to see over the premises.

Lady Anne, whose charm must have been great, if one is to go by her letters and writings, as well as the lively, intelligent face shown in her portrait, certainly managed to be shown round. Her sound sense and acuteness of perceiving beauty in what, to a turn of the eighteenth/nineteenth-century lady, might have seemed strange scenes, is marked:

'Mynheer Cloete took us into the wine-press hall; where the whole of our party made wry faces at the idea of drinking wine that had been pressed from the grapes by three pairs of black feet; but the certainty that the fermentation would carry off every polluted particle settled that objection with me. What struck me most was the beautiful antique forms,

Cape Town in 1867, with Table Mountain — not wearing its 'tablecloth of cloud' — centre right, the Lion's Head peak on the far right. The Dutch Reformed Church, on the left, with superb interior woodwork, is the oldest to have been established there. The town houses, with their eighteenth-century elegant lines, are quite different in style from the gabled country houses, although a few of the latter may still be picked out, dating from former times. The vineyards begin among the foothills of the mountains left of centre. Little wonder that Anthony Trollope was impressed!

45

Lady Anne Barnard

perpetually changing and perpetually graceful, of the three bronze figures, half-naked, who were dancing in the wine-press and beating the drum (as it were) with their feet to some other instrument in perfect time. Of these presses there were four, with three slaves each. Into the first the grapes were tossed in large quantities, and the slaves danced on them softly, the wine running out from a hole at the bottom of the barrel, pure and clear — this was done to slow music. A quicker and stronger measure began when the same grapes were danced on over again. The third process gone through was that of passing the pulp and skins through a sieve, and this produced the richest wine of the three; but the different sorts were ultimately mixed together by Mynheer Cloete, who told us it has been the practise of his forefathers to keep them separate and sell them at different prices, but he found the wine was improved by mixing.'

Today's visitor, walking up from the superb house and the wine museum that is now in the former cellar — though this is above ground — to the vineyard of Groot Constantia, arrives at the highest part of the vineyard and passes a large gracefully shaped marble basin, into which leaves from fragrant trees drop and around which there is nothing to be heard but birdsong — the Cape doves' croon urging everyone to 'Work *harder* — work *harder*!' This is known as 'Lady Anne Barnard's bath', but it seems very unlikely that, however much she might have liked to bathe, she ever did so there.

Lady Anne inevitably became involved as consultant and adviser in the love affairs of the young men and women in the small society around her. Always tender-hearted, she was also open-minded: 'altho' I never stand up for love and a cottage,' she wrote about one apparently unsuitable match, 'I have lived long enough to see that people may be happy in very different ways.' She was well aware that the climate — of which she never complained — might nevertheless bring on premature old age — she had grown up in the cooler, moister climate of Scotland and the cosmetics of her day didn't provide protection against the sun. But she enjoyed planting a variety of seeds at 'Paradise' and then, in 1800, she wrote home in October that: 'Our vines will make us eight or ten leagueurs of wine this year, but Van Rhenin, who takes all the trouble of making it, is to have the half of the wine.' She was beginning to pack up for the Barnard's return to England and was practical: '. . . plants of different sorts in packing cases, and pots, to be ready for a sea voyage.' But before they left, the Barnards spent 'two days and a night' on the top of Table Mountain 'pitching our tent there with all sorts of conveniences, our bed, chairs, tables, telescopes; our cook and about twenty coolies.' She'd been up there before and 'did the honors' to Barnard. They saw the eclipse of the sun.

They went 'home', then Barnard was sent out again and, in October 1807, he died at the Cape while on an excursion. Lady Anne, having felt anxious about him, had delayed sailing there herself for fear she should pass him on his way back. She herself died in 1825, aged seventy-four. Her charm wafts down the years and, although she says 'I have had the spell of bad pens thrown over me at my birth', it is only sad that she did not write even more — and that she has, so far, not been the subject of a more detailed study than *Lady Anne Barnard at the Cape of Good Hope*, by Dorothea Fairbridge (Cambridge University Press, 1924).

Anthony Trollope wrote:

'It was in April of last year, 1877, that I first formed a plan of paying an immediate visit to South Africa. The idea that I would one day do so had long loomed in the distance before me. Except the South African group I had seen all our great groups of Colonies . . . and had written books about them all — except South Africa. To "do" South Africa had for some years been on my mind, till at last there was growing on me the consciousness that I was becoming too old for any more such "doing".'

He had, indeed, 'done' parts of North America 'in which our cousins, the descendants of our forefathers, are living and still speaking our language', but this may have been some attempt at counteracting the adverse criticisms of his mother who, poor woman, had become very much the supporter and wage earner of the family and had aroused great antagonism by the book she had poured out — as with many of her books, written at night, with a kettle making yet more tea, while she watched over some sick child — which was

Anthony Trollope

sharply critical of much that she saw in the United States. Anthony Trollope, however, was impelled to visit South Africa because of the troubled situation there where 'we were told that English interference and English interference only could save the country from internecine quarrels between black men and white men'. He would not, by undertaking such a trip, be losing writing time on his novels, for he set himself to complete a certain number of words daily, no matter where he was or what he was doing. (He does not appear to have suffered from travel ailments or seasickness).

He admitted that his arrival was a disappointment for it was a Sunday morning and misty, so 'neither the Table Mountain nor the Lion be seen' —

he remarks tartly that 'Landseer's lions lie straight'. Then he had to remain 'standing at the gate of the dockyard for an hour and a quarter waiting for a Customs House officer to tell me that my things did not need examining'. He had a better view when he left though: 'by that time the hospitality of the citizens had put me in good humour' twelve days later. However, he didn't really care much for the place, and the post office (in which, in Britain, he had worked for thirty years) met with only qualified approval — he didn't care for the protective grills which made him think the officials regarded the public as enemies, though he enjoyed many of the public buildings and the town club. But the countryside around 'is hardly to be beaten for picturesque beauty.... I was taken down to Constantia where I visited one of the few grape growers among whom the vineyards of this district are divided. I found him with his family living in a fine old Dutch residence .... Here he keeps a few ostriches, makes a good deal of wine, and has around him as lovely scenery as the eye of man can want.' But the man 'complained bitterly of the regulations', chiefly, it seems, concerning the problems involved with labour.

A little later he went into the country in what was then midsummer and Trollope:

'... prepared myself to keep watch and ward against musquitoes and comforted myself by thinking how cool it would be on my return journey, in the Bay of Biscay for instance, on the first of January. I had heard, or perhaps had fancied, that the South African musquito would be very venomous and also ubiquitous. I may as well say here as elsewhere that I found him to be but a poor creature as compared with other musquitoes, — the musquito of the United States for instance. The South African December, which had now come, tallies with June on the other side of the line, — and in June the musquito of Washington is as a roaring lion.'

His first visit then was made to 'The Paarl, to see the vineyards and orange groves, and also the ostriches'. He wasn't always impressed by the grandeur of 'countries of large area, such as South Africa, the United States, the interior of Australia, and Russia generally, — of which I speak only from hearsay'. But he enjoyed Paarl, whose 'prettinesses, however, come from the works of man almost as much as from those of Nature'. He admired the eight miles of the long main street and the oak trees and 'graceful' houses and 'it was evident from the great number of churches that they all went to church very often'. A Dutchman 'whose homestead in the middle of the town was bosomed among oaks' was visited: 'His vineyard was a miracle of neatness, and covered perhaps a dozen acres' where he found the wine so cheap that he thought, if he lived at 'The Paarl' he would prefer to farm ostriches. Those entertaining him expressed the hope that there would be a 'reduction of the duties, so that Cape wine may be consumed more freely in England. I endeavoured to explain that England cannot take wine from the Colonies at a lower rate of duty than from foreign countries. I did not say anything as to the existing prejudice against South African sherries.' Trollope was then taken to two other farms in one of which they went into the house and were given wine:

'... that was some years old. It certainly was very good, resembling a fine port that was just beginning to feel its age in the diminution of its body. We enquired whether wine such as that was for sale, but were told that no such wine was to be bought from any grower of grapes. The farmers would keep a little for their own use, and that they would never sell. Neither do the merchants keep it, — not finding it worth their while to be long out of their money, — nor the consumers, there being no commodity of cellarage in the usual houses at the Colony. It has not been the practice to keep wine, — and consequently the drinker seldom has given to him the power of judging whether the Cape wines may or may not become good. At dinner tables at the Cape hosts will apologize for putting on their tables the wines of the Colony, telling their guests that that other bottle contains real sherry or the like. I am inclined to think that the Cape wines have hardly yet had a fair chance, and have been partly led to this opinion of the excellence of that which I drank at Great Draghenstern.'

In saying goodbye to another farmer, Trollope wrote that he 'seemed to me to be as well off as a man need be in this world. Perhaps it was that I envied him his oaks, and his mountains, and his old wine, — and the remaining oranges.'

In a later summary of wine and brandy production, Trollope deprecated the small amount — only 695 gallons (33 hectolitres) — that was imported by Britain, though he also commented that much was obviously sent 'to the other districts of South Africa by inland carriages, so that the Customs House knows nothing about it'. He was also surprised that 'less than one seventh' of the amount of wine produced in 1875 was exported 'seeing that the Cape Colony is particularly productive in grapes. . . . Much no doubt is due to the fact that the merchants have not as yet found it worth their while to store their wines for any lengthened period.'

Trollope finished his substantial book when sailing home, actually in the Bay of Biscay. His observations are detailed and fair, his little adventures sometimes amusing, his remarks about the economy and problems of the country both sensible and, in many respects, relevant to the present day. Possibly those who enjoy his novels think of him as a mild, almost naive man, but he was a first-rate commentator and reporter too, never avoiding hardship or even danger when concerned with giving an account of countries far outside the quiet scenes in which his fictional characters played out their parts.

PVP

THE REVOLUTION 'DOWN UNDER'

Ross Brown doesn't look like a young man who has been at close quarters with a revolution. As a member of one of Australia's historic wine dynasties, he might have found this revolution difficult to endure. Not at all! The past twenty years have not only effected radical changes in wine-making, vine cultivation and the structure of the Australian wine industry, but Australia's drinking habits have also been transformed. Changes have been impelled, from grape cuttings to what's in the glass.

Brown Brothers of Milawa are an independent family concern, of which there are still several energetically in business. It was families like these who founded the Australian wine business, often planting a patch of vines, like an allotment, adjacent to wherever they had set up their home, thus starting business or cultivation in the huge new continent. James Graham, a Scot who had been in Canada, bought land at Milawa when it was first open to offer; there he built a Canadian-style high barn as well as laying out a vineyard in 1857. His daughter Rebecca married George Harry Brown, who'd come to Milawa and planted vines too. It was their second son, John Francis, who really concentrated on wine-making from his first vintage in 1899. It's his son, John Charles — the eldest son is now always christened John — who, with *his* four sons, continues the tradition, each of the four concentrating on a different section of the business. It might be the theme of one of those bulky family sagas, except that there don't appear to have been either any refusals to get involved with wine, or dramatic domestic conflicts.

John Francis Brown, who made his first wine at Milawa in 1889.

John Brown Senior with Pat, his wife, on his left. Left to right: Ross with his wife, Judy, sitting in front of him; Peter with wife Jan standing alongside him; John Junior with wife June on his left; Roger with wife Elu sitting in front of him. In 1989 the family and firm of Brown celebrate their centenary.

Today, John Charles Brown, himself an only son, is a gentle patriarch, son John Graham Brown is the wine-maker, Peter Brown the viticulturalist, Ross Brown deals with marketing, and Roger Brown with propagation and harvesting. It would, the outsider may suppose, have been easy and indeed routine for such a family to have continued their proud traditions and, maybe, have coasted along, secure, like a few of the other wine families, in making fine wine without excessive effort.

Far from it! The Browns are certainly traditionalists, maintaining their proud past, but they soar into the twenty-first century whenever possible even if the results of their explorations and innovations then swoop, boomerang-like, back to the garden-encircled modest country house at Milawa — where the Canadian-style barn now houses the maturing fortified wines. This is why young Ross is able to speak both for his family and for his contemporaries in the Australian wine industry.

After World War II, many different peoples arrived in Australia, often from wine countries: among them Greeks, Italians, Yugoslavs. Restaurants of many different styles began to open, staffed by people who brought their own traditions of food and drink to this country that can yield up a cornucopia of produce, and proved an inspiration to many; for example the Polish settlers, who could now extend or create their own lifestyles. In the 1950s Australia enjoyed a period of affluence: those who had gone overseas often returned with not only a wish to enjoy 'the good life' but with experiences of different ways of eating and drinking. No longer did Australia look over its shoulder at Europe, in so many ways life was richer and more challenging than in those war-torn countries, and so definite Australian styles of living and entertaining began to evolve.

Brown Brothers have always been famous for the wide variety of grapes that they grow and utilize, and with which they experiment. Ross Brown points out that even the famous classic grapes respond differently in Australia, which is a whole continent, not merely a set of regions within the boundaries of a single country. Generalizations about 'Australian wine' are, therefore, meaningless. The individuality of the wines comes via the personality of the maker. It is Australian wine-makers, whose energy is admired by all overseas visitors, who continue to explore and exploit the natural resources of their country; they experiment with new methods, they try out the potential of grapes that may seem 'new': for example, Ross cites the Mondeuse, a variety that is too tannic for widespread use in France, but which can yield satisfactorily in Australia. Brown Brothers have sometimes been teased about the '57 varieties' they are said to plant — at least, admits Ross, there are certainly thirty-five different ones definitely in use.

Australians, who may compete with each other in business as regards wine, are willing to share knowledge and findings. If someone thinks a particular site may be planted with a grape variety that will yield satisfactorily, there is no reason why the grower shouldn't go ahead (though, it should be said, there are overall checks on vineyards and installations) so as to further overall progress. The freedom that Australian wine-makers enjoy is one of the contributing impulses to their dynamism and it also means that, being flexible, their produce can cater for the different demands of the export markets. For example, the Chenin Blanc, a popular variety throughout south-east Asia and in Japan, may not appeal to some other buyers; the Australian Sauvignon Blanc apparently isn't of much appeal in the US because of its pronounced bouquet and flavour, although it is precisely this very 'herbaceousness' that the Browns like to stress when describing this wine.

The different vineyards that are owned by the Browns — at Mystic Park, Whitlands and King Valley — in addition to Milawa, mean that the exploitation of varietal potential can be made in the context of cross-sections of soil and climate. Indeed, some grape names may seem unfamiliar to European-trained palates — Ruby Cabernet, Mataro, Bonvedro, Flora, Orange Muscat. There can be pleasant surprises too, as was found with the Columbard, not regarded by many as a quality vine in the northern hemisphere, but making wines of pleasant refinement in Australia.

Ross Brown reiterates constantly that, in Australia, it is essential to develop the flavour and fruit of the grape according to the different regions; the fruit character must be investigated and, he says, the 'natural personality of the grape' has continually to be discovered and exploited. The family tradition stresses that retention of the fruit's definition must be maintained and, thanks to refrigeration, there need now be no loss of flavour due to oxidation, as once used to happen in Australia and which resulted in their wines attracting adverse comments and descriptions.

This recent revolution of quality, plus the great work of the wine colleges at Roseworthy and Wogga, has meant that, soon, there will probably have to be another basic change in pricing. Ross now finds that, in the UK, the cost does not always reflect the quality of the Australian wines. Finer Australian wines may, when exported, have their prices increased, though some of the 'everyday' bottles may become cheaper.

Australia also enjoys the enthusiasm of a wine-drinking public, manifest in front page newspaper headlines reporting on wines at the various wine shows. Wine isn't merely big business, it is 'news' and news that is followed by all sections of society. A taxi driver, hearing that Ross is in the wine business, will engage him in conversation — rather as Paris taxi drivers are said to participate in talk with fashion editors during the showings of the couture houses.

As all the Brown wives are both interested and creative as regards entertaining, it is no surprise that Ross finds the Australian public more alert to the possibilities of partnering wines and dishes. One glossy publication recently commented that, these days, it is no longer routine to have just one wine served throughout the meal — each course now gets its appropriate (or discussed) accompaniment. One member of the Brown family, whom they won't name, even asserts that it's possible to serve a 'soft and generous Shiraz' with a not too aggressive curry!

Wine, as Ross repeats, must begin with fruit; fine wine must be based on perfectly ripe, sound fruit which, depending on the vineyard, can reflect its environment which, he admits, can in some hands be 'rowdy and noisy', although not from his establishment! The flagship wines of the sweet types, plus the great Muscats for which nearby Rutherglen is renowned, are never in abundant supply; a run on them might be a tragedy and exhaust reserves. A quotation from Brown Brothers' account of themselves is relevant to Australian traditions in general: 'the longer the period of ripening, the greater intensity of flavour and aroma of the grape and the better balance of its sugar and acids.' It is impossible not to believe that, with families such as this in business — many members of them also influential in the mighty concerns where firms are reshuffled like playing cards — Australia is 'ripening' towards great future vintages.

PVP

THE WINES OF BORDEAUX — MY OWN CLASSIFICATION

by Clive Coates

Is there any need for a classification of the wines of Bordeaux? Why do we have this almost insatiable desire to tabulate and place into some sort of pecking order everything we come across — especially something as delicately poised, as changeable and as changing and, ultimately, as personally sensual as an appreciation of the relative merit of a bottle of wine?

Yet I would argue that it is quite natural. Instinctively, given two glasses of similar wine, we will taste, compare and contrast. In so doing we will form a value judgment on them both. We will (probably) prefer one to the other. It is part of the appreciation and enjoyment of wine. Part, too, of the fun — and wine drinking *should* be fun — is to relate our experiences to others round the table, to compare our notes and argue our differences. A healthy agreement to differ is part of civilized participation in what André Simon called 'The Art of Good Living'.

So — naturally we classify. Also, as consumers, we need classifications. There are many, many wines; each year brings new and different vintages. We need help so as to spend our money wisely for, it is only too clear, high prices do not necessarily indicate top quality, nor do reasonable prices signify mediocrity. Reputations of fine wines may rise or fall as the result of the raising or lowering of standards. We, the buying public, need to be told. And, indeed, why should dedication and expertise *not* be rewarded, in a competition, by a top place or a gold medal? I need hardly add that any such awards will assist the proprietor in marketing his product.

But there is an important trap to be avoided. There are no absolutes. The majority of 'experts' — and I deliberately put the word into inverted commas, it is one seldom applied by those who really know something about wine to themselves — may tell us that Wine A is better than Wine B. If our personal taste reacts and decides differently, who cares? It's our opinion and our money. Our view is just as valid as that of the next man. And life would be very dull if we all preferred the same wine.

Earlier classifications:

If some of what I am now to state seems too much of a repetition of what has so often been written, I plead that there is always a 'first time' — both for the reader beginning to be interested in Bordeaux and for the claret lover of a lifetime who may have forgotten some of the past history.

The top wines of Bordeaux have been classified since the time when they became individual wines, sold under the name of the estate making them, more than 300 years ago. The famous classification of the red and white wines of Bordeaux, produced by a committee of brokers, ratified by the Chamber of Commerce and then exhibited at the Exposition Universelle de Paris in 1855 was, albeit more official, only the latest, then, in a long line of lists drawn up by those who had been involved in selling or writing about the local wines over the previous century and a half. Individuals as assorted as J Bruneval, supplier to the cellar of the future King George II of England in 1723, and Thomas Jefferson, the future President of the United States who, as Ambassador to France and being himself a vine grower in his home state of Virginia, made an extensive tour of the French vineyards during 1787; brokers such as Abraham Lawton in 1815; and writers such as Pagieurre (another broker, whose *Classifications et Descriptions des Vins de Bordeaux* appeared in 1828), Wilhelm Franck (his *Traité sur les Vins du Médoc etc* appeared in various editions from 1824 until 1860), the English schoolmaster Charles Cocks and his French collaborator, Féret, not to mention others such as André Jullien and Alastair Henderson — all of whom wrote in the decades immediately prior to 1855 and some of whom borrowed from each other; each of these provide us with their impressions of the hierarchy of the time, in other words, what they then thought were 'the best' wines of Bordeaux.

What is fascinating is not only to see the rise and fall of the reputations of individual properties, but to note the consistency of views; British writers were not always inclined to agree with their French opposite numbers, but on this aspect of the subject they usually did. From the very beginning of any attempt at classification, the four growths of Haut-Brion, Lafite, Margaux and Latour reign supreme. The consistent second growths are Léoville and

Château Haut Brion, at Pessac in the Graves, the 'odd man out' in the 1855 classification of the red wines.

Rauzan, both then undivided estates, also Gruaud-Larose, later to be joined at this level and surpassed by Brane-Mouton, the original name of the property later famous as Mouton-Rothschild. Other properties — Calon-Ségur, the then undivided Pichon, Kirwan, Lascombes, Brane-Cantenac, Durfort-Vivens, and Ducru-Beaucaillou — have equally venerable histories. Cos d'Estournel and, even later, Montrose, appear almost as interlopers. Moreover, these early lists were not restricted to the Médoc (plus Haut-Brion); La Mission Haut-Brion and Pape-Clément (both in ecclesiastical hands until the French Revolution of 1789) are also quoted in earlier classifications, plus neighbouring properties which have since disappeared into the concrete sprawl of the Bordeaux suburbs.

The 1855 Classification:
What has to be categorically emphasized about the 1855 classification is that it was not merely a classification of the Médoc, with Haut-Brion somehow smuggled in 'on the old-boy network', as Edmund Penning-Rowsell puts it, because it was too important to be left out. The classification was of the top red wines of Bordeaux. These were the wines which, then, had the highest reputations and which fetched the highest prices. The Libournais wines, just as much as those of Léognan and elsewhere in the Graves, were not considered good enough.

Moreover, the list was compiled in 1855 in order of merit within the different categories — first growth down to fifth growth. So Mouton was preferred to Rauzan and Léoville, both properties by this time having been divided; Giscours was preferred to Kirwan and Issan, St Pierre to Talbot, and Beychevelle and Pontet-Canet were preferred to Grand-Puy-Lacoste and Lynch-Bages. And Lafite was considered to be the finest of all.

The top white wines were also classified. Dry white wine was not, then, a sought after commodity. All the 'crus classés', headed by Yquem in a category of its own, came from the Sauternes and Barsac areas and produced *vin liquoreux*.

1855 Classification of Red Wines (as originally given)

PREMIERS CRUS/1st GROWTHS

Ch Lafite	*Pauillac*
Ch Margaux	*Margaux*
Ch Latour	*Pauillac*
Ch Haut Brion	*Pessac (Graves)*
Ch Mouton-Rothschild	*Pauillac (since 1973)*

In 1973 a decree of the French Ministry of Agriculture was issued, whereby the first five wines of the first growths were stated to be of equal worth and it was said that their names should henceforth be given in alphabetical order — that is:
Château Lafite Rothschild
Château Latour

Château Margaux
Château Mouton Rothschild
and 'by assimilation' (because it is in the Graves and not the Médoc):
Château Haut Brion

DEUXIÉMES CRUS/2nd GROWTHS

Ch Rausan-Ségla	Margaux
Ch Rauzan-Gassies	Margaux
Ch Léoville-Lascases	St Julien
Ch Léoville-Poyferré	St Julien
Ch Léoville-Barton	St Julien
Ch Durfort-Vivens	Margaux
Ch Lascombes	Margaux
Ch Gruaud-Larose	St Julien
Ch Brane-Cantenac	Cantenac
Ch Pichon-Longueville	Pauillac
Ch Pichon-Longueville-Lalande	Pauillac
Ch Ducru-Beaucaillou	St Julien
Ch Cos d'Estournel	St Estèphe
Ch Montrose	St Estèphe

TROISIÈMES CRUS/3rd GROWTHS

Ch Kirwan	Cantenac
Ch d'Issan	Cantenac
Ch Lagrange	St Julien
Ch Langoa	St Julien
Ch Giscours	Labarde
Ch Malescot-St-Exupéry	Margaux
Ch Cantenac-Brown	Cantenac
Ch Palmer	Cantenac
Ch Grand La Lagune	Ludon
Ch Desmirail	Margaux
Ch Calon-Ségur	St Estèphe
Ch Ferrière	Margaux
Ch Marquis d'Alesme-Becker	Margaux
Ch Boyd-Cantenac	Margaux

QUATRIÈMES CRUS/4th GROWTHS

Ch St-Pierre-Sevaistre	St Julien
Ch St-Pierre-Bontemps	St Julien
Ch Branaire-Ducru	St Julien
Ch Talbot	St Julien
Ch Duhart-Milon	Pauillac
Ch Pouget	Cantenac
Ch La Tour-Carnet	St Laurent
Ch Lafon-Rochet	St Estèphe
Ch Beychevelle	St Julien
Ch Le Prieuré-Lichine	Cantenac
Ch Marquis-de-Terme	Margaux

CINQUÈMES CRUS/5th GROWTHS

Ch Pontet-Canet	*Pauillac*
Ch Batailley	*Pauillac*
Ch Haut Batailley	*Pauillac*
Ch Grand-Puy-Lacoste	*Pauillac*
Ch Grand-Puy-Ducasse	*Pauillac*
Ch Lynch-Bages	*Pauillac*
Ch Lynch-Moussas	*Pauillac*
Ch Dauzac	*Labarde*
Ch Mouton d'Armailhacq (*now* Mouton Baronne Philippe)	*Pauillac*
Ch du Tertre	*Arsac*
Ch Haut-Bages-Liberal	*Pauillac*
Ch Pédesclaux	*Pauillac*
Ch Belgrave	*St Laurent*
Ch Camensac	*St Laurent*
Ch Cos-Labory	*St Estèphe*
Ch Clerc-Milon-Mondon	*Pauillac*
Ch Croizet-Bages	*Pauillac*
Ch Cantemerle	*Macau*

1855 Classification of White Wines

GRAND PREMIER CRU

Ch Yquem	*Sauternes*

PREMIERS CRUS/1st GROWTHS

Ch La Tour-Blanche	*Bommes*
Ch Peyraguey (Clos Haut-Peyraguey)	*Bommes*
(Lafaurie-Peyraguey)	*Bommes*
Ch Rayne-Vigneau	*Bommes*
Ch Suduiraut	*Preignac*
Ch Coutet	*Barsac*
Ch Climens	*Barsac*
Ch Guiraud	*Fargues*
Ch Rabaud (Rabaud-Promis)	*Bommes*
(Sigalas-Rabaud)	*Bommes*
Ch Rieussec	*Barsac*

DEUXIÈMES CRUS/2nd GROWTHS

Ch Myrat	*Barsac*
Ch Doisy	
(Doisy-Daëne)	*Barsac*
(Doisy-Védrines)	*Barsac*
(Doisy-Dubroca)	*Barsac*
Ch Peixotto (part of Rabaud-Promis)	*Bommes*
Ch d'Arche	*Sauternes*
Ch Filhot	*Sauternes*
Ch Broustet	*Barsac*
Ch Nairac	*Barsac*
Ch Caillou	*Barsac*

Ch Suau	*Barsac*
Ch de Malle	*Preignac*
Ch Romer (2 proprietors)	*Fargues*
Ch Lamothe	*Sauternes*
Ch Lamothe-Berguey	*Sauternes*

1959 Classification of White Graves*

Ch Bouscaut	*Cadaujac*
Ch Carbonnieux	*Léognan*
Ch Olivier	*Léognan*
Domaine de Chevalier	*Léognan*
Ch Malartic-Lagravière	*Léognan*
Ch La Tour Martillac	*Martillac*
Ch Laville Haut Brion	*Talence*
Ch Couhins	*Villenave-d'Ornon*

*__Haut Brion Blanc__ was not included in this classification at the request of the proprietor.

Changes since 1855:

Since 1855 there has, sadly, been no revised classification and what was produced more than 130 years ago has, inevitably, become out of date and misleading. Moreover, there have been extensive changes in vineyard ownership, especially in the five communes which made up the appellation of Margaux.

Some properties have disappeared from view; others have been split; yet more exist in different locations and are radically different in style from that of the property that was classified in 1855. After fifty years of lobbying, the late Baron Philippe managed to get Mouton-Rothschild elevated to first growth status in 1973. Since the 1950s there have been several rumours, if not tentative proposals, of large scale revisions of the classification. These have come to nothing, due to inertia from those owners who are content with their position today as laid down in 1855, also as a consequence of the antagonism of those properties threatened with declassification and, also, due to the lack of a political will to establish an authority which could, at need, defend itself against the inevitable consequences of its actions.

Yes, the Graves has been separately classified (a revision is now five years overdue), as has Saint-Émilion. But what is needed is an official, revised classification of all the red wines of Bordeaux in a single list, one which, moreover, would itself be updated every twenty years or so.

Unofficial Classifications:

One or two intrepid spirits have, meanwhile, produced their own classifications. Alexis Lichine's version, first published in the late 1960s, has appeared in subsequent editions of his *Encylopedia of Wines & Spirits* ever since (the most recent edition, the seventh, published by Cassell, appeared in October 1987). Alexis is too kind to Brane-Cantenac, Pichon-Baron and Pape Clément, each of which he rates alongside 'super seconds' such as Ducru-Beaucaillou and Léoville-Lascases. He is cruel to Canon and Vieux Château

Two-handled Greek kylix, dating from the fifth to the fourth
century BC, one of the exhibits from the 'Cups and glasses' room
at the impressive Martini & Rossi wine museum at Pessione,
near Turin.

Riquewihr 'the pearl of Alsace', in the foothills of the Vosges mountains, with the vineyards rising steeply and directly from the outskirts of the village.

The variations in the terrain in Alsace necessitate angling the
rows of vines so that they enjoy maximum exposure to the
morning sun. The local reference to Alsace says it is 'Three
castles on one hill, three churches in one churchyard, three
villages in one valley'.

Certan, which he deems the equal of Trottevieille and Gazin in his third category. He is indulgent to his beloved Prieuré-Lichine, which has an asterisk (denoting a wine which is 'considered better than its peers' in this same third category) as, rightly, do Canon and Vieux Château Certan. There are numerous other idiosyncrasies in this classification.

Alexis Lichine's Classification of Bordeaux

Crus Hors Classe (Outstanding Growths)

HAUT-MÉDOC

Ch Lafite-Rothschild *(Pauillac)*
Ch Latour *(Pauillac)*
Ch Margaux *(Margaux)*
Ch Mouton-Rothschild *(Pauillac)*

GRAVES

Ch Haut-Brion *(Pessac, Graves)*

SAINT-ÉMILION

Ch Ausone
Ch Cheval-Blanc

POMEROL

Ch Pétrus

Crus Exceptionnels (Exceptional Growths)

HAUT-MÉDOC

Ch Brane-Cantenac *(Cantenac-Margaux)*
Ch Cos d'Estournel *(Saint-Estèphe)*
Ch Ducru-Beaucaillou *(Saint-Julien)*
Ch Gruaud-Larose *(Saint-Julien)*
Ch Lascombes *(Margaux)*
Ch Léoville-Barton *(Saint-Julien)*
Ch Léoville-Las-Cases *(Saint-Julien)*
Ch Léoville Poyferré *(Saint-Julien)*
Ch Lynch-Bages *(Pauillac)*
Ch Montrose *(Saint-Estèphe)*
Ch Palmer *(Cantenac-Margaux)*
Ch Pichon Longueville, Comtesse de Lalande *(Pauillac)*
Ch Pichon-Longueville-Baron *(Pauillac)*

GRAVES

Domaine de Chevalier *(Léognan)*
Ch La Mission-Haut-Brion *(Talence)*
Ch Pape-Clément *(Pessac)*

SAINT-ÉMILION

Ch Figeac
Ch Magdelaine

POMEROL

Ch La Conseillante
Ch l'Évangile
Ch Lafleur
Ch La Fleur-Pétrus
Ch Trotanoy

Grands Crus (Great Growths)

HAUT-MÉDOC

Ch Beychevelle *(Saint-Julien)*
Ch Boyd-Cantenac *(Cantenac-Margaux)*
Ch Branaire-Ducru *(Saint-Julien)*
Ch Calon-Ségur *(Saint-Estèphe)*
Ch Cantemerle *(Haut-Médoc)*
Ch Cantenac-Brown *(Cantenac-Margaux)*
*Ch Giscours *(Labarde-Margaux)*
Ch d'Issan *(Cantenac-Margaux)*
Ch La Lagune *(Haut-Médoc)*
Ch Malescot-Saint-Exupéry *(Margaux)*
Ch Mouton-Baronne-Philippe *(Pauillac)*
*Ch Prieuré-Lichine *(Cantenac-Margaux)*
Ch Rausan-Ségla *(Margaux)*
Ch Talbot *(Saint-Julien)*

GRAVES

Ch Haut-Bailly (*Léognan*)

SAINT-ÉMILION

Ch Beau-Séjour-Bécot
Ch Bélair
*Ch Canon
Clos Fourtet
Ch La Gaffelière
Ch Pavie
Ch Trottevieille

POMEROL

Ch Gazin
Ch Latour-Pomerol
*Ch Petit-Village
*Vieux-Château-Certan
Ch Nénin

Crus Supérieurs (Superior Growths)

HAUT-MÉDOC

Ch Batailley (*Pauillac*)
Ch Chasse-Spleen (*Moulis*)
Ch Clerc-Milon-Rothschild (*Pauillac*)
Ch Duhart-Milon-Rothschild (*Pauillac*)
Ch Durfort-Vivens (*Cantenac-Margaux*)
Ch Gloria (*Saint-Julien*)
Ch Grand-Puy-Lacoste (*Pauillac*)
Ch Haut-Batailley (*Pauillac*)
Ch Kirwan (*Cantenac-Margaux*)
Ch Lagrange (*Saint-Julien*)
Ch Langoa-Barton (*Saint-Julien*)
Ch Marquis d'Alesme-Becker (*Margaux*)
Ch Marquis de Terme (*Margaux*)
Ch Pontet-Canet (*Pauillac*)
Ch Rauzan-Gassies (*Margaux*)
Ch La Tour-Carnet (*Haut-Médoc*)

GRAVES

Ch Carbonnieux (*Léognan*)
Ch de Fieuzal (*Léognan*)
Ch La Louvière (*Léognan*)
*Ch Malartic-Lagravière (*Léognan*)
Ch Smith Haut-Lafitte (*Martillac*)

SAINT ÉMILION

Ch l'Angélus
Ch Balestard-la-Tonnelle
Ch Beauséjour-Duffau-Lagarosse
Ch Cadet-Piola
Ch Canon-la-Gaffelière
Ch La Clotte
Ch Croque-Michotte
Ch Curé-Bon-la-Madeleine
Ch La Dominique
Ch Larcis-Ducasse
Ch Larmande
Ch Soutard
Ch Troplong-Mondot
Ch Villemaurine

POMEROL

Ch Beauregard
Ch Certan-Giraud
*Ch Certan-de-May
Clos de l'Église
Clos de l'Église-Clinet
Ch Le Gay
Ch Lagrange
Ch La Pointe

Bons Crus (Good Growths)

HAUT-MÉDOC

Ch d'Agassac (*Haut-Médoc*)
*Ch Angludet (*Cantenac-Margaux*)
Ch Beau-Site (*Saint-Estèphe*)
Ch Beau-Site Haut-Vignoble (*Saint-Estèphe*)
Ch Bélair-Marquis d'Aligre (*Soussans-Margaux*)
Ch Belgrave (*Saint-Laurent*)
*Ch de Camensac (*Haut-Médoc*)

* Pp 65–7 these wines are considered better than their peers in this classification.

Note: All Saint-Émilion and Pomerol châteaux classified pp 65–7 bear the strict commune designations of Saint-Émilion and Pomerol respectively.

Ch Citran *(Haut-Médoc)*
Ch Cos-Labory *(Saint-Estèphe)*
*Ch Croizet-Bages *(Pauillac)*
Ch Dauzac *(Margaux)*
Ch Ferrière *(Margaux)*
Ch Fourcas-Dupré *(Listrac)*
Ch Fourcas-Hosten *(Listrac)*
Ch Grand-Puy-Ducasse *(Pauillac)*
Ch Gressier-Grand-Poujeaux *(Moulis)*
Ch Hanteillan *(Haut-Médoc)*
Ch Haut-Bages-Libéral *(Pauillac)*
Ch Haut-Marbuzet *(Saint-Estèphe)*
Ch Labégorce *(Margaux)*
Ch Labégorce-Zedé *(Margaux)*
Ch Lafon-Rochet *(Saint-Estèphe)*
Ch Lamarque *(Haut-Médoc)*
Ch Lanessan *(Haut-Médoc)*
Ch Lynch-Moussas *(Pauillac)*
Ch Marbuzet *(Saint-Estèphe)*
Ch Maucaillou *(Moulis)*
*Ch Les Ormes-de-Pez *(Saint-Estèphe)*
Ch Pédesclaux *(Pauillac)*
*Ch de Pez *(Saint-Estèphe)*
Ch Phélan-Ségur *(Saint-Estèphe)*
Ch Pouget *(Cantenac-Margaux)*
Ch Poujeaux *(Moulis)*
*Ch Saint-Pierre *(Saint-Julien)*
Ch Siran *(Labarde-Margaux)*
Ch du Tertre *(Arsac-Margaux)*
Ch La Tour-de-Mons *(Soussans-Margaux)*
Ch Villegeorge *(Haut-Médoc)*

GRAVES

Ch Bouscaut *(Cadaujac)*
Ch Larrivet-Haut-Brion *(Léognan)*
Ch La Tour-Haut-Brion *(Talence)*
Ch La Tour-Martillac *(Martillac)*

SAINT ÉMILION

Ch l'Arrosée
Ch Bellevue

Ch Berliquet
Ch Cap-de-Mourlin
Domaine du Châtelet
Clos des Jacobins
Ch Corbin *(Giraud)*
Ch Corbin *(Manuel)*
Ch Corbin-Michotte
Ch Coutet
Ch Dassault
Couvent-des-Jacobins
Ch La Fleur-Pourret
Ch Franc-Mayne
Ch Grâce-Dieu-Les-Menuts
Ch Grand-Barrail-Lamarzelle-Figeac
Ch Grand-Corbin
Ch Grand-Corbin-Despagne
Ch Grand-Mayne
Ch Grand Pontet
Ch Guadet-St Julien
Ch Laroque
Ch Moulin-du-Cadet
Ch Pavie-Decesse
Ch Pavie-Macquin
Ch Saint-Georges-Côte-Pavie
Ch Tertre-Daugay
Ch La Tour-Figeac
Ch La Tour-du-Pin-Figeac
Ch Trimoulet
Ch Yon-Figeac

POMEROL

Ch Bourgneuf-Vayron
Ch La Cabanne
Ch Le Caillou
*Ch Clinet
Clos du Clocher
Ch La Croix
Ch La Croix-de-Gay
Clos de l'Église
Ch l'Enclos
Ch Gombaude-Guillot
Ch La Grave-Trignant-de-Boisset
Ch Guillot
Ch Moulinet
Ch Rouget
*Clos René
Ch de Sales
Ch du Tailhas
Ch Taillefer
Ch Vraye-Croix-de-Gay

Robert Parker Jnr in his *Bordeaux, The Definitive Guide* (Dorling Kindersley, 1986) has also produced his personal version of a classification. It runs to one hundred growths, divided into five categories, and is based in the main on the performance of the wines between 1975 and 1983. There are fifteen first growths, the 'super seconds', as well as the established firsts. Surprisingly, space is found for Gruaud-Larose and Trotanoy, but not for Lafleur, Figeac, or Cos d'Estournel. Parker is generous to Giscours, Montrose and Léoville-Barton, all of which are among his fifteen second growths, and also to La Mission Haut-Brion and La Tour Haut-Brion, which did not produce very good wine in the six vintages prior to the Haut-Brion acquisition of both properties in 1983. He is cruel to Domaine de Chevalier and Vieux Château Certan, which deserve a rating better than third. Surely these estates produce far better wines today than Boyd-Cantenac and Cantemerle? And he totally ignores Fronsac.

If minor Médocs, such as Potensac, can scrape into the list of fifth growths, a place must be found for Canon-Moueix and Canon-de-Brem.

There are many other anomalies. Most of the Graves *crus classés* fail to be admitted. Cadet-Piola, Clos de Jacobins, Soutard, La Dominique and L'Arrosée are in, but others of Saint-Émilion's *grands crus classés* — the obvious candidate is Larmande, but what of Pavie-Decesse, La Tour Figeac, La Tour du Pin Figeac-Moueix, Le Serre, Curé-Bon-La-Madelaine, Beauséjour-Bécot and others ? — are not.

Robert Parker's Classification of the Top Châteaux of Bordeaux

FIRST GROWTHS (15)
Ausone *(St-Emilion)*
Cheval Blanc *(St-Emilion)*
Ducru-Beaucaillou *(St-Julien)*
Gruaud-Larose *(St-Julien)*
Haut-Brion *(Graves)*
Lafite-Rothschild *(Pauillac)*
Latour *(Pauillac)*
Léoville-Las Cases *(St-Julien)*
Margaux *(Margaux)*
La Mission-Haut-Brion *(Graves)*
Mouton-Rothschild *(Pauillac)*
Palmer *(Margaux)*
Pétrus *(Pomerol)*
Pichon Lalande *(Pauillac)*
Trotanoy *(Pomerol)*

SECOND GROWTHS (15)
Canon *(St-Emilion)*
Certan de May *(Pomerol)*
La Conseillante *(Pomerol)*
Cos d'Estournel *(St-Estèphe)*
Branaire-Ducru *(St-Julien)*
L'Evangile *(Pomerol)*

Figeac *(St-Emilion)*
Giscours *(Margaux)*
Lafleur *(Pomerol)*
La Lagune *(Ludon)*
Latour à Pomerol *(Pomerol)*
Léoville-Barton *(St-Julien)*
Lynch-Bages *(Pauillac)*
Magdelaine *(St.-Emilion)*
Montrose *(St-Estèphe)*

THIRD GROWTHS (11)
Beychevelle *(St-Julien)*
Boyd-Cantenac *(Margaux)*
Cantemerle *(Macau)*
Domaine de Chevalier *(Graves)*
Grand-Puy-Lacoste *(Pauillac)*
d'Issan *(Margaux)*
Lafleur-Pétrus *(Pomerol)*
Langoa-Barton *(St-Julien)*
La Tour-Haut-Brion *(Graves)*
Talbot *(St-Julien)*
Vieux Château Certan *(Pomerol)*

FOURTH GROWTHS (10)
L'Arrosée (St-Emilion)
Calon-Ségur (St-Estèphe)
La Dominique (St-Emilion)
Gloria (St-Julien)
Haut-Bailly (Graves)
Lascombes (Margaux)
Léoville-Poyferré (St-Julien)
de Pez (St-Estèphe)
Prieuré-Lichine (Margaux)
St-Pierre (St-Julien)

FIFTH GROWTHS (52)
Batailley (Pauillac)
Belair (St-Emilion)
Bon Pasteur (Pomerol)
Brane-Cantenac (Margaux)
Brillette (Moulis)
Cadet-Piola (St-Emilion)
Camensac (Haut-Médoc)
Cantenac-Brown (Margaux)
Certan-Giraud (Pomerol)
Chasse-Spleen (Moulis)
Clerc-Milon-Rothschild (Pauillac)

Clos des Jacobins (St-Emilion)
Clos-René (Pomerol)
Duhart-Milon-Rothschild Durfort-
Vivens (Margaux)
L'Eglise Clinet (Pomerol)
L'Enclos (Pomerol)
Fonbadet (Pauillac)
Les Forts de Latour (Pauillac)
Fourcas-Hosten (Listrac)
Le Gay (Pomerol)
Grand-Puy-Ducasse (Pauillac)
La Grave Trigant de Boisset
(Pomerol)
Kirwan (Margaux)
Haut-Bages-Libéral (Pauillac)
Haut-Batailley (Pauillac)
Lafon-Rochet (St-Estèphe)
Haut-Marbuzet (St-Estèphe)
Lanessan (Haut-Médoc)
La Louvière (Graves)
Malescot St-Exupéry (Margaux)
Maucaillou (Moulis)
Meyney (St-Estèphe)
Mouton-Baronne-Philippe (Pauillac)

'Le Bol de Cristal' by Chardin, 1758/9, showing the use of the 'solitaire', by means of which a single glass can be washed and dried on the diner's napkin, facilitating the service of a number of wines — and still in use at a table in at least one Bordeaux estate.

Les Ormes-de-Pez *(St-Estèphe)*
Pape-Clément *(Graves)*
Pavie *(St-Emilion)*
Pavillon Rouge de Margaux
Petit-Village *(Pomerol)*
Pichon Baron Longueville
Le Pin *(Pomerol)*
Pontet-Canet *(Pauillac)*
Potensac *(Médoc)*

Poujeaux *(Moulis)*
Pouget *(Margaux)*
Rausan Ségla Rauzan-Gassies *(Margaux)*
Rouget *(Pomerol)*
de Sales *(Pomerol)*
Sociando-Mallet *(Haut-Médoc)*
Soutard *(St-Emilion)*
du Tertre *(Margaux)*

The Clive Coates Classification:

It is, of course, easy to pick holes in other peoples' versions. My own list, published in my book *Claret* (Century, 1982) contains a serious omission. I inadvertently missed out Grand-Puy-Lacoste and have been apologizing to the Borie family ever since! It is also, in retrospect, I find, too biased in favour of the Médoc and the Graves. So here is my revised version. This is based on the quality, reputation and prices of the properties concerned over the past fifteen years or so and with particular reference to their performance in the five years between 1982 and 1986. The wines are listed in alphabetical order within each category. Second wines have not been included.

My classification does not pretend to be either infallible or definitive. It is a personal view of this recurrently discussed topic. I hope, therefore, that it may provoke some further interesting discussion.

Clive Coates' Classification of Bordeaux

First Growths

The Undisputed Top Wines of Bordeaux

Médoc
Ch Lafite
Ch Latour
Ch Margaux
Ch Mouton-Rothschild

Graves
Ch Haut-Brion

Saint-Emilion
Ch Ausone
Ch Cheval-Blanc

Pomerol
Ch Pétrus

Outstanding Growths

These are the super seconds, wines which, more than occasionally, produce wine of first-growth quality. One could argue very forcibly that in terms of absolute quality (if there is such a thing), some at least should be included in the category above. Prices, however, push the First Growths into a category apart.

Médoc
Ch Ducru-Beaucaillou
Ch Cos D'Estournel
Ch Léoville-Lascases

Ch Palmer
Ch Pichon-Longueville,
Comtesse de Lalande

Graves
Domaine de Chevalier
Ch La Mission Haut-Brion

Saint-Emilion
Ch Canon
Ch Figeac
Ch Magdelaine

Pomerol
Vieux Ch Certan
Ch Certan de May
Ch La Conseillante
Ch L'Evangile
Ch Lafleur
Ch Trotanoy

Exceptional Growths

These wines are often as fine as those in the category above and many are clearly of equal standing as a general rule if not as prestigious or as expensive.

Médoc
Ch Beychevelle
Ch Branaire
Ch Cantemerle
Ch Clerc-Milon
Ch Gruaud-Larose
Ch Grand-Puy-Lacoste
Ch D'Issan
Ch La Lagune
Ch Léoville-Barton
Ch Léoville-Poyferré
Ch Lynch-Bages
Ch Pichon-Longueville-Baron
Ch Rausan-Ségla
Ch Saint-Pierre

Graves
Ch de Fieuzal
Ch Haut-Bailly
Ch Malartic-Lagraviére
Ch Pape-Clément

Saint-Emilion
Ch Belair
Ch La Gaffeliére
Ch Pavie

Pomerol
Ch L'Eglise-Clinet
Ch La Fleur-Pétrus
Ch Latour à Pomerol
Ch Petit-Village
Le Pin

Very Fine Growths

Many of these regularly produce wine in the 'Exceptional' category and some, I am sure, will join the ranks above before too long.

Médoc
Ch D'Angludet
Ch Batailley
Ch Boyd-Cantenac
Ch Brane-Cantenac
Ch Calon-Ségur
Ch Chasse-Spleen
Ch Cos-Labory
Ch Desmirail
Ch Duhart-Milon
Ch Durfort-Vivens
Ch Fonbadet
Ch Giscours
Ch Gloria

Ch Grand-Puy Ducasse
Ch Haut-Bages-Libéral
Ch Haut-Batailley
Ch Haut-Marbuzet
Ch Kirwan
Ch Labegorce-Zédé
Ch Lafon-Rochet
Ch Lagrange
Ch Lalande-Borie
Ch Langoa-Barton
Ch Lanessan
Ch Lascombes
Ch Malescot

Ch Marquis-D'Alesme
Ch Marquis-de-Terme
Ch Mouton-Baronne-Philipe
Ch Montrose
Ch de Pez
Ch Pontet-Canet
Ch Pouget
Ch Poujeaux
Ch Prieuré-Lichine
Ch Talbot
Ch du Tertre
Ch La Tour De Mons

Graves
Ch Bouscaut
Ch Carbonnieux
Ch Larrivet-Haut-Brion
Ch La Louvière
Ch La Tour Haut-Brion
Ch La Tour Martillac

Saint-Emilion
Ch L'Angélus
Ch L'Arrosée
Ch Beauséjour-Bécot
Ch Beauséjour-Duffau-Lagarrosse
Ch Cadet-Piola
Ch Canon-La-Gaffelière
Ch Curé-Bon-la-Madelaine

Ch Dassault
Ch La Dominique
Ch Fonroque
Clos Fourtet
Ch Larcis-Ducasse
Ch Larmande
Ch Pavie-Decesse
Ch La Serre
Ch Soutard
Ch Tertre-Daugay
Ch La Tour-Figeac
Ch Troplong-Mondot
Ch Trottevieille

Pomerol
Ch Le Bon-Pasteur
Ch Certan-Guiraud
Ch Clos du Clocher
Clos L'Eglise
Ch Le Gay
Ch Gazin
Ch La Grave-Trigant-de-Boisset
Ch Lagrange
Ch La Pointe
Clos René

Fronsac
Ch Canon *(Moueix)*
Ch Canon-de-Brem

3 WINE AS INSPIRATION IN WORKS OF ART

BOWLS FOR IMBIBERS

by Sally Kevill-Davies

'Immortal Punch
That elevates the Soul,
It makes us Demi Gods
When O'er a Flowing Bowl'
(From a Delftware bowl, dated 1755)

Punch, introduced to England during the second half of the seventeenth century by the merchants of the East India Company, consisted of five ingredients: brandy or rum, heated and mixed with water; sugar; citrus juice; and spice. The name is thought to allude to the Sanskrit word *panche*, meaning 'five'.

In 1746 the Earl of Warwick gave a 'Dallas' style alfresco banquet, where a marble basin was filled with punch which included '80 pints of lemon juice . . . one thousand three hundredweight of sugar . . . and five pounds of nutmeg'. It was served by a boy who floated on the surface in a small rosewood boat. George IV's typically sybaritic version known as 'Regent's Punch' called for 'three bottles of Champagne, two of Madeira, one of Hock, one of Curaçao, one quart of Brandy, one pint of Rum and two bottles of Seltzer-water, flavoured with four pounds of bloom raisins, Seville oranges, lemons, white sugar-candy and diluted with iced green tea instead of water'.

However lethal the ingredients, punch was vastly popular. After four bowls, James Boswell became 'merry to a high degree . . . of which passed I have no recollection of any accuracy'. Hogarth's topers, clustered round their punch bowl in 'A Midnight Modern Conversation', have provided us, with their raucous posturing and convivial collapse, with an enduring icon of eighteenth-century masculine society, and the perfect Victorian Christmas, described by Dickens in *A Christmas Carol* (1843), was not complete without 'seething bowls of punch that made the chamber dim with their delicious steam'.

The bowls from which this irresistible liquid was served — with horn, bone, or ebony and silver ladles — were made in a wide range of materials and sizes. By the end of the seventeenth century trade between China and the west was rapidly increasing. While Queen Mary (daughter of James II and wife to King William 'of Orange') was infecting England with 'Chinamania' or a passion for oriental porcelain, the holds of the East Indiamen, packed with fragile cargoes of tea and silk, were desperate for 'kintledge' or ballast, to make the ships seaworthy. An East India Company order dated 28 January 1702 directed ships' masters that 'it must be your first care to provide kintledge commoditye to stiffen your ship and make her sail worthy . . . with heavy goods proper for that purpose . . . china ware of the useful sorts, especially plates and dishes which stow close. Buy us also some large, some middling, some smaller punch bowls . . . . What hollow chinaware you buy fill up with sago or other more profitable commoditye.'

By 1710 English prototypes were being sent to China to be copied by Chinese potters and among the tea, dinner and dessert services sent to

Chelsea punch bowl of 1770

England were many punch bowls. Some were painted in the Chinese taste, with long-tailed birds, rockwork and flowering peony branches. By the 1730s and 1740s colours were enhanced by the pink enamel introduced to the Chinese by the Jesuits, which gave its name to the style of decoration known as *famille rose*. Blue and white dragons, pagodas on islands, misty mountains and fishermen in sampans also helped to provide the English with an impossibly romantic vision of Cathay, which was later to find its apogee in the Royal Pavilion at Brighton.

More elaborately painted bowls with 'mandarin' figures showed Chinese culture sentimentalized for the European taste, with scenes of venerable patriarchs, mischievous boys, beautiful maidens and merry peasants, dressed in brocaded robes, and engaged in aimless but pleasurable pursuits.

Always skilful copyists, the Chinese were flooded with orders for bowls decorated in the English idiom. Captains of merchantmen ordered portraits of their ships with red ensigns fluttering, and banners with 'Success to' and the ship's name. Merchants ordered bowls painted with the 'Hongs' or European trading posts in Canton, each identifiable by their national flag. In 1769 William Hickey described the port of Canton as 'strikingly grand, and at the same time picturesque ... the scene upon the water is as busy as the Thames below London Bridge ... each factory having the flag of its station on a lofty ensign before it.'

Many more pictures were copied from contemporary engravings sent out to China, including bowls made for the English squirearchy, with scenes of huntsmen, horses and hounds eternally engaged in hot pursuit round the sides. The Chinese interpretation of Europeans was always comical, and bowls painted with the Judgement of Paris show the three goddesses with eccentric anatomical details, including ribcages of Herculean proportions, being judged by a bemused Paris. Scenes from Ovid's *Metamorphoses* and Aesop's *Fables* exist, as do Masonic bowls, and bucolic images of English country life show slant-eyed shepherdesses dallying with Chinamen disguised as haymakers or cherry pickers. Some topographical scenes depict minutely observed views of the Mansion House and Ironmongers' Hall, both in the City of London, and the Palace of Versailles. Bowls with political overtones include those with subjects supporting or opposing the Jacobite cause, or the Wilkes affair, and a few rare examples, for male eyes only, are painted with a 'surprise' concealed under the rim. This was the age of unbridled bawdiness, when men took every possible opportunity to guffaw in groups around a snuff box with a titillating scene hidden inside the lid, or a watch with a stimulating movement, which not only told the time, but showed couples engaged in their own rhythmic movements. Members of the She-Romps Club even dragged passing girls into the precincts of the Club and forced them to walk on their hands so that their skirts fell about their ears. Scenes such as this provided the Chinese decorators with inspiration, and an acrobatic milkmaid without her drawers on the foot of a Chinese punch bowl could be seen as an alternative origin for the jovial salutation 'Bottoms up!'

Aristocratic families sent out drawings of their coats of arms to be copied onto services, which often included punch bowls. The bowls are handsome and imposing, although terrible mistakes occurred and stories (some perhaps apocryphal) abound of the slavish copying of jotted down instructions onto the finished pieces and the mischievous switching of mottoes en route to China, so that a service with the motto 'Think and Thank' was returned two years later inscribed 'Stink and Stank'.

In 1784 the Americans entered the market and began ordering their own bowls painted in sepia with oval vignettes of the Delaware River or Mount Vernon. The American eagle was a very popular motif, as were also the arms of New York and the Society of Cincinnati.

From the start, tin-glazed earthenware, or Delftware, was a popular medium for punch bowls. Principally associated with the Dutch town of Delft, after which it takes its name, it was introduced into England by Dutch potters at the end of the sixteenth century, and was renowned for its soft earthenware body, covered with an opaque milky-white glaze. The earliest English example is dated 1681 and most early bowls were decorated in chinoiserie style or, perhaps, with the arms of a City Livery Company. Later, bowls were painted on the exterior with landscapes, animals, birds, flowers and figures in blue and polychrome.

During the eighteenth century many Delft bowls, particularly from the trading ports of Bristol and Liverpool, were painted with ships, often dated and bearing such inscriptions as: 'God Prosper the THOS. and HANNAH Where Ever She Goes, 1764' and 'Success to the Emsworth, John Sheperd Master, 1757'.

A number of bowls with patriotic or political inscriptions are known, including those commemorating the Crosby and Oliver affair of 1771, and others promoting election candidates, with the words '[Name] For Ever.' The former refers to the occasion when two magistrates from the City of London, Brass Crosby and Richard Oliver, were sent to the Tower of London for acquitting some printers who had been charged with the offence of publishing parliamentary debates. After they were released, in May 1771, they were accorded the status of folk heroes. Probably the best known, however, are those celebrating John Wilkes' publication in 1764 of a scurrilous attack on the King's Speech in his Journal *The North Briton*, a publication of such anarchic venom and popularity that its owner rapidly became the subject of a cause célèbre: such bowls are inscribed 'Wilkes and Liberty' or 'No 45', a reference to the edition of *The North Briton* and not to the 1745 rebellion of Prince Charles Edward Stuart. Jacobite bowls were made, however, as were others loyal to George II, inscribed 'No Pretender 1746' after Bonnie Prince Charlie's defeat at the Battle of Culloden.

Bowls to celebrate betrothals and marriages abound, inscribed with the names of the couples and the year of their marriage and, occasionally, with a verse, poignant in its sweetness and simplicity: 'My heart is Fix'd, I cannot range, I like my choice too well to Change'. Bowls to commemorate a christening are also found and sickly babies were often baptized at home in the family punch bowl in the first days of their uncertain life, before being taken to church some months later for a second baptism, when their fragile life was no longer thought to be in danger.

By far the most common of the inscribed Delftware bowls, however, are those which evoke all the rowdy good humour of the tavern and the club: 'A little more spirit would make this punch good'; 'Fill this Bowl Landlord'; 'One Bowl More and Then. ...'; or 'Drink Fair Don't Sware [sic]' are often found, along with other extravert exhortations in rambling and misspelt doggerel sounding, literally, punch-drunk! Large bowls were difficult to fire in English porcelain, so much softer and less stable than its Chinese counterpart, and although bowls of eight or nine inches (about twenty or twenty-three centimetres) were made by most of the English porcelain factories, the lack of inscriptions makes it difficult to ascribe their use, particularly in relation to punch, although some larger examples do exist.

Punch bowls also occur made in Staffordshire salt-glazed stoneware, brown-glazed Nottingham stoneware and Sunderland lustreware of the first half of the nineteenth century. Fine cream-coloured earthenware, known as creamware, was manufactured in large quantities during the last quarter of the eighteenth century in Leeds, and also by Josiah Wedgwood at his factory in Etruria in Staffordshire, and it was also used for punch bowls, often with a black transfer-printed decoration.

Glass bowls are found from the end of the seventeenth to the nineteenth century and later examples of these often have engraved decoration.

Wooden bowls, usually of turned *lignum vitae* (the term, meaning 'wood of life', refers to two tropical American trees whose wood is very hard and attractively stripey), are also known as wassail bowls; this word, from Old English, meaning 'Be of health!' became associated with Christmas — hence the carol 'Here we come a-wassailing' — and refreshments offered to the singers who went from house to house or, sometimes, into the orchard to serenade the fruit trees so that they 'may bear Full many a plum and many a pear' (a somewhat pagan survival this). Wassail bowls sometimes have covers with a knob on the top, in the form of a spice box — to season the wassail itself — and occasionally they are found with turned spindles, to hold upturned dipper cups when these were not in use for drinking.

Silver punch bowls were for the tables of the aristocracy. Late seventeenth-century examples have engraved chinoiserie birds and figures, while slightly later ones have armorial engravings and rims ribbed for greater strength; they sometimes had a detachable 'coronet', which turned them into a wine glass cooler or 'Monteith', when required. The term was first used in 1683, by Anthony à Wood, an eccentric Oxford diarist and antiquarian, who noted that 'this year in the Summer-time came up a vessel or bason notched at the brims to let drinking vessels hang there by the foot so that the body or drinking place might hang into the water to cool them. Such a bason was called a "Monteigh" from a fantastical Scot called Monsieur Monteigh who at that time, or a little before, wore the bottoms of his cloaks or coats, so notched.' Our image of eighteenth-century dinners is of sauces and conversation congealed with the cold, but we forget the heat that must have been generated by the scores of candles, open fires, braziers and chafing dishes. Winter ice, gathered from frozen lakes and ponds and stored in subterranean ice-houses, thatched with turf, was at a premium and to chill glasses in iced water was considered fashionable and efficacious. Early silver examples of this kind of cooler were circular, with eight wide notches round the rim, and had gadrooned sides. Later examples were oval, with notches sometimes in the shape of Victorian scrolls, and double lion mask handles. Monteiths are also found made in copper, brass, toleware, Delftware, creamware, Chinese porcelain and Sheffield plate. Also known as Pontypool or Usk-ware, because of the locality of its origin, toleware was tin-plated sheet iron laboriously covered with a hard-glossed heat-resistant varnish, which could then be painted with a variety of scenes.

Individual wine glass coolers became fashionable after they were used at the Coronation Banquet of George III in 1761. They were subsequently banned from court because those with Jacobite sympathies had been seen raising their charged glasses and passing them over the coolers during the Loyal Toast to the sovereign — thus symbolically drinking to 'The King — over the water'; the swift gesture was less defiant and provocative than actually waving a glass over a large cooler or water jug. These individual coolers were only restored to court and fashionable tables by King Edward VII in 1905. They were known as 'water-glasses' until about 1790 and were often accompanied by 'water-plates'. Clearly, they were not always correctly used and in 1766 Tobias Smollett, in his *Travels* thundered that he 'knew of no custom more beastly than that of using water-glasses in which polite Society spirt, and squirt, and spue the filthy scourings of their gums'. Not to be confused with plain circular 'wash hand glasses', otherwise known as fingerbowls, coolers had either one or two lips in the rim on which to rest the stems of the glasses so that the bowls came down into the water. Some were plain, others cut with facets, flutes and neo-classical border decoration; amethyst and Bristol blue glass examples are known, the latter sometimes with a gilt border around the rim. Nineteenth-century instructions to butlers stipulated that 'hock and champagne glasses are to be placed in the cooler, two wine glasses upon the table'. The use of an individual cooler facilitated the service of several wines, for sometimes these bowls are known as 'solitaires', the diner rinses his glass, dries it with his napkin and can use it again for a different wine. (I have been informed that 'solitaires' were and probably still are in use at Château Langoa-Barton, in the Médoc.) Bowls of

Large glass punch bowl, dated 1790

this type tend usually to be somewhat deeper than ordinary fingerbowls, because the length of the stem of the wine glass necessitated this.

Once the ladies had left the table to drink tea in the drawing-room, it was time for the sideboard cupboard to be opened and another bowl, larger and with one handle, would be passed round with the port. Most self-respecting sideboards contained at least one chamberpot in one of the cupboards, although other pots could be concealed in compartments in the panelling of the dining-room, or in classical pedestals conceived as columns or surmounted by urns, which flanked the sideboard. A French visitor with a fancy name and sensitive manner, François de la Richefoucauld-Liancourt, noted with disgust that 'nothing is hidden, I think it most indecent'. But alcohol is a diuretic and the chamberpot had become as much a part of eighteenth-century life as the punch bowl.

'Since Drinking has Power
To Give us Relief
Come Fill up the Bowl,
& a Pox on all Grief.
If that won't do,
We'll have Another,
& so we'll Proceed
From one Bowl to the Other'
(From an English Delft punch bowl, dated 1740)

SMALL SILVER IN THE SERVICE OF WINE

by Judith Banister

Since man first learned to extract silver from its ore and to alloy it as a lustrous grey and durable metal, it has been inextricably linked with wine. From Europe to Cathay cups, bowls, flasks and ewers were in demand from at least the third millenium BC, and centuries later the Romans, Anglo-Saxons, Normans and, in England, the Plantagenet 'royals', used the metal lavishly for all kinds of drinking and serving vessels, as can be judged from the archaeological finds and the many chance survivals that are to be seen in numerous museums in various countries as well as Britain.

By the sixteenth century, the art of the Renaissance made even more lavish use of silver — often enhanced with gilding — some examples happily surviving in public and private collections. There was, of course, no tradition then of collecting old silver; those who could afford it had their cups, bowls, beakers and jugs remade as fashion dictated new styles. It was only rarely that a 'cupboardful of plate', such as Samuel Pepys boasted in the seventeenth century, remained intact, though those that did were probably preserved as a type of bank, which would provide so much bullion to be converted into coinage in time of emergency, whether personal or public — such as the Civil War (the conflict between the Crown and the Parliamentarians in Britain in the mid seventeenth century.) Many families and institutions had their plate melted down at this time.

Even so, the present-day collector of English silver has a reasonably large choice, even of seventeenth-century date, if his subject is small silver in the service of wine. For our ancestors silver, whether for ecclesiastical, ceremonial or domestic use, had the advantage of being a safe metal, that did not taint the liquid, as well as being hard-wearing, beautiful — and unbreakable.

The 'King's coming into his own again' occurred in 1660. Charles II's return from exile saw an upsurge in domestic silver of all kinds, much of it concentrated on articles made specifically for wine — setting aside those used for beer, punch and spirit-based liquors — there survive examples of objects great and small, from the capacious wine cisterns and fountains, coolers, jugs and flagons, to goblets, beakers, tumblers, sugar caskets and accessories such as corkscrews, wine funnels, and wine tasters. A good cellar, whether of imported or homemade wines (and these latter were a major part of the gentlewoman's repertoire, as E Smith's *The Compleat Housewife*, first published in the 1720s and in its eighteenth edition by 1773, so cogently reveals) was the aim of all who aspired to be gentlemen. For the most part, in the seventeenth century wine was still matured solely in cask, so that when, on 19 January 1663, Pepys visited a Mr Povey and saw his wine cellar 'where upon several shelves there stood bottles of all sorts of wine, new and old, with labels pasted upon each bottle', he was most impressed. Indeed, by the late autumn of the same year he had, perhaps not unexpectedly, imitated the

Wager cup in silver gilt by Joseph Angel, 1827. The girl's skirt forms another cup which, when the figure is upended, must be emptied as well as the cup suspended between the boughs — slightly 'naughty'.

Small wine cup of 1655, with matted flower decoration and 'trumpet' foot (because of the shape).

ambitious politician Povey and went 'to Mr Rawlinson's and saw some of my Bottles made with my Crest upon them, filled with wine, about five or six dozen.' These bottles, which probably had glass seals bearing the crest on their shoulders, allowed the quality of the wine to be judged more easily, although it still needed to be tasted (or tested) before decanting.

The 'taster', perhaps because it was relatively small and light, as well as being a personal piece of silver used by vintner, wine cooper, cellarman or householder alike to judge the wine drawn from cask or jar, has survived, even pre-Civil War examples existing, though, unhappily, there are none as early as that recorded in 1420 as 'a tastour of selver with myn own merke ymade in ye bottom'. One of the earliest tasters known is that of 1631 in the Jackson Collection (in Cardiff), engraved with the name 'John Hine', perhaps a vintner; not a few, well into the nineteenth century, bear such inscriptions, sometimes adding the title or address of the taster's owner.

Recently, some doubt has been expressed about applying the term 'wine taster' to the little two-handled bowls or saucer-like dishes, of which large numbers, dating from about 1610 to around 1700, are still available to collectors. One of the first to doubt was Michael Clayton, in his *Dictionary* (Country Life Books, 1971), while Philippa Glanville, in her *Silver in England* (Unwin Hyman, 1987) firmly refers to them as 'saucers' or 'dram cups', both authors, it appears, restricting the term 'wine taster' to the one-eared variety in the French style (the *tastevin* familiar to many today and now mainly associated with Burgundy), or else the small bowl with a domed centre (such

There can, however, be no doubt about the latter type of 'taster', of which a few pre-Restoration examples have survived. A particularly interesting example of 1647 was found some years ago on the foreshore of the River Thames, near Southwark Bridge; it is typical in form, four inches (about ten

Small two-handled dish, dating from 1659, during the Commonwealth, chased with bunches of grapes and bearing the maker's mark 'HB' in monogram. It may have been used as a 'taster' by a housewife, in the days when many establishments made their own 'wines' from a variety of produce.

centimetres) in diameter and weighing two point eight ounces Troy (eighty-seven grams), maker's mark 'WT' between two annulets, and is engraved with the name 'Edward Drury'. The domed centre enabled the vintner to judge the colour and clarity of the wine and the pattern remained popular well into the nineteenth century, though with the arrival of the Huguenot craftsmen at the end of the seventeenth century (when so many left France in order to practise their religion in freedom) a few tasters were then made in the continental style, often with a single handle formed as a ring, a shell, or a coiled snake.

The small, two-handled 'dram cup' or 'saucer' should not, perhaps, be wholly discounted as a piece of silver used in conjunction with the cellar or the kitchen, especially when examples are decorated with bunches of grapes and vine leaves. This type of 'tester' may have been used by the housewife to judge the clarity and colour of her own homemade wines, or, it would now be correct to term them, many of them 'country wines', as these, made from a variety of fruits and farm produce, exercised her skill. It is interesting to note that, of the small two-handled saucer dishes that are nowadays often called wine tasters, made between about 1650 and 1685, not a few were obviously treasured in households and, later, re-engraved, even as late as 1710, with names and initials, being, presumably, family heirlooms; one of these, engraved 'Simon Yorke' was left by the will of Elizabeth Yorke of Erddig to 'my nephew' in 1636.

An essential in the cellar was the wine funnel — for bottling or decanting. Most early examples, dating from the 1680s, were quite small, light and plain, of conical form with a straight funnel, between two and a half and four and a half inches (six to eleven centimetres) in height and weighing between a half and two ounces Troy (fifteen to sixty-two grams). Like the wine taster, the funnel was apparently considered a personal piece of plate and often bore the owner's initials or, in grander households, a crest or armorials. It is possible that the very small funnels were used for decanting toilet waters rather than wine. The conical style continued well into the eighteenth century, the more familiar pattern with a compressed bowl and curved spout not appearing until the middle of the century, soon to be followed by the two-piece variety, which allowed for easier cleaning. Being functional, most funnels were plain, with perhaps a rounded rim and border to the base of the bowl, though occasionally, by the end of the century, a fluted stem might be a feature or, even, a bowl might be fluted and ogee-shaped. Bowls generally were finely pierced and sometimes a muslin was inserted between the bowl and funnel. By 1800 funnels were generally larger and heavier and were sometimes accompanied by a stand; the average size was between five and six inches (twelve point seven to fifteen point two centimetres) in height, weighing perhaps five or six ounces (140 or 170 grams), but an exception must surely be the eleven and three-quarter inches (thirty centimetres), thirteen point three ounces Troy (155–186 grams), funnel with a chased anthemion mount applied to the bowl (anthemion signifies a floral design): this was made by Paul Storr in 1816 for Rundell, Bridge & Rundell, perhaps being intended for use with a magnum decanter holding the equivalent of two bottles.

Once bottled or decanted the wine needed to be labelled and, with improved glass being made, the fashion grew for silver bottle tickets or wine labels to be used to indicate the contents of the vessels in the dining-room. The earliest type, dating from the 1730s, was of cartouche shape, either plain or chased with vine motifs, the name being boldly engraved in the centre. Few bear more than the maker's mark and the lion passant, until the advent of the duty mark in 1784 and most were made by smallworkers, early London makers of note being Sandylands Drinkwater and Richard Binley and his widow Margaret. As the century progressed so did the range of styles made, either singly or in sets, and to silver were added labels in old Sheffield plate, the problem of engraving revealing the copper base being overcome by blacking in the letters of the inscription.

Many of the decanter labels from the latter half of the eighteenth century had the wine names pierced instead of engraved and, by the early 1800s, massive cut glass decanters and claret jugs brought in the fashion for massive, often gilded, labels. The period also saw heavy cast shells, quatrefoils, crowned Royal lions and other highly decorative patterns, the wine names being pierced or sometimes applied, as well as the plethora of designs — grand and not so grand — that poured out of the smallworkers' shops from London to Edinburgh and every other silversmithing centre in Britain, not forgetting the 'toymen' of Birmingham and the silversmiths of Dublin.

Much rarer than the decanter labels were silver-mounted corks, though these only rarely featured the wine name, most simply alluding to wine by use of vine branches of grapes or, perhaps, a boy on a barrel. These stoppers usually had a screw-thread between the upper part and a base mount, so that the cork could be replaced as necessary.

For the butler — literally the man in charge of the cellar — a corkscrew was as vital as his taster and funnel. The bottle-screw, as it was first known, is occasionally of silver and Dr Jonathan Swift actually had one of gold, which he bequeathed to the Reverend Mr Robert Grattan, who had originally given it to him. The usual form, unchanged basically until the invention of the patent versions that allowed the screw to continue turning after reaching the bottom of the cork and so extract the cork without pulling it, was a screw with a T-shaped handle, a pattern that was often made in miniature in silver for inclusion in travelling sets, so necessary for those journeying to places where cups, spoons and forks and other tableware might be 'doubtful'.

A rarity from the cellar was the wine syphon, of which several of about 1750, made by the silversmith Thomas Harache, are recorded, the cellarman using the mouthpiece to draw the wine along the curved tube. One example has the additional refinement of a tap, which can be turned one half-turn to open or close the pipe. A similar tap was incorporated in a wine syphon with pump action made by smallworkers Phipps and Robinson in 1809. Another rarity is the barrel tap or spigot, devised probably at the end of the eighteenth century: one example of 1798 was exhibited at Goldsmiths' Hall in the City of London in 1983; it had a small bore, suggesting its use was for wine rather than ale, and with a detachable head so that it could not be used by thirsty servants. The idea was developed in 1874, when William H Ryder of Ellis Street, Birmingham, registered his design for 'A plug and perforator for Tap or Cock' with a long pin and tap which could be used to penetrate Champagne corks and draw off the wine.

Once out of cask or bottle and even after the development of good lead crystal glass by Ravenscroft, many drinkers preferred to use silver cups for wine, silver being renowned for its purity as well as being less fragile than glass — though the never-to-be unfashionable Samuel Pepys recorded in 1666 that he was buying drinking glasses and on 13 November recorded having a 'glass of wine'. Nonetheless, the admirer of English silver has a wide range of cups suitable for wine to choose from, ranging from small tumblers — round-based cups which literally tumble back to upright if knocked — to 'beakers full of the warm south' and elegant baluster-stemmed wine cups. At least today's oenophile, whether using silver or glass for his wine, has no need of the sugar casket to ameliorate the taste of rough and maybe somewhat uncertain products of his cellar!

Tumbler — self-righting if tipped — dated 1693, with the maker's mark 'SH' in monogram, probably the initials of Samuel Hood, and showing a typical inscription of the period, with surname above, and the initials of the husband and wife below.

SCRATCHING THE SURFACE

by Nicholas Rootes

The drinking glass has played an important part in history — sometimes more than is appreciated. It is the means whereby we convey drink to our mouths and, as such, it has been raised on countless occasions to cement the bonds of friendship, to commemorate past events or toast future success. The glass, appropriately engraved, has emerged as an ideal medium for transmitting symbolic messages of goodwill and it has been used for this purpose since antiquity.

The Romans of Classical times commemorated the achievements of champion charioteers and gladiators by drinking copious quantities of wine from glasses engraved in a way to honour the victor and, after a lapse of several centuries during the Dark Ages, European craftsmen rediscovered engraving and developed new techniques. From the sixteenth century onwards the art of glass engraving was revived and drinking glasses of all shapes and sizes were engraved, to suit a variety of purposes.

There were armorial and masonic emblems, often engraved on large goblets, suitable for passing round among a number of people assembled together. There were engravings that commemorated monarchs, living or deceased; engravings showing or referring to statesmen, to battles and to treaties; other engravings might be family recordings of births, baptisms and marriages. There were glasses specially engraved for clubs and associations, countless drinking glasses being commissioned for members, and, of course, there were glasses that were engraved simply to display the exuberance of decoration and the skill of the craftsman.

Several techniques existed for creating different types of an engraved effect. Wheel engraving was described in the first century AD. The principle is straightforward: a copper wheel, coated with an abrasive material, is rotated on a lathe and when a glass vessel is held up to the wheel its surface is incised. Diamond-point engraving is even less complicated: a hand-tool with a diamond nib is used to scratch a design on the surface of the glass. Of course, easy as it sounds, nothing would be achieved without the creative skill of the artist who, at worst, breaks the glass — and at best creates a masterpiece.

Stipple engraving is a newer technique, pioneered in Holland during the early eighteenth century. The surface of the glass is tapped with a sharp instrument to build up a picture made of thousands of dots. As in newsprint, tone is created by the density of the dots but, since the medium is glass, refraction imparts an etherial quality to great effect.

Before the invention of lead glass, engraving was a hazardous business, as the lime soda glass made by the Murano glasshouses in north Italy, which was both exported and subsequently copied throughout Europe, was brittle and liable to break. Nevertheless, engraving was attempted. Glassware had been made in Venice from around AD 450, when glassmakers from Aquileia fled

German royal armorial goblet with cover, engraved in Potsdam about 1720–23, bearing the motto and arms of George I of England, first of the Hanoverian kings.

there escaping from Attila the Hun. In 1292 glassmakers were forced to remove their establishments from Venice itself to Murano by edict, because the presence of their furnaces was a definite fire risk, which, on the nearby island of Murano, was lessened. A Bohemian priest, Johannes Methesius, observed in 1562 that 'Nowadays all sorts of festooning and handsome lines are drawn on the nice and bright Venetian glass.' Indeed, Bohemia, at that time part of the Austrian Hapsburg Empire and now part of Czechoslovakia, became the centre for the revival of engraving techniques so long forgotten. It was entirely appropriate that the Bohemians enjoyed engraving their drinking glasses so much — given their fantastic thirst (a tradition that persists, via beer drinking, to this day) and also their fondness for producing differently decorated beakers with which to toast every sort of social occasion. There were 'Welcome' cups to be drunk to the health of guests arriving, there were 'Come again' cups to be raised to those leaving, as well as many moments in between the beginning and end of some celebration that would call for glasses being raised to salute the company.

Kaspar Lehmann is credited with the reintroduction of wheel engraving at the end of the eighteenth century and, in recognition of his services, the Emperor Rudolf II rewarded him with the hereditary title of Glass Engraver to the Imperial Court. Perhaps because of the expense of glass, royal patronage was essential in those early days and when Rudolf II moved his court to Vienna from Prague in 1612, that city's importance as a glassmaking centre declined. However, the fashion for engraved glass was spreading and Lehmann's one-time pupil, Georg Schwanhardt, moved to Nuremberg in 1622 and there combined the effects of wheel and diamond-point engraving to decorate vessels with landscapes framed in baroque scrollwork.

Despite the extraordinary engraving skills displayed by Lehmann and Schwanhardt, working on soda lime glass was a limiting factor. Then, in 1685, it was discovered that glass could be made more durable and brilliant in appearance by replacing soda — the alkali ingredient in glass — with potash. This permitted greater scope in engraving techniques and, in particular, the development of wheel engraving designs in high relief and, also, the reverse of this — *intaglio*, where the ground is left in relief and the design is deeply engraved, or *hochschnitt* and *tiefschnitt* as the Germans succinctly describe the processes. The two leading practitioners of this style were the brothers Friedrich and Martin Winter, who decorated drinking vessels, such as *pokals* in this manner: the *pokal* was a typ of large goblet with a cover and it was used like a loving cup. When filled with drink, it would be passed ceremoniously around from one member of the company to another, to symbolize the bond of friendship existing between the guests at a gathering.

Dissatisfaction with soda lime glass also spurred English glassmakers to experiment with new ingredients. Before the development of 'lead' glass by George Ravenscroft, English glassmaking was derivative of the Venetian style and large quantities of drinking glasses were imported from Venice. Jacopo Verzelini's 'Crutched Friars Glasshouse' in London produced glasses which were engraved, probably by Anthony de Lysle, between 1577 and 1586, but it was not until 1681, when Ravenscroft's lead glass was finally perfected, that engraving techniques developed beyond the use of diamond-point.

Just as Venetian glass had become prized throughout Europe, the fame of lead glass now extended beyond the boundaries of Britain, particularly to the

Low Countries. Diamond-point engraving on brittle Dutch glass had already been practised during the seventeenth century by keen amateurs, such as Anna Roemers Visscher and Willem Jacobz Van Heemskerk, both of whom worked in a calligraphic style inscribing the glasses they decorated with an intertwining script. The new generation, however, began to engrave in lead glass blocks imported from England. Jacob Sang worked in Amsterdam until his death, in 1783, wheel engraving drinking glasses from Newcastle with motifs that commemorated family events — such as the birth of a baby, or a marriage. Frans Greenwood, a skilled amateur engraver, pioneered stipple engraving, copying his designs from contemporary prints — and once Frans Greenwood had shown what could be done with stipple engraving, others followed. The most talented worker and artist was David Wolff, a painter by training, whose work dates from the last quarter of the eighteenth century; he made his own designs and specialized in portraits of notable people. Followers of his style were numerous and many engravings, which are not directly attributable to him, are generically referred to as 'Wolff glass.' As might be expected from a sophisticated mercantile society, the wealthy Dutch were keen to commission and collect engraved glasses and, in the paintings of the period, many types of drinking glasses are shown.

Meanwhile, in England, politics, as well as thirst, inspired a proliferation of engraved drinking glasses. During the first half of the eighteenth century and even beyond, there was strong support for the restoration of the Stuart line of succession, which had been ousted by the 'Glorious Revolution' of 1688, when King James II fled from England to France, giving way to 'King Billy' — William of Orange and his wife, Mary, James's daughter.

Henceforth, many a Scotsman — the Scots had been adherents to the Stuarts since the middle of the seventeenth century and the Civil War — plus sympathetic Englishmen who found themselves unable to accept the claim to the throne of William, son of the English Princess Mary of England and husband to the daughter of James's first wife, split allegiance. 'Divine right' of the 'anointed king' and his progeny was still respected and strong: those who were henceforth to be known as 'Jacobites' — loyal to the Stuarts — would continue to pledge themselves to this cause; conversely, patriots loyal to the newly established monarchy — William and Mary — toasted King William. This split of allegiance in which, it should not be forgotten, many still believe today, is something that is commemorated even after the centuries in that easily shattered commodity — glass.

The 1715 and 1745 uprisings of the Jacobites may have been fought and lost in the field, but, for many years after these defeats, the Stuarts were remembered and toasted at table in glasses appropriately engraved, even though to pledge support to the Stuarts in such a way was a treasonable offence, punishable by death. The symbolic Jacobite engravings on glass conveyed messages of support for the cause to those who were familiar with the interpretation of the signs: a wheel-engraved rose, with one or two buds springing from the stem, was the most common emblem used, the rose signifying the Crown of England (harking back, maybe, to the Tudor linked white and red roses); the buds represented the Old Pretender and the Young Pretender — more romantically known as Bonnie Prince Charlie. Carnations, sunflowers and thistles were other Jacobite emblems and creatures, such as birds, butterflies and bees, symbolized 'the return of the soul' — or of the movement, in reference to Charles Edward Stuart.

Each Jacobite club or society, of which there were many (there are still some to this day), had its own motto and every member was supplied with his own drinking glass. One of the most famous was the Cycle Club, where each glass was engraved with a star and the word *Fiat* meaning 'May it come to pass' (ie the restoration of the Stuarts) and each member kissed his glass upon making his solemn pledge of loyalty. Similarly the Oak Society, which met at The Crown and Anchor Inn in the Strand in London, adopted the word *Redeat* as its motto — 'Let him return!' Other glasses carried a portrait of Prince Charlie in full Highland dress, and the motto *Audientor Ibo* which may be translated as 'I shall go more boldly'.

The rarest and earliest type of 'Jacobite' glass, however, that is still in existence is the 'Amen' glass, of which there are probably no more than thirty extant. Typically, such a glass will be engraved with the Stuart royal cypher 'JR 8', set beneath a crown and reversed, in reference to the Old Pretender, James Edward Stuart, as James VIII of Scotland. This engraving is accompanied by two or more verses of the Jacobite hymn, which is an altered version of the present British National Anthem, with a final 'amen'.

But even at table the Jacobites were outmanoeuvred via glass, for the Protestant supporters of William and Mary retaliated with glasses engraved with emblems commemorating William's victory over James II at the Battle of the Boyne in 1690. Such glasses were usually decorated with an equestrian portrait of the monarch and an inscription, or with a Williamite emblem, such as an orange tree. The way in which men tacitly indicated their allegiance at table — such as by passing their glasses over a water jug or cooler ('the King — over the water!') is indicated elsewhere in this book.

But the link between drink and politics was not merely confined to issues such as the succession of the monarchy. Protests against the Earl of Bute's cider tax were also engraved on glass when this was instigated in 1763. At this time, the popular radical, John Wilkes (1727–1797) was a thorn in the side of the government of the day and, although cider had been previously deemed to be a somewhat humble country drink, it became a 'radical-chic' symbol of opposition to the government's policies: cider was therefore temporarily elevated to fashionable status (it had always enjoyed prestige in the regions where it was made) and it was drunk out of glasses that were engraved with the words 'No excise'.

Happily, the majority of people drank simply for the enjoyment of drinking and, consequently, many glasses were engraved with appropriate symbols of their intended contents, or else purely for the sake of decoration. These glasses, commonly referred to as 'flowered' glassware, were popular in eighteenth-century England. Ale glasses — which, in the days when ale might be high in alcoholic strength, were often on tall stems with small bowls — were often wheel engraved with ears of barley and hop blooms; cider glasses might have engravings of apple boughs, or the codlin moth; wine glasses show vine leaves and bunches of grapes. Other glasses might be decorated with flowers or floral festoons. The ale glasses of the eighteenth century had small bowls, usually of an elongated funnel shape, because of the strength of the liquor. Cider glasses from the same period often have 'bucket' bowls.

The first records of glassmaking in North America date back to the beginning of the seventeenth century, but European glass was imported, in

'Sir Bourchier Wrey' by George Knapton, 1744, the bowl bearing an inscription from one of the *Odes* of Horace to the effect that 'It is sweet on occasion to play the fool'.

Wine in Paintings
Three pictures selected by Robert Cumming illustrate totally different aspects of wine as shown in works of art.
Right below 'The Marriage Feast at Cana' by Murillo
Overleaf above 'Maidservant Drawing Wine' by Gerard Dou
Overleaf below 'A La Mie' by Henri de Toulouse-Lautrec

Wine is seldom the central feature in works of art, except for still life studies. It does often form a focal point of light and different texture. In Murillo's 'The Marriage Feast at Cana' the occasion of the first miracle of Jesus, when, at the wedding feast after the wine ran out, Jesus turned the water in nearby jars into the best wine of all, the servants are using water pots of a fairly modest size, instead of the big jars that were customarily available for ablutions in a Jewish household in New Testament times. Domestic occupations have often been interesting to painters and although there is nothing to indicate the type of wine that is being drawn from the cask in Gerard Dou's painting, this is also something visitors to wine regions may often still see. The obviously coarse 'gros rouge' in Toulouse-Lautrec's painting stresses the poverty and pathos of the situation: the title refers to the 'crumb' (*mie*) of the loaf and, in this context, signifies something of no value.

Jacobite goblet, dating from about 1750, with a portrait of Charles Edward Stuart in Highland dress, with the motto *Audientor ibo* 'I shall go forth more boldly'.

quantity, until American glass began to be produced in 1827, when the New England Glass Company started to manufacture press-moulded glass in Cambridge, Massachusetts. Before the invention of mass-produced glassware, the embryonic North American industry was influenced by the migration of a number of German glassmakers, who arrived in the country during the second half of the eighteenth century. Henry William Stiegel and John Frederick Amelung were among the most influential and important of these; both of them produced — among other vessels — drinking glasses that were finely engraved and derivative of the European, particularly Bohemian, style. Amelung's most famous piece was a giant *pokal* or loving cup, made and engraved in 1788 and sent over to Germany so as to demonstrate to his backers the quality of the output of his factory.

The Bohemian style was demonstrated in the next century by Louis F Vaugel, another German immigrant, who worked for thirty-two years as master glassmaker to the New England Glass Company. His early engravings were on uncoloured glass, but later he engraved ruby coloured 'flash' glass —

A massive goblet, dated 1940, engraved in diamond-point by Laurence Whistler, after a design made by his brother, Rex Whistler, who was killed in World War II. The view is of Godmersham Park, Kent.

that is, glass which has been dipped in molten coloured glass, which forms a thin layer over the body of the vessel. When engraved, the 'flashing' is cut away, to reveal the glass underneath, the design contrasting with the coloured outer layer. This decorative effect was typical of the German Biedermeier style, which revived the fortunes of Bohemian glass factories in the first half of the nineteenth century.

The twentieth century has been a fertile period for engraved glass internationally, some of the best work resulting from the commissioning of designs from artists and sculptors by leading glass manufacturers. In 1916, the Swedish establishment Orrefors employed two artists, Simon Gate and Edward Gald, to design their glassware. Then, in 1933, Steuben Glass Inc, at Corning in New York State, began a similar experiment: the sculptor Sidney B Waugh was engaged to exploit the inherent beauty of a newly developed crystal glass with imaginative design. Many of the wares from this establishment were engraved and Waugh's designs began to receive international acclaim. Waugh's first works for Steuben were shown at the Paris Exhibition of 1937, where they attracted a great deal of attention, including that of the artist Henri Matisse, who agreed to make a design to be engraved on glass.

Another artist who has worked on Steuben glass is Laurence Whistler, who is also a poet and writer; it is he who has been responsible for the revival of interest in stipple engraving in England. Since the 1930s he has been an independent engraver, at first often working on old glass, but after World War II (in which his brother, the distinguished artist Rex Whistler, was killed) he has been decorating shapes mainly blown to his own specification. His early work was usually inscriptional or emblematic, but since then he has turned his hand to depicting English country houses and landscapes.

The progress of European history can, to a great extent, be traced by studying the engravings on drinking glasses. It would be reasonable to assume that the days of overtly political glass engraving are over, but then — what the future has in store is anybody's guess! Engraved goblets are currently enjoying popularity as commemorative gifts, for weddings, anniversaries of various kinds, or retirement presentations to distinguished persons who have contributed to the arts and academic institutions, for christenings and for occasions when a group of people wish to honour a friend or colleague who already may 'have everything'. Recently, the eminent wine writer, Cyril Ray, founder and first President of the British Circle of Wine Writers, was presented with an engraved glass on his eightieth birthday — Bella Spurrier the wife of the chairman of the Circle did the engraving! Even a simple inscription can enhance what is anyway a beautiful object — a glass drinking vessel.

A WINDOW OF WINE

The Editor finds a treasure at Vintners' Hall

Some works of art give such an impression of rightness, inevitability, that they seem to have come into existence instantaneously, with a wave of the creator's hand. The new window in Vintners' Hall, in the City of London, is like this. The delicate definition of the engraving, the detail that progressively rewards the eye, all seem as if they might have emanated in a moment from the magical atmosphere conjured up by fine wines during a good dinner.

In fact it was at one of the dinners of the Vintners' Company that the window had its inception. The then Master of The Vintners Company, M H Fairbank, was sitting next to Paul Wates, chairman of Wates in the City; this mighty building concern had been working in association with the Vintners' Company, developing parts of the property in the vicinity of the Hall. This section of the bank of the River Thames has been involved with wine since early medieval times, when the Bordeaux wine fleet would arrive in the autumn with the new vintage; the first Charter of the Vintners' Company (15 July 1364) was a grant of monopoly for trade with Gascony, the English having the right to buy herring and cloth for resale to the Gascons from the south west of France (an area which of course then belonged to the English crown). The Hall itself was destroyed in the Great Fire of London in 1666, but rebuilt, although building and rebuilding in the small area of 'Vintry Ward' as it is described in John Stow's *Survey* of 1598, made the environs somewhat chaotic, even prior to the fortunately slight damage of World War II, after which the Victorian glass was removed from the Hall windows.

Paul Wates apparently looked up at one of the tall windows, with its plain glass, and remarked 'Something should be done.' So, together with the Vintners' Company, the idea of the window began. Michael Fairbank had become familiar with the work of Hugh Whitwell, who had engraved glass at Sutton Vallence and other places, after himself leaving a post in the promotional department of one of the big drink organizations; he was an innovator in that he evolved his engravings so that, as windows, they can be viewed from the front, light coming through from outside. People inside the building can therefore examine them both in daylight or by artificial light. Hugh, albeit an unorthodox worker in glass engraving, already knew and admired a designer who, even while still young, had made a reputation and been awarded many honours in the world of glass, notably in her native New Zealand. This was Beverley Shore Bennett, an artist whose grandfather had always worked in stained glass. The personal histories of both Hugh Whitwell and Beverley Shore Bennett are as fascinating as their work. Both had created works of art in churches, Beverley's including windows in Christchurch, at Russell in the Bay of Islands, and nave windows now being completed for the Cathedral in Napier, among many others.

The Vintners' Hall window is described by Beverley as 'a celebration of wine, not the wine itself, but all the aspects which go into its creation: the

vines ... the people, the creation of the wine itself; the miracle which represents the transformation of water, earth and sunshine into wine.'

Michael Fairbank is having prepared a detailed written 'key' or plan to the whole window, which will be in the shape of a bottle, with handles, so that visitors can examine the panels, though as the Hall is being closed for cleaning, it will not be until 1990 that the window can be seen in its superb setting. It is a sight worth waiting for! The different shades that the engraver has managed to convey make it quite definite as to which of the grape varieties shown is white, which black, and the swans almost dazzle with the 'whiter than white' of their plumage. At the top of the window there are the initials 'J C'. Apparently Mrs Shore Bennett explained that she had hoped that we humans might find the Christian Saviour revealed through humble things, as in 'Love Joy' by the seventeenth-century writer and divine, George Herbert:

'As on a window late I cast mine eye,
I saw a vine drop grapes with J and C
Annealed on every branch. One standing by
Ask'd what it meant. I who am never loth
To spend my judgement said, It seemed to me
To be the bodie and the letters both
Of Joy and Charitie. Sir you have not missed,
The man reply'd: It figures Jesus Christ.'

Mrs Shore Bennett, who in 1977 was installed as the first woman lay Canon of Wellington Cathedral, hesitated when mentioning this to the Vintners' Company who, she wondered, might be unwilling to make such a declaration of a specific religious faith — but the initials did also stand for 'Joy and Charity', both properties of wine, she said. The Vintners' were delighted by both the window and the sentiments: thus the window is 'signed' in this way.

Although the panels are immediately understandable to any wine lover, it is perhaps of interest to add some information about the other symbols shown. The swans at the base, each proudly bearing a bunch of grapes around its neck, are part of the arms of the Vintners' Company. They have owned swans on the River Thames since before records were kept, the Junior Warden caring for the birds (particularly essential in some of the severe winters of the past, when they had to be taken out of the river). The Swan Marker is in charge of putting two 'nicks' on the beak of each bird, to denote who owns it. (These markings are, nowadays, carefully done so as to avoid any suffering — although the task of those doing the marking is by no means without perils, as anyone who has seen an angry swan charging will know!) Swans belonging to the Dyers' Company bear a single nick on their beaks, those of the Sovereign are unmarked. The cygnets are marked at the annual July 'Swan Upping' and there is a 'Swan Feast' every year in November. Those who have eaten swan report that it can be pleasant, but is somewhat gamey and fishy and Dr Andrew Boorde, in the sixteenth century, commented — one senses with the voice of experience — that 'old swans be very difficult of digestion'.

The panel depicting St Martin of Tours and the beggar is of great interest. Martin is the Company's patron Saint. A Roman soldier, he was approached by a beggar (seen kneeling gracefully before him here) but, having no money, he divided his cloak with the poor man. And that night Jesus appeared to him in a dream to say that He had been the beggar. Martin is associated with numerous legends to do with wine, and the churches dedicated to him and, in France, the villages incorporating his name, are very numerous. The figure of Martin, already haloed, is sturdy, his sandals Roman army issue, good for walking.

The various activities to do with tending the vine and producing wine are clearly shown; the vines in the semicircle at the top are, from left to right, the Sauvignon Blanc, Gamay, Palomino, Pinot Noir. On the left side, from the top, they are Riesling, Cabernet, Sauvignon, Chardonnay; on the right, Pinot Noir, Chenin Blanc, Merlot. Looking at the window while sitting quietly in the Hall where, so often, I've attended wonderful receptions, tastings, luncheons, dinners — and, gazing for inspiration up at the mighty chandeliers, heard lectures and, done exams in the past — I did slightly regret that the Muscat, the Gewurztraminer and, possibly the oldest grape of all, the Shiraz or Syrah, are omitted. But just as, in the world of wine, there is never time, space, the right people nor the appropriate wines, so this is only a minute regret.

There was, though, a discovery that particularly delighted me. Right at the bottom of the window, before the vines begin to climb upwards, there is one short, downward-pointing tendril, spirally coiled, as vine tendrils grow . . . . It was mid morning and I hadn't even thought of having a glass of wine . . . . There, at the base of the glorious window, is the perfect design for a corkscrew. Yet it took centuries before man saw the significance of much that God put before our eyes — even down to the ideal instrument for opening a bottle.

As I left Vintners' Hall, I couldn't help but chant to myself a stanza whose author I've never known:

> 'God made man —
> Frail as a bubble;
> God made love —
> Love made trouble.
> God made the vine —
> Was it a sin
> That man made wine
> To drown trouble in?'

4 WINE UNDER THE HAMMER

HEUBLEIN AND THE US WINE AUCTION SCENE

by Michael Broadbent

Without more ado, I must credit that vast drinks conglomerate, Heublein —
now, incidentally, British-owned — with the emergence of the New World
wine auctions. Whether this was a corporate idea, dreamed up by their public
relations men, or the brain child of Alexander C (Sandy) McNally, I know
not. All I do quite clearly remember was a transatlantic telephone call, with
Sandy reminding me that we had met over lunch at John Harvey's
establishment in King Street, St James's in London several years before — and
would I consider doing a wine auction for Heublein in the States?

Shortly afterwards, we met in Paris and, a month or so later, a Christie's
wine catalogue look-alike appeared, to summon the newly emergent
American world of wine buffs to 'The Premier American Sale of Finest and
Rarest Wines'. In my innocence, I assumed that 'Premier' in this mouthful of a
title meant the first of what was intended to be a sequence of such events. I
have since learned that most American organizers have this optimistic —
somewhat presumptuous — approach and I always groan inwardly when I
am invited to participate in 'the first' great charity auction or 'international
[which often turns out to be local] total wine experience' weekend. Well, as it
happened, 'Premier' on this first occasion did mean first, thereafter the title
changed to 'Premiere' (sic). No matter: from a successful standing start, it
soon became the leading wine event in the States.

The first sale was held in Chicago in May 1969. This for the same reason
that Christie's hold their frequent wine auctions there now: the liquor laws of
the State of Illinois are more liberal and the licensed trade more open-minded
than in most other states of the Union — though I do recall the then President
of the Teamsters' Union threatening an injunction; his truck drivers thought
they would be put out of business if wine auctions took a hold of the trade!
Happily, despite an ugly moment or two, the first sale went ahead as planned.
It was preceded by a good deal of publicity and I had my baptism of fire in
New York. I had arrived on an afternoon flight from London — my first-ever
trip to the States — and was met by the Heublein publicity machine .... After
a short night's sleep there was a breakfast interview, followed by a radio
interview down near City Hall. Meanwhile, CBS (or was it NBC?) were
setting up lights and cameras in a Heublein warehouse for my first TV
performance, which was not very inspiring. I was hungry. No one had
remembered to provide anything to eat so, with empty stomachs, we were
then rushed to La Guardia Airport to board a mid-afternoon flight to
Chicago, just as the plane doors were closing. Quick change and shave for me,
then dinner with a senior lady wine columnist, after which I was taken by the
one surviving Heublein PR man to a local television studio for what turned
out to be a live late night chat show — and I was last on. By this time I was

Broadbent at the rostrum during one of the Heublein auctions in the US.

exhausted and not in the best of tempers. We got away at about 1.30 in the morning. But it taught me a lesson ....

The day before the sale itself there was a mammoth tasting in the ballroom of the Continental Plaza Hotel. By London standards, a startlingly large array of wines was laid out on a great square or, rather, oblong arrangement of tables; at the far end was a long table on a dais upon which stood a dozen or so old rarities. This was to be the pattern for all pre-sale tastings and I must say that they were always extremely well organized. I have long admired the efficiency and professionalism of American hotels and the waiters, even the old hands, do listen to instructions and co-operate willingly. When the doors opened — usually I had to badger Sandy to let the public in on the dot, whether or not we had finished our pretasting — it was difficult to contain the flood: not just amateur 'wine buffs', but restaurateurs, retailers, wholesalers and, of course, the press. Throughout the day Sandy and I would take it in turn to open and decant the oldest bottles, pouring a minute quantity into the glass of each of the starry-eyed tasters who had queued patiently for a sniff and taste. It was a new — or, rather, old — 'wine wonderland'. Even the act of skimming a capsule, drawing a cork and decanting — done with running commentary — was reverentially watched and listened to. What we English 'pros' took for granted was quite new to this ardent band of American wine lovers. Heady days!

But these tastings were wearing. A long day. What I always hoped for was a good night's sleep, for the day of the auction itself was even more taxing. Although by May '69 I had been conducting wine auctions for a couple of years at Christie's (the first sale I took was at the very end of the opening season of the new wine department) I was still pretty nervous and sat, white-faced, yawning for oxygen and wondering why on earth I had let myself in for such an ordeal. I had, of course, done my homework, putting into the auctioneer's catalogue what are referred to in North America as 'sealed bids' (in Britain these are 'Commissions' to bid) noting reserve prices and so forth, so, when I stepped up to the rostrum, in tailcoat, red carnation in buttonhole, looking more English than the English, and actually started, the nerves disappeared as I concentrated on numbers.

Every bidder in the room had pre-registered and had been given a numbered 'paddle' for identification, a great boon, as I have a notoriously bad memory for names and, in any case, virtually all the bidders were unknown to me; registering bidders and bidding with numbered cards is now commonplace, but at King Street, St James's in London this procedure was not introduced until comparatively recent times.

Even at the first Heublein sale, publicity seekers, usually members of the trade, would ask me beforehand what the 'star' lot might be, their intention being to concentrate on this, hoping that the price they paid would be the highest in the sale, perhaps establishing a record. I regarded this as fair game, though strange and, certainly, a feature totally absent from the more frequent and lower-keyed wine sales at Christie's in London. After all, the whole Heublein event was keyed to publicity, Heublein themselves were spending a great deal, with the ultimate aim of publicizing the company, their own main brands and the wines of their overseas suppliers; the title page of the catalogue made it quite plain that the auction was 'Presented by the Wine Companies of Heublein, Inc' and it was self-evident that wines and wineries not handled by Heublein would not get a look in. Initially, this was neither noticed nor resented. Later, though, it was. Indeed, the regularly touted succession of wines from the Inglenook and Beaulieu vineyards, from Bouchard Père et Fils and Paul Jaboulet Aîné and other either wholly-owned or agency-related companies, did eventually make the pre-sale tastings and sales a bit repetitive. Happily, the eager beavering of Sandy McNally unearthed quite a few one-off cellars and collections of older and more obviously exciting wines.

Before we leave the subject of publicity, it is only fair to admit that this was, too, the main attraction for Christie's. Right from the start I was persuaded that these Heublein sales would provide excellent 'exposure' and it was on the basis of this that my services were originally provided without fee, but with all the expenses being met. It *was* excellent exposure. 'J Michael Broadbent' as I am known in the US 'of Christie's, London', received a great deal of publicity through this novel media event; there was always television coverage, masses of interviews took place, endless articles appeared, but over and above this the real value to Christie's was the opportunity of being seen by and of meeting all branches of the then fast-expanding US wine trade and wealthy 'collectors'. Eventually, after some mild bluffing, even threatening to engage a competitor, Heublein agreed to pay Christie's a substantial fee for my services. Honour was satisfied.

Sandy McNally and I *were* the sale. I regarded myself as the conductor, he the orchestrator, and the programme was provided by the wine. Sandy's catalogues were brilliantly conceived and well executed, though his purple prose tended to be a bit, well, un-Christiefied: 'These rare remaining bottles … are, after long consideration, being offered generously by the Marquise des Pins …. This gesture marks the closing of one era and the dawning of a new one.' Though, on second thoughts, the first James Christie, founder of the firm in 1766, would have felt quite at home with this sort of puff.

To put the Heublein wine auctions into perspective: at the first all day sale the total hammer price was $55,632, compared with Christie's United Kingdom wine sales total for the 1968–69 season of just over half a million pounds sterling. Heublein returned to Chicago the following May and their 1970 knockdown total doubled to $106,128, an almost identical figure in pounds sterling to that of the six 'Fine Wine' category sales at Christie's in London. But the total sold was around 75% of what was offered, as compared to our 92% sold at King Street. The third Heublein sale in 1971 was held in San Francisco. Quite clearly now the momentum had gathered force, for the sale total doubled again to a dizzy $230,751 (ours in London had risen during the full 1970–71 season to £710,000).

San Francisco was a popular venue. We all felt closer to wine. After all, the heart of the Napa Valley was under two hours' drive away. The ballroom of the St Francis Hotel throbbed with anticipation and it was there that the first really startling and record price was achieved.

One of the lots consisted of a single bottle of Château Lafite of the 1846 vintage. I think I opened the bidding around $400 and, unlike Chicago, where bidding was sometimes hesitant and bidders needed a little coaxing, it seemed to take off. At about $2,000 most of the frantic paddle waving had eased up and, shortly after, just two bidders were left in the running. There were about 800 people in the room and they went strangely silent as my bid steps climbed remorselessly. Apart from the usual slight worry about losing count, what made this particularly tricky was that the two bidders were both sited centre left and one was sitting directly behind the other. Well, eventually — it seemed ages but was only a couple of minutes from the start — the bottle sold for $5,000. The shock-haired young buyer was immediately pounced on by reporters and cameramen. When the hubbub had quietened down a little the sale proceeded.

The following spring my office door in St James's opened to reveal a rather tidier young man, with an extremely beautiful girl in tow. He told me that he was a wine merchant in Boston, that his father had initially been appalled at the price — but that it had turned out to be the best $5,000 they had ever spent. They now had an exalted reputation in that most staid of North American cities; he had his own wine column in the *Boston Globe* and appeared on local television. Only one drawback, he said: he was now expected to wear a tie!

Heublein dominated the US wine scene, but they were not the only firm to hold an annual wine auction. A notable family-owned Texan department store, Sakowitz, jumped onto the bandwagon in 1970, but nearly missed their footing. Another firm conducted the first wine auction for them in Houston in 1970. From 1971 I took over, but their sales, held in the autumn, were low-key evening affairs; they were hampered by Texan licensing laws and Sakowitz had not only to own the stock but, as retailers, could only sell to the private consumer. There were excitements, however, including some that rebounded, such as the record price paid for a jeroboam of Mouton-

Rothschild 1929 by a newly married lady. She immediately telephoned her husband, who was not at all understanding. He flew into a rage — and into Houston. Alas, although the lady respected her contract, her husband did not and the bottle, paid for, remained in Sakowitz' cellars for several years after their divorce.

Apart from the razzmatazz, which, I confess, I enjoyed, it was fun for me to visit different cities in the US. Thanks to Heublein's muscle, local licensing difficulties seemed to evaporate and they — and I — travelled around. After the first two sales in Chicago and the third, already mentioned, in San Francisco, 1972 saw us at the Lincoln Center in New York, in 1973 in Atlanta, Georgia, in 1974 back to Chicago, 1975 at the Waldorf Astoria, New York, 1977 in New Orleans, a favourite spot for the wine fraternity and in those days still relatively unspoiled; then in 1978 back in Atlanta, 1979 in Chicago again, 1980 at the elegant Stanford Court in San Francisco, in New Orleans in 1981 — when it was in the process of being tarted up, but May is anyway a beautiful time of year there.

By 1982, the fourteenth Heublein sale, the novelty had worn off and, as an auction, it started to conflict with Christie's own serious and professional activities in Chicago. I resigned as auctioneer, the fifteenth Heublein sale being conducted in Los Angeles by Reeder Butterfield whose firm, incidentally, now holds its own wine auctions in California. By then I think that the cost of the operation was proving a burden — as it was indeed to me — for not only did the tastings and auctions take place in large and expensive hotels, but big pre-sale tastings were also held in other cities. Even with catalogues costing $40.00, the expenses of tastings could not be covered and, towards the end of this period, I am told that, although many people attended the tastings, few remained for the sale the following day.

My resignation was, a few years later, followed by that of Sandy McNally — so the heart and soul of the original enterprise had disappeared. Though I grimaced a little at the time, I, for one, will miss Sandy's catalogues: well composed, beautifully illustrated, exorbitantly lavish descriptions of cellars and wines: 'in the secret Bouchard family crypt located midst the inmost recesses of honeycombed caverns undermined deep beneath the medieval bastions of Beaune, reposes the time capsule treasure cache of family-to-son bottles, access to which remote *caveau* is as elusive as Edgar Allen Poe's "Cask of Amontillado", and the cellarmaster, who is pledged to secrecy.' Well, Sandy was eventually allowed in, for, according to the 1974 catalogue, he 'gasped, because of the dank air, fumbled and recovered composure as the cork was drawn from a bottle of Beaune, Clos de la Mouche, 1864 ... the precious potion poured, tawny-red like the blood of a long-sleeping giant awaked as Brigadoon to breathe an instant in another age. The pulse quickens and the nostrils flare ....!' All great fun. Privileged tasters were allowed a pre-sale sniff and sip — and the truth of the matter is that these previously undisturbed (save for recorking) bottles of pre-phylloxera Burgundies of Bouchard Père et Fils were, indeed still are, unbelievably beautiful. But, even after a full page of McNally prose, the two bottles offered at the 1974 auction fetched what now seems a very modest price, $420 and $400 respectively. Last May, in 1988, at a special Burgundy sale at Christie's in London a bottle of the Bouchard 1864 Le Montrachet from the same cellars sold for £1600. I admit to longing to lift chunks from Sandy's Heublein catalogue before that

It shouldn't happen to J Michael Broadbent!

sale, but finally resorted to writing more down to earth tasting notes that I had made earlier at some of the Heublein pre-sale tastings.

By and large, when Americans — by which I mean North Americans — do this sort of thing, they do it well. The Napa Valley wine auctions are a case in point: they started in 1981 and are an example of the 'First Annual' already referred to. Everything about this was spectacular, particularly the setting, a sort of tree-lined glade in a little valley near St Helena; a vast marquee and a large, very happy, colourful crowd. That year there were two small problems: the beautifully designed catalogue fell apart (bindings were improved thereafter) and the heat, 110°F (44°C) in the shade, was almost overwhelming. I had my feet in a bucket of iced water and had to sip water every four or five lots. Despite this it went well; all the valley seemed to put itself out, winery owners offered hospitality and their staff donned designer aprons to marshal bidders. Though this, like the Heublein events, was a big promotional exercise, the essential difference was that the total proceeds, less expenses, were donated to three hospitals in the Valley. I conducted the first six of these annual auctions, the hospitals eventually benefitting to the tune of more than $400,000 per sale.

I cannot end this piece about wine auctions in the United States without again mentioning Christie's. Apart from one excursion into Washington, they have all been held in Chicago. We opened in April, 1981 and, under the extremely capable management of Michael Davis (who, despite being American, proves that good cataloguing does not need hyperbole!) has expanded to five major sales a year. Over the past three years I have noted that the percentage sold is even higher than here, at home in King Street, which means that they must be the most effective of all wine sales. But what I most like about them is that they are fun to conduct: the audience — for this is what it is — have come to Chicago for a full day out devoted to wine, often bringing their wives for the marvellous shopping and to see the art galleries that are on hand in the 'windy city'. The audiences here are quicker to respond and certainly more respectful than the regulars who attend sales in our 'Great Rooms' in King Street, St James's. And they laugh when I make little jokes .... Very rewarding!

AUCTIONS IN GERMANY

by Peter Hallgarten

Wine auctions are nothing new. There may well have been bids placed and *amphorae* knocked down to the stewards of wealthy households in the *agora* (market places) of the various Greek states. In Roman times sales were well documented: no doubt that where the Romans planted vineyards they also introduced their various marketing systems. Pliny the Younger (Epistle VIII, 2) refers to the sale of wine 'on the vine' — an anticipation of the practice of buying *sur souche*, or anticipating the vintage, which is not officially permitted today. By the time of Marcus Porcius Cato — 'Cato the Censor' — (234–149 BC) there were rules in force specifying terms of sale of grapes prior to the vintage: the *lex vini pendentis* stipulated that the buyer of the grapes had to leave to the seller the 'marc' and lees of the wine when the fruit had been pressed, and he had to take away the wine itself during the first days of October, or otherwise the wine could be dealt with as the seller desired. Obviously a sale could not be an unregulated free for all.

During the Middle Ages and up to the present century it was usual for wine growers to present their wines for sale to the trade either in markets — which of course might be part of a general sale of the local agricultural produce — or else potential buyers would visit the various viticultural regions, selecting what they required and buying it on the spot. This was when brokers started to introduce buyers — who might be complete strangers to an area, possibly not even easily able to communicate with the growers; the brokers, in return for an agreed commission, would then ensure that the wine was kept pure and was eventually delivered to the purchaser in perfect condition.

The wine trade, as we know it today, really only developed in the nineteenth century. But sales of wine took place in Germany earlier by auction, first on the Mosel, then in the Rheingau; some also took place in Frankfurt and, eventually, in the Rheinpfalz. Such sales, however, were not regular features of the regional trade until much later. These events began to deal with wines that came onto the market subject to special conditions — the disposal of bankrupt stock, wines available at the dissolution of estates, sales held by executors on behalf of a deceased. In such circumstances, large quantities of wine could be sold in a very short time, usually at bargain prices — which naturally attracted the attention of those who heard of such bargains in time to go and try to buy them. The first recorded date of an auction announcement is that of the 1757 Trierer Wochenblaettchen. But, it should not be forgotten, during the seventeenth century there was an active trade in wines from the Mosel and Saar with both Holland and England; other exports went to both the Far East and the West Indies. Trade, in spite of many apparently adverse circumstances such as wars and customs exigencies, was, once established, continuous. Those who seem to suppose that it was only in the reign of Queen Victoria that the British began to enjoy and prize fine German wines should study the history of the German exports prior to this! In addition, the advent in the eighteenth century of the Hanoverian rulers to the English throne brought German wines, which the 'Four Georges' both knew and enjoyed, into the pattern of fashionable drinking, both at the English court and in the dining-rooms of these who were loyal to the established monarchy.

K von Vorster, an academic viticulturalist, (*Rheingauer Weibau*, 1765) wrote about the sales of wines with their casks, also mentioning that old casks were best for these wines. One of the most interesting Rheinpfalz auctions took place in Dürkheim in 1781, when seventy-four *Fuder* (each *Fuder*, the local cask, contained 1,320 bottles), all wines in cask of fourteen vintages, were sold, covering the vintages of 1766–1780. Seven years later, at a sale announced as 'due to war' (wars ravaged different regions of Germany during this period), there were fifteen *Fuder* of the 1784–1787 vintages sold at auction.

Apparently, after this time, some communes began to sell their young wines annually, providing a wonderful opportunity for tasters to overindulge and then appear at the sale, after tasting each wine from the cask, somewhat the worse for wear! As there was an obvious risk of someone bidding when drunk — which would have made bids null and void — buyers were allowed two days' grace in which their offer might be cancelled; the bidder, however, was responsible for any of 'his' wine that had been consumed during the tastings.

In these early days wines were sold only under the names of their villages and their vintages; but by 1805 wine-lovers (*Liebhaber*) were invited to attend a Rheingau auction where six *Stück* (140 dozen each) of Marko-brunner were offered, as well as one *Stück* of Rauenthaler Berg and three *Stück* from Eltville — the first recorded offer of a *Lage* wine, or that from a specific plot. The terms of this sale were strict: tasting took place in the morning and buyers had the option as to whether they accepted the wine in cask or bottle. Bottling had to be done within eight days of the sale, payment being made after bottling. For cask wines, the purchaser had to take delivery of the wine immediately or, if winter weather was too inclement for the safe transport of the wine to the purchaser, then it had to be delivered within at least four weeks of the date of the sale.

By the 1820s regular auctions were being arranged by large estates, in particular those of Graf von Schönborn and also the Nassauer'sche Domaine, this being obviously a very satisfactory method for disposing of large quantities of good wine. The Domaine initiated the trend for standard conditions of sale in the 1830s.

By the 1850s an even better routine was developed. Wines were presented for tasting one month before the sale; small samples might be drawn for sending to potential buyers who couldn't travel from afar to be present at the official tasting, with further samples being available on the actual day of the sale. From that time, the wines were named in greater detail and some of the *Lage* wines began to gain their reputations. Later, samples of wines were given out at the sales as each lot was offered. Much wine was consumed at these auctions, which made the procedure expensive for the growers, but it did give them the opportunity then to taste the wines of their neighbours — and competitors!

1903 poster for an auction of Mosel, Saar, Ruwer wines at Trier

Opposite
Château Margaux, built at the beginning of the nineteenth century by the Bordelais architect Louis Combes, who also designed the superb pillared *chai*. The buildings and the entire estate have recently undergone considerable rehabilitation.

The sale of wine in and with cask eventually came to an end; this was originally due to the shortage of wood during the late nineteenth century. Indeed, it became established practice to sell without the cask when it was proved that old wood produced much better wine than new wood. Although wines were stored in *Fuder*, or even larger casks, lots were offered in *Logel* (forty litres (8.4 gallons), sometimes more), so that each wine inevitably had several buyers, often at very different prices from the first lot to the last one.

During World War I wine was very scarce and auction prices were incredibly high. Many merchants started to sell by auction and eventually the German Government decreed that only producers were allowed to sell in this way and this regulation is still in force — only producers can auction wines, although the Federal States can, for special occasions, grant licenses to do so.

No regular auctions took place in Germany during World War II. Until the 1950s such auctions were generally for cask wines, mainly from recent vintages. When a wine was accepted for entry to an auction, the cask was sealed and it remained closed until, at the sale, the auctioneer gave permission for the seal to be removed, to be replaced by the seal of the buyer. Buyers were given the option of either bottling the wine themselves, these wines then being labelled 'growth of — ' with the grower's name inserted, or else having the wine bottled in the producer's cellar (*Originalabfüllung*, a term now changed to *Erzeugerabfüllung*); but everything, after the actual knock-down, took place at the risk of the buyer.

Nowadays, auctions centre on bottled wines and very little cask wine is ever offered without the cask-sealing procedures, this being a sign of honesty in dealing.

Only certified brokers are allowed to bid at the auctions and, until twenty years ago, buying was only permitted if on behalf of a trader; more recently brokers have accepted purchase mandates from private persons, particularly as the parcels of the more expensive wines are usually split by the purchaser with one or more 'underbidders'. As bids can only be made by a broker on the spot, this can give rise to furious signalling across the room, in racecourse bookmakers' style, as buyers concern themselves not only with direct bidding but also with the splitting of some sought after parcel. Such negotiations while bidding is taking place can hoist prices to unexpected heights on occasion.

Originally, brokers received three per cent commission from the vendor; but this was changed in the 1950s, so that both parties now pay, the split usually being two per cent the buyer, three per cent the vendor, official terms being established between the brokers' organization and the association of the growers. As will be understood, the broker plays a very important part in the procedure and is an essential intermediary.

Up to 1933 the wines to be auctioned were valued by three brokers and the average estimated by them became the official reserve price. Once a wine is accepted for auction, the grower has no right to sell elsewhere, should he disagree with the valuation, or for any other reason. No only does this stress the role of the broker, it puts even more responsibility on those involved with offering the wine for sale. An example of this occurred when my grandfather, Arthur, was on one occasion asked to advise and assist Schloss Johannisberg; he subsequently found fault with one cask of wine — which had already been sent up for auction. But as this wine couldn't be withdrawn from the sale and

Panorama of the roofs of St Émilion, with the curved tawny tiles
typical of the southern regions of France. The steep up and down
streets make this one of the most interesting as well as most
picturesque and historic wine towns of the south west.

as the administrator of the estate didn't want it to fall into other hands, my grandfather bought it in, albeit for a very high price ... because, as may be imagined 'If Arthur is bidding, it must be very special!'

The most important and certainly the most publicized sale these days is the annual auction of 'Der Grosser Ring', of the Mosel-Saar-Ruwer growers. Formed in 1908 by the Oberbürgermeister (Lord Mayor) of Trier, the Ring brought together the wines of several estates which had regularly sold their wines by auction through three separate organizations. Initially, all these growers' wines had to be offered for these sales. This rule was amended in 1965, however, allowing the member growers to supply their visitors direct.

By 1910, too, a national organization had been formed: Verband der Deutschen Naturweinversteigerer, the VDN; their symbol, which continues in use for the present German National Quality Wines Association, is now the VDP (Verband Deutscher Prädikatsweinversteigerer) and includes members from all viticultural regions.

From the beginning only growers with the best sites were included and wines that are offered at auction at Trier are always one hundred per cent Riesling. Until 1968 sales were by *Fuder* (the traditional Mosel cask of 1000 litres or 210 gallons), but since then offers are in 'lots' of bottles. A strict system of self-monitoring is used and only special and, usually, fairly rare wines are auctioned. With the introduction of the 1971 German Wine Law, the Grosser Ring members are now permitted to offer QbA (chaptalized) wines. Although some of the finest estates are members, producing some

Part of the scene at the 1910 auction of the Grosser Ring in Trier

250,000 cases per vintage, the magnificent wines of the Trier church properties and the Freidrich Wilhelm Gymnasium are not offered.

Some staggering prices have been paid for outstanding wines over the years, a very high proportion of them coming from the Saar. The highest ever recorded was for a 1976 Trockenbeerenauslese at DM 1150, an Eiswein at ten per cent higher, and — an unusual rarity — a 1933 Bernkasteler Doctor Spätlese at DM 1500.

The most picturesque auctions are still held within the hallowed walls of the magnificent cellars of the Kloster Eberbach, a perfect setting in which buyers can overbid! The most outstanding prices have been DM 35,000 for a bottle of 1893 Nerobuerger Trockenbeerenauslese and DM 11,000 for a bottle of 1920 Steinberger Trockenbeerenauslese. More normal prices range around DM 35 for good vintage Auslesen and up to DM 600 per bottle for parcels of that very small production — Eiswein.

These days few villages have auctions, where what are described, perhaps too modestly, as 'lesser wines' are offered, although many of these are, often, better value than some of their more famous brethren. Annual Rheinhessen auctions include wines from four villages — Nierstein, Alsheim, Mettenheim and Guntersblum. Attendance, for which usually a minimal fee must be paid, can be both interesting and enjoyable, as well as providing an excellent opportunity to get an idea of vintages and the localized production. Fortunately only small quantities of the finest wines are auctioned — the bidding being fast and furious!

It is perhaps worth stressing that the German auctions do not have an influence on the general valuations of wines and vintages — as do the much publicized auctions elsewhere, such as at the Hospices de Beaune in Burgundy. The Grosser Ring auctions can be very friendly, almost social, affairs; the big tasting takes place in the morning and the inevitable speculation about prices follows among those participating. The auction itself begins at one o'clock (1300 hours). Depending on the overall programme, the sale can last for five or six hours, particularly when wines of a great vintage are being offered. The auctioneer will be joined on the platform at each stage by the grower, so that he can accept or reject any final bid that comes below the reserve at the nod or shake of the grower's head. Normally, the auctioneer will taste every wine as it is offered and he can — if he wishes — interject his own positive comments. As the bidding rises he will conclude 'Zum Ersten, zum Zweiten' ('first — second') and, occasionally, 'Niemand mehr?' ('No one else?'), then 'Zum Dritten' ('third'!) and then he hits the desk before him with his wooden gavel. Then the auctioneer names the successful bidder, also the names and the quantities that have been negotiated with the underbidders during the sale of that particular lot.

Wine lovers looking at old photographs of the Grosser Ring sales will note the portly gentlemen around the tables with, before them, small, squat tumblers — and no spittoons! These days stemmed glasses with small bowls are usually in place of the tiny tumblers. At the morning tastings of the Grosser Ring tasting spittoons are provided; at the sale itself the sample is swallowed — any surplus thereafter being poured away.

At contemporary sales, regulations are strict. Ordinary wine-lovers can only attend if they are admitted by a broker or grower. As has been mentioned only accredited brokers are allowed to bid, but they may do so on behalf of

anyone who instructs them. Visitors wanting to buy are able to accompany brokers to a sale — entrance to which of course the broker will have arranged for them — but seats must be reserved in advance and, naturally, anyone attending a sale as a guest is expected to purchase something from their host during the sale. A recent auction in Bernkastel is an example of the way in which the overall controls are maintained: all wines must have an official quality control number, must be guaranteed to have been produced from approved vine varities and they must be offered for sale in bottles complete with labels and cartons ready for despatch. The buyer of the first batch of a lot that contains several of the same wine has the right to buy all the wine at the same price. Commission for the broker is three per cent from the vendor and two per cent from the purchaser. Payment must be made within six weeks of the date of the sale anyway; unpaid amounts are charged interest at two per cent above that of the bank discount rate. The recent Bernkastel auction, which took place on 1 September 1988, featured the wines of good but not world-renowned growers, who offered as many as 43,394 bottles and 330 half bottles from ten vintages, in seventy-three lots, the lots usually being of several hundred bottles each — from 200 to 1200. The older and rarer wines were offered in lots from twenty-four bottles. The wine that achieved top price was a 1985 Beerenauslese, at DM 90 (about £30) per bottle.

The auctions have done much to publicize Germany's fine wines in the past but, in recent years, the image of some of these has suffered and members of

Members of the Grosser Ring in one of the William Morris rooms at the Victoria and Albert Museum, June 1988.

the Grosser Ring, among others, have acted to establish that Germany's best is superb in the eyes of the world. So, in the summer of 1988, members came to conduct a tasting in the Victoria and Albert Museum in London, in one of the most impressive rooms, with nineteenth-century glass in the tall windows, pillars encrusted with antique tiles and walls bearing designs and pictorial representations from the time when the great German wines held a proud place in royal and fashionable dining-rooms. Most of the wines then shown, both to members of the UK wine trade and the press, were selected from the personal stocks of the growers who participated and were programmed to show the depth of flavour and distinctive character in mature wines of quality in good vintages. The spaciousness of the surroundings and the unusual decor provided a special and suitable atmosphere for those attending to appraise the differing styles of fine wines produced along the Mosel and Saar.

It is sometimes remarked that the high prices attained by certain wines at the great auctions, including those of Germany, are 'hyped up' — unrealistically pushed to limits where the publicity will attract attention throughout the world. A wine, like any other commodity offered for sale, must be in demand — both by those who may *want* to buy it and by those whose interest and interests affect their reactions to its disposal. I can only speak from my own experience — from tasting the 1920 Steinberger TBA, about which my notes read: 'Last tasted 29.2.60. Deep golden, phenomenal fruit salad nose, rich yet very well balanced acidity and sweetness, absolute "nectar of the gods"!' Refrigerated and regularly tasted, the final drops were tried in September 1960, when I noted 'Very dark chocolate colour, strong, peachy aroma, very *edel* (noble) finish — the most remarkable wine I have ever tasted.'

(NB In noting the prices of the wines, approximately one-third of the price given in DM should give an adequate price in pounds sterling. But of course, what was a price ten years or more ago might be much more in today's valuation!)

GOING, GOING — WHAT?

by David Wolfe

Good things come in threes, says the superstition. So number three was due and the end of the day was near.

Number one had been the vintage port, the reason for my presence at the country house auction. The bottles were unlabelled but, while awaiting the invention of lasers, I had prudently equipped myself with a powerful narrow beam torch so as to read the branded corks through the dark glass of the bottle-necks. When my bid of five shillings (25 new pence) a bottle succeeded, I knew I had a bargain. For the ports were Taylor's and Graham's, of the vintages 1927, 1924 and 1920.

Good thing number two was picking up the wine racks. The porter, for a small contribution to his own cellar fund, had shown me the cellars where the port had lain. He said that the racks had not been catalogued for the sale and, if I could take them away, I was welcome to do so. Another contribution had seen them loaded into the van.

A

CATALOGUE
Of all the REAL GENUINE
HOUSEHOLD FURNITURE,
China, Stock of Wines, Spirituous-Liquors,
Live and Dead Stock, &c.

o f

MR. WILSON,
INN-KEEPER and FARMER,
AT THE
WHITE-HART and POST-OFFICE,
in *Petersfield, Hampshire.*
CONSISTING OF

Damask, Morine and Cotton, in Beds and Window-Curtains, Mahogany, Rose-wood, and Walnut-tree Tables, Bureaus, Desks and Book-Cases, Double Chests of Drawers, Pier, Sconce and Chimney-Glasses, Carpets, and exceeding good Kitchen Furniture, Coppers, Lead Cisterns, &c. Three Post-Chaise and Harness, two Mares, (one of which is with Foal) a Colt, a Cow and Calf, a Quantity of old Hay, and various other Effects.

Which will be Sold by AUCTION, by

MR. CHRISTIE,
(On the Premises)

On TUESDAY the 28th of MARCH, and
Two following Days.

To be viewed on SATURDAY and MONDAY, the 25th and 27 of this Instant, and to the Time of Sale, which will begin at Twelve o'Clock each Day.

CATALOGUES may be had (*gratis*) at the Place of Sale, at the Post-Offices in the following Towns, viz. Kingston, Guildford, Portsmouth, Southampton, Winchester, Alton, Haslemere, Alresford, Hartford-Bridge, Midhurst, Liphook, and at Mr. Christie's, Pall Mall, London.

The third good thing was towards the end of the sale, when the oddments of wine came up: two dozen very mixed bottles of Liebfraumilch, straw-wrapped Chianti, dusty Orange Bitters, some dubious English-bottled claret and Burgundy, and a few healthy products from the chemist's were to be sold. The auctioneer asked for a bid of a pound. No response. He tried ten shillings (50p). Still not a flicker of interest.

'Will anyone offer half a crown [12.5p]?' he pleaded.

A strangled yelp from the back started the bidding. From the back again, but on the other side of the great marquee, came the next bid. Now they came freely from either side, first in sixpenny steps, then a shilling at a time. A rustle of movement from behind drew attention to the first bidder, slowly advancing down the aisle, but not that slowly considering his apparent age. His clothes seemed to have been matured by years of working on and with his father, the soil.

The bidding had reached two pounds, and the rival bidder was coming down the other aisle. He too was short, bespectacled and about the same age as the other man. In fact they looked remarkably alike. By the time both reached the auctioneer's podium, the bid was nine pounds and little could be heard above the laughter. The onlookers knew the bidders. They were the local poachers, twin brothers who shared a cottage. When they recognized each other there was a short silence. From the ensuing conversation I learned several interesting words in the Essex dialect on such subjects as ancestry, character and personal habits.

It was a world away from the professionalism of the Hospices de Beaune auction, where distinguished figures from the world's wine and catering trades bid for fine young Burgundies from the vineyards that have been donated over the past centuries for the support of the Hospices. Here, the bidding is limited in time by the life of two tapers, the first of them lit as the first bid for each lot is made, the final bid coinciding with the last flicker of the second taper. These tapers seem to be made of an unusual mixture of wax and rubber. The auctioneer, who refreshes himself during the long afternoon with draughts from a bottle of Meursault under his table, has two assistants to ensure that no bid is missed from the crowd packed into the covered market in the centre of Beaune and these colleagues will also identify the bidders — many of whom, of course, they know from past years. There was, however, one occasion when they were asked not to identify those bidding . . . .

The two members of the British wine trade had come into the auction hall after lunching together. The repast had been well matched to their more than ample frames and justice had been done — and could be seen to have been done — to the wines of Burgundy. They sat side by side, each with an arm across the other's shoulders; the embrace was as much for mutual support as to show mutual friendship. A lot came up on whose excellent quality they seemed agreed. Naturally they bid for it, each in turn waving his free, outside arm. Only the auctioneer's altruism came between them and a new record price for a Hospices de Beaune wine.

It was recently announced that the highest price for a German wine was achieved at Eberbach, where a bottle of Johannisberger Riesling from Schloss Schönborn was sold for DM 53,000 — about £18,000. Though this is small beer compared with the record £105,000 paid for a bottle of Château Lafite, bearing the initials 'Th.J', sold at Christie's in December 1985. Auctioneers

A

CATALOGUE

OF

THE GENUINE STOCK

O F

Excellent Choice Wines,

The Property of the Right Honourable

EARL of KERRY,

At his MANSION, on the East Side of

PORTMAN-SQUARE;

CONSISTING OF

CHAMPAGNE, BURGUNDY, OLD HOCK

of the Year 1719, MADEIRA, fin

OLD PORT, CAPE, &c. &c. &c.

Which will be Sold by Auction,

By Meff. Chriftie and Anfell.

On the PREMISES,

On *THURSDAY, APRIL 2,* 1778.

To be tafted at the Time of Sale, which will begin One o'Clock.

Catalogues may be had on the Premifes, and at Mr CHRISTIE and ANSELL's, *Pall Mall.*

like record prices because of the publicity they create. I would be the last to criticize because, when I bought a bottle of Château d'Yquem 1869 at a Bordeaux auction, the ensuing publicity, which owed more to the price paid than to the rarity and beauty of the wine, generated a lot of business. Because it was then believed that this was a world record the bottle, with this writer in a supporting rôle, appeared on BBC radio and television and was shown in the British press. It could not then be admitted but now it can safely be revealed that the auctioneer, Monsieur Balaresque, had been bidding against me on behalf of the Château; his instructions were to obtain the bottle at any price. But my bid was the equivalent of £30 and, as he said with a wry shrug, 'There must be a limit.'

If I once paid what was a record high price, I equally vividly recall being present when the 1974 slump in claret prices reached its nadir. It was during the last session of the Christie's/Bass Charrington sale in London, one of the great big sales, when the ballroom of Quaglino's restaurant in St James's had to be taken for the event so as to accommodate the 800 or so bidders. The huge room, which had been as full as a New York deli sandwich, was now as thin as its British Rail nominal equivalent. The wine, if you choose to dignify it by that name, was Château Margaux 1972. No one had and has a lower regard for this disgusting vintage than I. Had it not been for the boom that preceded the depression, it would have been quietly and cheaply sold off as poor quality Bordeaux rouge. But it was still hard to believe that Château Margaux 1972 could sell at only £9 per dozen in bond. Perhaps there is a lesson to be learned from this.

Although a successful bid is a source of great pleasure to the bidder, not everyone enjoys buying cheaply. This was very apparent in the case of — let us call him Mr Green, a regular buyer at Christie's. He collected fine claret, with a taste for the first growths; an erratic taste, it must be said, because he often bought wines spurned by some discriminating buyers: Château Cheval Blanc 1945, for example, half of which had to be pasteurized because the fermentation went wrong; or Château Latour in vintages such as 1953 and 1947, when it was less successful than its peers.

Mr Green was normally stern of aspect. While he was bidding, even at a wine auction, his manner and countenance reflected his trade of diamond dealer. After a successful bid, he smiled. It was an entirely benevolent smile which he would bestow on the whole room as he swung round in his seat. The odd thing was that a purchase of something good at a low price produced only a first degree glow. A decent wine for which he had paid highly evoked a beam of satisfaction. But when an indifferent wine was knocked down to him at an exorbitant figure, the unearthly beauty of his smile lit up the day for all on whom it shone.

There is a gratification in the auction room which exceeds even that of a successful bid. It is the quintessential *schadenfreude* of seeing your business rival or, better still, your customer, paying too much. But dealers should beware of offering a customer more of a wine which he has just bought at auction; if the price is higher, he will refuse it and boast of how little he paid earlier, if it is lower he will feel foolish and buy nothing, since to do so would be to admit his folly. Worst of all is to offer it at the same price. He will be convinced that something fishy is going on.

My own folly in once paying too much was the subject of comment by a senior member of the wine trade. It was at one of the sales of old wine, run by Monsieur Balaresque, in the draughty warehouse dignified by the name of *salle des ventes* in Bordeaux. I had swept up most of the château-bottled Sauternes of '29, '28, '24 and '20, and was feeling well pleased as 'Mr Black' approached.

'You must be mad!' he said 'You don't pay thirty shillings [£1.50] a bottle for these wines. That's the retail price in London.'

This may suggest that I am referring to a distant era, but it was in fact as recently as the early 1960s.

The Bordeaux auctions were not at all like their English equivalents: sales started at ten o'clock; or half-past; or at ten minutes to three. They finished at five, or six and, once at least, at eight thirty. In St James's or in Bond Street in London the catalogue shows numbered lots, accurately describing the wine and its quality. The Bordeaux catalogues were innocent of lot numbers, they simply listed the château, vintage and the total quantity on offer. Lots were not sold in the printed order, either. Publicity was more important. The arrival of radio and television crews would be greeted by Monsieur Balaresque with 'Right — let us now deal with the Château Lafite-Rothschild.' Or it might be the Mouton-Rothschild. That eternal rivalry between the great estates was at its strongest in the auction room; both used every trick in the book and a few unrecorded stratagems to ensure that their wine achieved the top price in each vintage, with the maximum fanfare from the media.

In London, a bidder makes a bid and pays on the spot or, more usually, receives a bill a day or two later. Once it is paid the buyer collects the wine or has it delivered. In Bordeaux, the successful bidder would be handed a slip of paper, little larger than a cloakroom ticket, with a roughly scribbled abbreviated description and quantity; early next morning each of these had to be checked against a list of purchases and certified by a legal official, the *huissier*. Auctions, like every other aspect of French life, must help support the bureaucracy, so, when the bill (plus tax) was paid, you rushed back to the auction room with the stamped slips to collect your purchases. The slips were handed one by one to the porters, who sometimes brought the wine and sometimes brought their apologies for a lot that had disappeared. There were no refunds. The porters' stiff upper lips, when faced by these disappointments, furnished an admirable example to the notoriously excitable British.

Which was why you went early to the *huissier* and then rushed back to the auction room.

At one sale I bought a dozen Hermitage rouge 1868. As the Bordelais knew little of Rhône wine and cared less for such alien produce, it was very cheap. I had already 'lost' some lots when I handed the ticket for the Hermitage to a porter. He left to find it. After what seemed an eternity, another porter asked what I was waiting for. I told him and he too went away. It was several hours (actually at least three minutes) before one approached from the left, with the red Hermitage. Simultaneously, the other entered right, bearing a dozen white Hermitage of the same vintage. To my surprise, both red and white were in superb condition. These great wines proved both the longevity of Hermitage and the serendipitous pleasure of buying at auction.

But serendipity is not to be relied on. As you sit waiting for your lot to come up, you may notice something which is about to be sold far too cheaply. You bid in a hurry and only when you see the account do you realize that you have bought wine in bond, instead of duty paid; or that the wine was bottled not at the château but at Châteaudun.

If you attend an auction, the safest course is to bid only if you have priced the lot beforehand, unless you are a regular buyer, when you may be lucky enough to pick up a hint from the auctioneer that you are missing a bargain. This may be no more than a direct glance as he says 'No more bids? I am selling — '

The opposite sign may be an almost imperceptible quiver, that could be a negative shake of the head, as he catches your eye. But it is warning enough.

In these days of instant worldwide electronic communications, those actually attending a sale may find themselves outnumbered as well as outbid by electronic bidders in London, New York, or Sydney. This is a pity, for much of the pleasure of attending auctions is social and they are usually good-humoured events. I don't think modern technology could convey the voice of a famous auctioneer, now gone to the Great Rostrum in the Sky, when he was selling the stock of a bankrupt wine merchant. Fine wines went first, then the everyday wines and spirits, down to the beer and cider, then —

'We come now' — long pause — 'to — the — grrrapefruit juice.' Nor do I think that modern technology can accurately transmit an exchange I once heard in Christie's Great Rooms, when attending a sale was rather like going to the theatre (or pantomime) and taking part in the performance. The auctioneer had become a little confused and hesitatingly announced:

'It *is* lot three hundred and forty-three —'

'Oh no, it isn't!' roared the audience.

5 WINE IS FUN

AGAINST THE NEW PURITANS

by Auberon Waugh

The news that American activists in various States of the Union have successfully forced through a bill requiring wine to carry a 'health warning', like cigarettes, was broken to me by Mr Robert Mondavi, the great California wine maker, at a luncheon given in the Victoria and Albert Museum, of all places. It was an occasion for the wine trade and wine writers. There we sat, surrounded by the artefacts from nearly 2000 years of a Christian civilization which was nurtured and sustained by the grape — the only really worthwhile civilization the world has ever known — to be informed that a handful of pipsqueak pressure groupers and health faddists in the youngest, brashest corner of the earth had decided that wine was bad for the health.

It is true, I suppose, that where there is no prospect of an eternal life hereafter — and can young Americans, looking at each other over their Pepsi Cola tins, honestly imagine that they have immortal souls? — health becomes paramount. The pleasures of life, its sorrows and joys, become subordinate to the overwhelming necessity of staying alive. Health becomes more than a fetish. It becomes a thoroughgoing religion, along with its High Priests, rituals and accompanying excesses of self-denial, superstition, evangelical fervour and suppression of dissent. It does not matter how miserable or uncomfortable your life is so long as you can somehow prolong it; you eat nothing but tasteless bran with a minimum of protein, you spend all your spare time working out at a gym or jogging fatuously and painfully along tarmac paths in a concrete wilderness, but at least you safeguard your health.

More alarmingly, you believe anything you are told by the huge industry which has sprung up to cater for such neuroses. Television programmes, newspaper articles, whole magazines devoted to the health lunacy may tell you one week that cauliflowers are suspected of containing a chemical which will make you blind, that water in which eggs have been boiled will give you warts if brought into contact with the skin, that goat cheese rind will block your urinary passages, that the 'eyes' of potatoes give you cancer, that aspirin produces internal haemorrhage. And you believe it all — until the next scare has you worrying about tinned peas, or rabbits' kidneys, or chickens' eggs.

All this is the recipe for a miserable, anxiety-ridden life, and quite possibly a short one. Those unaffected by such anxieties may feel a twinge of anger at the way unscrupulous people in the media and anxiety industries exploit them — but so long as the fetishists keep their anxieties to themselves, we may reasonably decide that it is nothing to do with us. It is only when they organize themselves into pressure groups and start trying to impose their neuroses on the rest of us that I feel it is time to call a halt. There comes a moment when stupidity, if allowed to flourish and assert itself, is more than a minor nuisance. It is an insult to God and man, a denial of reason and a threat to the equanimity which is the only glimpse we poor mortals are allowed of that much greater happiness which may (or may not) await us around the next twist or turn in our mortal coil. In other words, it is time we organized ourselves in defence against the health fanatics, the religious bigots and others who threaten one of the greatest pleasures of life on earth.

One of the greatest objections to calling a Crusade — or whatever the twentieth-century equivalent of a Crusade would be — is that it requires almost as much dedication — not to say fanaticism or bigotry — to oppose these ideas as it does to impose them. The homme moyen sensuel (or femme moyen sensuelle) loses out every time. All we want is a pleasant, easy-going life, with the possibility (but scarcely any certainty) of eternal happiness eventually. Religious fanatics may convince themselves that it is worth the risk to sacrifice something on earth for some noble cause, but your average wine drinker is not a religious fanatic. That is why the Christians lost the Crusades. The only weapon on our side in the eternal war against enthusiasts, fanatics and power maniacs is the great force of human inertia. That is surely the weapon we must deploy against the new Puritans on the health front.

The suggestion that wine, in moderate quantities, is bad for the health is self-evidently absurd. Wine is as old as human civilization, being a major feature of all recorded cultures as far back as 3000 BC. In immoderate quantities, of course, even water drives people mad. Alexis Lichine makes the point that human civilization began with wine, for the simple reason that viticulture requires at least a couple of years residence in the same spot. The nomadic aboriginal tribes of Australia, currently so much in the fashion, never stayed in the same place long enough to grow radishes, let alone vines. Or, if they stayed there, they were never intelligent enough to work out the advantages of planting.

For 5000 years the beneficial properties of wine have been recognized and acclaimed by very nearly the entire human race. The whole of human experience, combining the lifetime perceptions of nearly everyone who has ever lived — the same perceptions which have led us, by slow stages, to our present technological, agnostic culture — have led humanity to conclude that wine is a beneficial substance, however much capable of abuse. Must we now accept this insult from a handful of health faddists, and accept an obviously mendacious statement on every bottle of wine we buy, to the effect that wine is dangerous to women in pregnancy? Nearly every mother who has ever given birth, outside Islam (since the seventh century) and the few areas which wine has never reached, in peasant China, Scandinavia and the northern reaches of Russia, has been exposed to wine or some other version of ethyl alcohol. Are we to suppose that babies born to Arabs, Turks, Chinese or Russian peasants were healthier, cleverer or more long lived than those born in Christendom? The evidence would point otherwise.

It is true that the history of prohibitionism is nearly as old as the history of alcohol. Rulers tend by their nature to be opposed to anything which makes their subjects happy without reference to the ruler's wishes, and the urge to control alcohol is almost universal in the cybernetic process. Earliest efforts to ban alcohol — in China, Finland and Sweden — were almost always tied to some genuine epidemic of alcoholism, such as breaks out from time to time in cold climates whenever traditional systems of discipline are breaking down or being discredited. I have no doubt that the present draconian measures against alcoholism in the Soviet Union are tied to official acceptance of a general awareness that communism — the sustaining myth of Soviet society — does not actually work. But outside government, when a voluntary movement arises among the citizenry to deny fellow-citizens one of the greatest comforts that human ingenuity has yet devised, the motives are more mysterious and often more sinister.

The great Prohibition Movement in America began at the beginning of the nineteenth century when the ruling Protestant establishment began to feel itself threatened by the influx of Catholic Europeans and Irish. It was tied to a great religious revival which expressed itself in a need for various groups in the rootless, immigrant society of northern America to gang up against other groups. Outsiders had to be made outlaws, by hook or by crook. The American Prohibitionist Movement next caught on in Ulster, for much the same reasons. The Ulster Temperance Society, formed in 1829, next burgeoned in Scotland, where the Presbyterians had never previously imagined that by dint of moral outrage they might be able to force their bizarre preferences on the Episcopalian and Catholic minorities. It was not until the World Prohibition Conference of 1909 in London had set up the Prohibition Federation that a new leadership began to emerge, closely tied to the beginnings of the Women's Movement. Only a small proportion of the women who flocked to join the World Women's Christian Temperance Union in fifty countries were themselves the victims of violent or alcoholic husbands. But they sympathized with their sisters, in the first awakening of female solidarity, and to women untempted by wine it seemed a thoroughly good cause, both as a means of eradicating a social evil and of expressing a certain resentment against menfolk in general.

However, after the triumph of the Puritans and women of both sexes in 1919, when a temporary wartime ban on the conversion of grain to alcohol was made permanent in the Eighteenth Amendment to the American Constitution, with a total ban on the making, selling, transporting and possession of alcohol in any form, the Prohibitionists were finally confronted by the greater strength of human inertia. Without anyone opposing them on grounds of principle or scientific truth, they found that the religious and social arguments against alcohol were not, in practice, viable. Illegal stills sprang up everywhere and a huge criminal subculture based on the speakeasy and the illegal sale of liquor, made nonsense of everything the Puritans had hoped to achieve. After the Democratic victory of 1932, on an anti-Prohibitionist ticket, and the Twenty-first amendment repealing the Eighteenth a year later, the Puritans came to accept that neither religious dogma nor social theories were going to carry the day. Both had been discredited.

So now they come up with the health argument — 5000 years after humankind first recognized wine as one of the great blessings which the world has to offer. Gullibility about health is certainly as great a force now as religious gullibility ever was, but the inherent absurdity of trying to force good health on other people is even more apparent than the earlier absurdity of trying to force religious orthodoxy or a particular form of social organization on those who resist both.

In Britain, where the health fetish has not quite the same hold, the Puritans proceed by an entirely different route. There is a great and growing carnage on British roads as a result of alcohol abuse, they say; Britain is in the throes

1904 advertisement in a London paper

Carry Nation, smasher of many barrooms, poses before an appropriately named theatre in which she was appearing.

of an epidemic of drunkenness; violence and criminal assault are exploding in Drunken Britain. Never mind that the first two statements are direct untruths and the third a deliberate distortion of the truth. Just as people in the United States are prepared to believe the untruth that wine is bad for your health, so people in Britain are mysteriously prepared to believe that we are a nation of drunkards. In fact, we have one of the lowest rates of road deaths in the free world and it has actually been declining for the last fifteen years, despite an enormous increase in the volume of traffic. According to Mr Peter Bottomley, the Junior Transport Minister, who is actually in charge of the campaign against drunk driving, we have the best drink driving record in the world. We have one of the lowest alcohol consumption rates in Europe, and the increase in criminal violence is not related to any increase in alcohol consumption.

But for some strange reason, people want to believe these lies. All we can usefully do is to ignore them, safe in the knowledge that if ever the liars prevail and enact their ghastly proposals, commonsense will prevail and they will once again be discredited for the next fifty years. Meanwhile, it might be prudent to build up our wine cellars.

TRAVELLING WITH THE TRADE

by Margaret Howard

My first encounter with the niceties of wine tasting came about through broadcasting — and I should say that broadcasters are not renowned for their appreciation of the finer points of oenology. Drink is drink. It is either there to quench thirst or support flagging inspiration. The only time wine gets mentioned on the air these days is when, for some reason, it becomes 'an issue' — as when the French insisted that the Spaniards could not call *cava* Champagne, or when the anti-freeze got into — well, that's an old and sad story. Tell a broadcaster that there has been a good vintage, or that this is likely to be a particularly fine year for Burgundy and the eyes will glaze. No scandal — no story.

Though I'm not a total philistine. I've drunk saké in Tokyo, palm wine in Lagos — both of which I could have done without and neither of which prepared me in any way for the rigours of travelling with the wine trade when they're working.

My initiation was when I was working on a news magazine programme, beamed all round the world, the aim of which was to project Britain and Britain's achievements overseas. I was sent off to do a story on English wine. 'Go to the vineyards,' my editor said, 'collect a few samples and get some taster chappie to sample them.'

The 'taster chappie' I found was none other than Michael Broadbent, MW, of Christie's. He courteously agreed to sample my English wines and give me a commentary on same, so I duly arrived at those discreetly impressive portals. Looking back, I can't imagine what the head of the wine department thought of the inelegant individual, carrying a battered old tape machine. The glasses were ready. The bottles were uncorked. I then saw (and heard) for the first time a wine taster at work; the delicate twirl of the glass, the admiring look at the colour of the contents against the light, then the sip, the slurp — and finally the spit. How could such a point device man spit like that in my presence and over such a long distance! He commented on my Pilton Manor Riesling and the Beaulieu Rosé — but when I asked him what wine he would choose if he could have only one, he mentioned a small vineyard in California that was close to his heart (why didn't I note its name?) and there was I thinking that, if ever anybody was philistine about wine, the Americans were. (This was a while ago, I hasten to add, when the Americans, at least the ones I knew, were more into Martinis than Chardonnay).

From this apparently unpromising beginning I found myself in the years that followed a welcome guest of the infinitely hospitable and courteous group of people who compose the wine trade. Indeed, neither the editor of this book nor I can recollect exactly how we met, but some years ago I was summoned by her to come and collect her at Bordeaux airport, then found myself driving up the Médoc to the most hospitable and courteous

The gateway to Château Loudenne in the Médoc

personality of all — Martin Bamford, MW, then Président Directeur Général of Gilbey (France), who received us at Château Loudenne.

Loudenne was a complete surprise. I'd been to the châteaux of the Loire as a tourist in the sunshine, but Bordeaux, when I got there and throughout my stay, was drenched in rain. My first purchase was a pair of wellingtons, rubber boots made in Taiwan, but bought in the small town of Lesparre — and I certainly needed them when tramping around the vineyards. Soon I discovered how the Victorian Gilbey family came to Bordeaux — two British brothers emerging from the South African wars managing to buy themselves a piece of the action in the wine world, with such success that they were able to acquire their own vineyard with its fairytale château.

As the car scrunched up the gravel drive that October day, I glimpsed in the failing light just before sunset a fondant pink house, turretted in the French manner, but with a Union Jack flying from the flagpole on the lawn. There, to meet us, beaming and bowing in his Paris couture tweeds, was Martin. That was the beginning of a very special friendship.

The staff soon settled us in our allotted rooms, mine being the Red Room, with rich brocade wallpaper of the same hue on the walls. Not that you could see much of the walls, because they were covered with pictures and ceramics, and antiques of all kinds filled the room, collected, I learned later, at flea markets all over France; the bed, the sort you climb up into via a step stool, had a mahogany headboard and was, as I discovered in the two happy weeks I spent living at Loudenne, divinely comfortable. But there was no time for lingering that first night.

We were to meet in the drawing-room for pre-dinner drinks and, as this was a special occasion, Champagne was served. A colleague of Martin's from International Distillers & Vintners was also there; he was on the commercial side of the business and clearly brought serious matters in his baggage. Though none of that was allowed to intrude on the first of many memorable dinners at Loudenne, where I learned that it was quite normal to have eight glasses on the table in front of you — and that one managed to drink from them all without falling over as one rose. Mind you, it wasn't far to the Red Room!

I must have shown my interest to Martin, because next morning at half-past ten he had me on parade in the tasting room, sited within a folly-like building that I think may have been a dovecot, and was teaching me how to recognize the Merlot and the Cabernet Sauvignon. Martin tasted with the glee of a mouse confronted with a fine piece of cheddar. If he had had whiskers they would have been bristling. His judgements were precise and dauntingly certain. I noticed then that he did not make a great ado about what temperature the wine was, believing as he did that a good taster must know what a wine is like regardless of such refinements. Indeed, the delicate care with which my wine trade friends approach wine is often matched by the apparent casualness with which they may serve and drink it — no chi-chi for them! My experiences at Loudenne were valuable groundwork, for later I was privileged to be entertained to luncheon at Château Lafite, where five vintages were served, then later at Château Palmer, where I was introduced to the behind the scenes renowned vintage kitchen (maybe not as beautiful as that at Loudenne, which was Martin's pride, but the fare of the two estates was celebrated).

Opposite
Château Latour, Pauillac, seen from a less familiar angle than the well-known one with the dumpy tower (which is at the back of the house here), the *chai* being just glimpsed on the right.

The *GIN* Shop.

We also went to Château d'Angludet, as guests of Diana and Peter Sichel, Diana breeding horses there, a mutual interest, which made another contact between us, and I was delighted by the murals in the Angludet drawing-room, which show scenes of the *haute école* at the Spanish Riding School. On this visit we were treated as 'family' and dined in the kitchen when, as I put my nose into a glass, I said innocently 'This must be the Palmer '61 I've heard so much about?' at which my neighbour at table, John Davies, MW, leaped to his feet and shouted *'Chapeau! Chapeau! Chapeau à Margaret!'* For I had apparently done something rather clever by getting the vintage — an instance, I'm afraid, of fools rushing in. In fact John Davies, who was then running the hospitality side of Château Lascombes, later invited me there and made it his business to continue with my gastronomic education.

One cloudy, wet morning, he collected the editor and me from Mouton Rothschild, where we had been visiting the wine museum. By this time, I had, I must confess, the mother and father of all hangovers (the editor was astonished — 'We drank about the same amount!' 'Yes,' I replied 'but *you've* had more practice.') It was on this occasion that John Davies insisted that we must have foie gras for lunch.... Hurtling along the damp, flat, greyish-brown roads, towards a remote country hostelry, the thought of goose and grease was almost too much. Was I going to let the side down at last?

The restaurant was in a single-storey building, set amidst untended grass, the whole thing reminiscent of a 1930s tea-garden and I rather expected to see some of those concrete mushrooms, so beloved in gardens of the period. Inside, the place was more as I imagine a brothel might be, decked out in black and gilt. *Madame la patronne*, John Davies intimated, was something of a witch, with a respected facility for conjuring salads out of strange leaves. My inside went into overdrive and I was forced to squeak that I couldn't possibly eat *anything*, not even a dandelion leaf. 'Nonsense!' said John. 'You haven't had any foie gras yet — and this might be your last chance.' At this point *Madame la sorcière* appeared — and offered a potion. By now I was beyond caring *what* happened and meekly drank the black liquid she'd mixed up.... And, miracle of miracles, her spell worked! Soon I was in the dining-room, tucking in to the largest piece of foie gras imaginable. (The dandelion leaves in the salad were magic too!)

There were many more educative experiences that autumn. I met Bill Bolter, who went to Bordeaux to write a treatise on Montesquieu and stayed — to go into the wine trade. There was a trip to the Graves to stay at Château Rahoul, then Australian-owned, and being entertained by the talented Peter Vinding-Diers and his wife, Suzy: she was in charge of her own vintage kitchen, where she — at one time the chief theatre sister at a world famous English hospital — had to cook the traditional lunch for the pickers. One would see her checking the food, the plates, the cutlery — and echoes of 'scalpel, needle, suture' whatever, inevitably came to mind. A vintage lunch, served with as much wine as the vintagers care to drink, is a robust meal and much the same from estate to estate. There's a hearty soup, with wonderful French bread, some meat or poultry, often grilled over vine prunings, with a salad, followed by lots of cheese and, maybe, a fruit tart or some form of pastry.

One Sunday we had a mad dash from Loudenne to Martin Bamford's country cottage in the Lot region for a picnic of langoustines, with lashings of

Opposite above left
Fifteenth-century Flemish painting, part of a diptych, now in the beautiful Art Gallery at Melbourne, showing 'The Marriage at Cana' and the first Miracle. The humans are all types recognizable today, especially the cellarman, obviously remarking that he can't stretch the agreed order for wine just because someone has turned up with a pack of fishermen friends.

Opposite above right
The ancestor of the vat — a *dolium* from the eleventh century BC. It would have been sunk in the earth to keep the wine cool, but in the Martini & Rossi Museum it is shown free-standing to indicate its size.

Opposite below
Eighteenth-century establishment where cheap gin was purveyed, the result being the excesses, poverty and disease against which well-intentioned persons campaigned. It has been pertinently commented that at least some of the nutritional deficiencies of the time might not have been incurred by those who tippled gin and tea (now more freely available and cheapish) had the British adhered to beer, ale — and wine!

Château Rahoul blanc — quite a launch for a débutante such as myself!

As anyone with experience of being with those who love wine will know, one good thing inevitably leads to another. Soon, I found myself regarded as some sort of 'gifted amateur', invited to judge inter-university wine contests, appraise restaurant wine lists — and I was installed as a Compagnon du Beaujolais. This last honour was conferred in Bristol. The gentlemen of the Beaujolais wine order, wearing long green aprons and black Homburg-shaped hats, require the new Compagnons to swear an oath of allegiance and a promise to promote their splendid wine. They then dub you gently on each shoulder with a large vine branch which looks like a knobkerry and invite you to drink out of an *enormous* tastevin. This pleasing ordeal completed, you get a tastevin of your own and a large kiss on both cheeks from whoever presides over the Compagnons on this occasion.

A less happy occasion was when I was invited — almost impelled to go by the editor — to Alsace, where she, with the assistance of Christopher Fielden, was putting a book together. It's a beautiful part of the world and the blossom was out when I got there, but sadly a peculiar virus I had brought along with me destroyed my palate and I could neither eat nor drink. All I recall of the region is the Disney-like architecture — everyone seemed to live in gingerbread houses. And there was the family of wild boar that lived along the drive to the hotel where we all stayed. I would sit, languidly sunning myself on a bench and — at least behind wire fencing — they would all come truffling along as if it was every day that wild boars and English ladies shared the same patch. I went out with my friends — and would suddenly find I had to lie down or even be driven back to the hotel while they tackled the vineyards and the vines and wines. It was some years before I could even think of Alsace wines with anything approaching enthusiasm.

Then, one day, I did an interview on the radio about German wines, after which my friend John Lipitch, of the UK Wine Development Board, asked me to have lunch. In the wine bar we went to, he indicated a bottle of Alsace wine — in prospect it seemed doubly repellent to me. After all, I was getting the *fee* for the interview, he was buying the lunch. I told myself 'I shall start feeling sick —' and, as I put my nose into the glass I experienced a — well, something wonderful. The wine was utterly delicious (why didn't I have a notebook to put down what it was?). I saw what they'd all been on about, I revelled in it. My friends were very tactful — no one said 'I told you so' about this revelation.

Eventually I decided that I must take the whole 'wine thing' a touch more seriously. There had been too many coincidences bringing me into contact with the wine trade — perhaps the most curious being that my next door neighbour, James Rogers, is one of the finest tasters of our day. James, after being a member of the family firm of Cullens, now has his own business and, disdainfully, calls himself 'Rentapalate' in his rôle as consultant. We have been known to give dinner parties together, starting in one house for the apéritifs, progressing via our front gardens to the dining-room next door for the meal (and the wines) and then going back to where we started for the coffee — and whatever we drink then.

So — as it was clearly meant that I should know more about wine, I embarked on some basic training. Christopher Fielden, shipper, merchant, writer, asked me to go with him to France and Spain one chilly February. The

Opposite
Eguisheim, one of the *villages
fleuries* of Alsace, rival to
Riquewihr for fairy-tale charm.

boat to Santander was a brave option at that time of year, given that we had to go through the Bay of Biscay; but Neptune smiled on us and we sat down to the 'gourmet dinner' on board with many bottles of wine — just to get in training, of course, for what was to come. Our party included a man who made one of those cream liqueurs that have recently become fashionable and we all aimed at converging on the Barcelona 'Alimentaria', a food and wine 'fair' or exhibition. But there was a lot of ground to be covered before we got there.

Once ashore, it was all hands to the steering wheel to get us through the regions of Rioja, Navarra, Penedés, but my driving was not fast enough for the dairyman turned vintner, so I was excused. This was just as well. Travelling with the wine trade is gruelling enough, even if you are a passenger. To start with, there are the bottling lines. It is my opinion that when you have seen one bottling line, you have seen them all. The trouble is you *have* to see them all and make original and encouraging comments about them to the enthusiastic operator of the 'cave' who will also want to show you each shiny vat and every last temperature control unit. This routine (if you are travelling with Fielden) can start at eight o'clock in the morning and end at nightfall (the editor wryly comments that I've fortunately never — yet — been obliged to continue until midnight). But, even then, you may well be the guest of some kindly estate or establishment owner, who will insist on taking you through the whole business again, after dinner. Someone should bring out a phrasebook giving twenty different ways of saying 'How interesting!' in French, Spanish — and, for all I know, other languages.

But, bottling lines apart, on that trip I covered three major wine regions of Spain and six of the minor areas in south-west France. In Rioja, the cellars of Henri Forner at Marqués de Caceres were formidably modern and elegant. The wines of Rioja are amazingly good, especially to someone like me who was brought up to think that the only thing you drink from Spain is sherry . . . I wasn't offered sherry there once! More surprises were in store in Navarra, where, at a place called Olite, they have an experimental station: grape varieties completely foreign to the region are planted, just to see how they thrive. The research laboratories were bubbling with pipettes testing soil, machines filled with rootstock churning around. Down in the cellars we sampled strange concoctions and I heard these discussed with deep seriousness.

From Navarra we progressed to Vilafranca del Penedés, to meet the legendary Miguel Torres Snr, who, although now seventy-eight years old, is still most sprightly. He's an autocrat to his staff but a genial host to his guests. Following lunch, after which you might expect that most men of his age would want to take a siesta, he leapt to his feet, eager to show us the house where he'd been born, which is now preserved as a museum, then, at what I can only describe as a scamper, we went through a room full of copper vessels where the TORRES brandies are distilled. I was flagging a little myself by then, but the magnificent family, who all work in the firm, had other plans for me: Doña Margarita Torres, matriarch of the dynasty, was to take me out to dinner at one of the smartest restaurants in Barcelona. This lady is a stunning beauty and, like her husband, still much involved in the business, representing TORRES in the USSR. The day after she entertained me she was going to Morocco to see if she could open up trade there. Languages clearly come easily to her and our conversation was entirely in very idiomatic English, although Doña Margarita was modest about her grasp of the tongue; it is one thing to know a language, she said, but another to master it.

Christopher Fielden is an exacting travelling companion — and the answer to those who suppose such trips to be easygoing. He will say that we must be ready at eight in the morning and then be banging on one's door at half-past seven demanding to know why one hasn't come down to breakfast? Once he even finished doing my packing, so as to get me on the road to another bottling line.

I hope I do not seem ungrateful. The kindness and hospitality of our many hosts was immense, from those who had expected us — and treated us like royalty — to those unaware of our arrival, but who welcomed us all the same and showed us the fruits of their labour with such enthusiasm. I shall never forget the lady who, seeing me walking down the corridor of her chilly château in bare feet, stepped out of her own slippers and insisted on my wearing them. Then there was the young girl in the Pyrenees who, left in charge of the vineyard and the shop while her parents were away, within minutes of our totally unexpected visit, put on her coat and drove us in a special sort of four wheel drive high terrain vehicle up a slope suitable only for mountain goats, so that we might inspect her father's vines, grown from the — new to me — Irouléguy grape. The same young girl agreed to be interviewed for the BBC in English, arranged where we should stay for the night and, as we left, pressed on us bottles of the family's excellent *Poire* alcohol for each one of our party.

If that's how they treat univited guests in the Pyrenees, what must it be like to be expected — there and in so very many other places?

It was definitely a lucky day when I encountered the wine trade.

DONS DRINKING

by Alan Bell

The historic surroundings and long academic traditions of the two ancient English universities help to give them a high reputation in all matters relating to wine and food. When I moved to Oxford from Edinburgh some years ago, to take up a senior post in the university library, many Scottish friends seemed more curious about my gastronomic good fortune than solicitous for my professional prospects. It soon became apparent that the tradition of early buying, laying down and serving vintage wine is very much alive in Oxford, keenly maintained by some of the newer colleges as well as by the ancient foundations. There are elderly college butlers famous throughout the university for their knowledge and helpfulness, and among the wine stewards of the senior common rooms (the fellows of colleges responsible for ordering new stock) are many people of daunting erudition, to whom merchants themselves sometimes turn for advice. Here are scholars accustomed to the minute grading of exam papers, who out of habit apply the same analytical standards to a trade presentation of recent clarets and Burgundies. Not for these learned men the mere ticking, crossing, and starring of lesser mortals: I have seen whole essays written about inky young bourgeois clarets, complete with examiners' algebraic markings, and I once detected a neighbouring taster adding a footnote to his lengthy screed. The skill of the ancients is passed on to the younger generation, and undergraduates often feel the benefit. The annual Oxford-Cambridge student wine tasting competition is taken very seriously, not least by the London trade, who may well find some promising recruits among the competing teams of men and women.

Not all Oxford wining and dining is in the 'fine' category, however; some rarely even achieves the epithet 'good'. I was once invited to a college guest night with the somewhat disconcerting assurance that 'the catering is rather like a station hotel in Carlisle' — which turned out to be a very accurate prognosis. Years ago, I was a visitor at a college table while the fellows were interviewing a group of candidates for the college chaplaincy. My neighbour took one sip from his glass, turned to me, and said 'It would be a good test of these vicars to find out which of them could turn this "wine" into *wine*!'

High table drinking is not therefore always a glorious sequence of Tio Pepe, Troplong Mondot and Taylor, whatever the undergraduates at the long benches lower down the hall may think. Nor is high table food of uniformly high standard, however often the students may feel that the dons are getting the best cuts and they the knuckle ends. Colleges that have a reputation for good cooking tend to provide well for undergraduates and fellows alike. Excellence at high table usually means a high standard throughout the college kitchen; the chef and his staff try harder, and the young are attracted into communal dinner in hall, which keeps its traditional position as one of the centres of college life. They are much better fed there than on endless spaghetti and plonk in out-of-college lodgings, or pies in pubs. The high tables, at which the fellows of the individual college meet for luncheon or dinner as one of the perquisites of their fellowships, gain from this benevolent rationale, and a number of college chefs are regular prizewinners in various local competitions.

Lunches tend to be brisk, businesslike occasions. Simple fare — soup, chop, and cheese, for example, washed down with a half pint of beer (in some colleges from a seventeenth- or eighteenth-century tankard) — is provided, and there is stolidly tutorial conversation on the internal affairs of the college and its students. Guests are few. At dinner, with the food rather more elaborate and the pace more relaxed, the talk is somewhat different. The tradition of leisurely dining in college has received a knock from the preference of many married fellows for eating at home. At the opening of Evelyn Waugh's novel *Decline and Fall*, two bachelor dons cower from undergraduate revelries in the quadrangle, while their colleagues are 'all scattered over Boar's Hill and North Oxford at gay, contentious little parties'. That was written in 1928, and there has been a further decline since then, but dining continues resilient in a number of colleges in spite of such domestic pressures.

Dinner in college is a time for unwinding after exacting work in the library or the laboratory, and a convention against too serious a 'business' conversation often prevails. Visitors, who are encouraged particularly on weekly guest-nights during term, are often surprised by the apparent triviality of high table talk. Those who might have hoped for high matters of Church and State, or for the welterweight exposition of a new philosophical theory, will be disappointed. They might be treated, instead, say, to a widely ranging discussion of the changed dimensions of a Bath Oliver biscuit. Journalists have sometimes, merely on the basis of a few puzzling post-prandial trivialities, written whole articles on the decline of Oxford's academic standards. They are wrong, as they probably do not realize how far dinner-time is regarded as an occasion for relaxation, and they can all too easily

Was this typical of the masculine get-togethers of our ancestors? Though this gathering seems to be held in a country mansion rather than a college hall.

underestimate the underlying seriousness of tone. If it is dry cheese biscuits that are under discussion, it could well be that an economic historian, a curator of the university museum, a professor of engineering and a literary critic will each contribute something interesting, abstruse or amusing, and these mixtures of different specialisms are of the essence of college life. Gossip abounds, of course, and some are skilled in that characteristic Oxford mode that mixes the proprietorial and the feline in equal measure. Bores are by no means unknown either, both of the elderly repetitive and the stridently monologuist variety.

Feast nights occur from time to time, to commemorate founders and benefactors, or to entertain former members of the college at 'gaudies' (named from the Latin *gaudeamus* — 'let us rejoice'). On such occasions there is grander (though not necessarily better) food, more (and finer) wine, sometimes a chirp or two from the college choir, but not too many speeches. The grandest of the college silver will be in evidence, and a loving cup (in one college an unmanoeuvrable founder's drinking horn) will be ceremoniously passed round, charged with a secret brew concocted in the steward's pantry, definitely highly traditional but usually rather nasty.

On such feast days, dessert (see below) will probably follow the main meal at the same table. On lesser nights (though a few colleges have regrettably abandoned the tradition entirely) after a short closing grace the company will rise from the oak table of the college hall, and reconvene with different neighbours around the mahogany one of an adjacent common room. Some colleges split up into groups of twos or threes, messing (see below) at circular wine tables — which involves a great deal of passing to and fro, and restricts general conversation. Most common rooms have the nuts and wine (and sometimes, rather an innovation, cheese and chocolates) laid out on a single beautifully polished table. In common room, even more than in hall itself, candlelight is a great advantage. Muted by quietly glowing mahogany rather than intensified by white napery as in a tasting or decanting room, it provides a mellow light guaranteed to put a decande or aureole on the rim-colour of a glass even of middling claret, and to make each of the wines appear rather more consequential.

Table equipage varies from common room to common room. To help with further sustenance there are nutcrackers and grape-scissors of some elaborateness but doubtful efficiency. At least one college believes its silver apple-corer to be unique. 'Someone ought to patent this,' they say, as the frame descends on a Cox's pippin, leaving four neat quadrants with a candle-like core standing in the middle of the circular block. Little do they know that similar devices, in base metal, have long been available in any large kitchen supplier's. For *ablution* there are finger bowls ranging from pressed glass fishpaste jars to silver basins presented by former members of the common room. For *inhalation* there will be a snuff box to go round once, gently announcing the end of the dessert proceedings and hinting that it is time to withdraw yet again, for coffee. Nowadays, judging by the dryness of the contents of the box, snuff is more a matter of ceremony than of serious indulgence.

Much ingenuity is devoted to *locomotion*, to ensure that the wine is moved smoothly and promptly, with the minimum of effort. So far as I know, Oxford cannot boast one of those chain-driven or seesaw Georgian railways

Georgian table, with net underneath so that the 'empties' could be easily tossed away, and a frame on which a screen could be arranged so as to protect the topers seated around the fire. Flaps enable the table to be drawn up close to the hearth without the risk of full bottles falling off the edge and being broken.

going round a table to take the decanter on its way. One small college has on the mantelpiece of its former common room a pair of wooden coasters operated by cords at each side, which take the decanters a mere six feet to the other side of the fireplace. These are a reminder of the oppressive smallness of the fellowship in the days when conversation died away in petty college squabbles or major rows, leaving senior and junior fellow at right and left to chug the wine back and forth in silence or torpor. Another college solves the problem of moving the wine by equipping the junior fellow dining with a pair of staves, one crook-ended and one crutch-ended. Some deft wrist-work with these push-me-pull-yous can ensure that the silver boat with its twin decanters is kept on its way, nudged from under the negligent nose of some garrulous visiting dignitary whom it might have been uncivil to buzz too markedly with a 'The wine is with you, sir.'

Many of the colleges at Oxford (and Cambridge) are famous for their cellars of vintage port. Oxford tends to be rather sensitive on the subject, and has been so since the historian Edward Gibbon's remarks in his *Autobiography* about the 'dull and deep potations' of the fellows of Magdalen during his brief career as an undergraduate there in the 1750s. Gibbon's asides on these men 'sunk in port and prejudice' have rankled for generations. In the mid eighteenth century, such remarks were justified; in Rowlandson's caricatures of academic life the punch bowl is often in evidence. It was then customary for colleges to buy their port by the pipe and to bottle it in their own cellars. World War I put paid to this practice, but colleges' bottles with named seals have survived from the old days to become collectors items, though many others were broken up to be set in cement on top of college walls to deter climbers-in.

Even now, 'port-swilling dons' (sometimes 'claret-swilling' to match a prevalent Social-Democratical tone in much Oxford politics) make an easy journalistic cliché when older universities are contrasted with more 'progressive' (and less sociable, probably wineless) institutions. There is an unfortunate misunderstanding abroad, too, that the fellows are pouring away their ancient endowments. In fact, although their food is provided by the colleges, the cost of the wine at high table and in common room is shared between those drinking, and at prices that balance the wisdom of the forefathers with the necessities of college accounting. Bursars and wine stewards rarely see eye to eye about replenishments.

In fact, less and less port seems to be taken at dessert nowadays. When the decanters go round, many seem to prefer continuing with the red table wine (or a different claret) to venturing on to something heavier. Madeira is usually offered, too (though rarely of a quality to match the vintage port), and it has a small following. In summer, many colleges will provide a good (sometimes a really excellent, and well aged) Sauternes, which can look its best against fine silver and glowing mahogany in the evening light. Port, however, does seem to be less in demand than it used to be. All too often one hears that old saw 'I do like port, but unfortunately port doesn't like me'. It usually comes from those who forget how port is usually given the blame for all that goes before (and after), just as it is the oysters that are conveniently blamed for the results of an entire banquet. The answer, surely, would be to show some restraint earlier, the better to enjoy the fine vintage port that common room will offer. It is often magnificent wine, beautifully and appropriately served as well.

William IV mahogany gout stool and Victorian ditto, raising and protecting the sensitive limb: essential in the days when for many gout had to be endured rather than treated.

This decline in port drinking is regrettable, though it does have the advantage for traditionalists that college stocks are conserved a while longer. No college has yet been know to complain of a port 'lake', though there have occasionally been sales of overstocks for the benefit of the continuing cellar — and perhaps of the college building fund, as well.

Is it too donnish to seek an abstract explanation for the moratorium that fashion seems to have temporarily decreed to reduce port consumption in the ancient universities? The Cambridge classicist F M Cornford's *Microcosmographia Academica* defined the committee man's view that the right moment has not *yet* arrived for any given course of action, as 'the principle of unripe time'. Such a delaying tactic is much more welcome in the cellar than in the committee room, particularly for a wine that should be venerable (though never hoary). There are therefore some advantages in a change of fashion that puts a temporary brake on consumption. The principle of unripe port scarcely bears thinking about.

Editorial note: The 'dessert' referred to should be understood in the sense of the Shorter Oxford Dictionary's definition, which seems to have originated in 1600. The word derives from the old French *desservir* — to remove what has been served, to clear the table.... A course of fruit, sweetmeats etc served after a dinner or supper; the last course at an entertainment.' The Shorter Oxford gives a second meaning: 'In U S often including pies, etc, 1848.' At a traditional British dinner the cloth — always laid on such an occasion — will be cleared, together with anything remaining from the meal, while the fruits and nuts will remain, the polished surface of the table facilitating the circulation of the decanters.

The use of the term 'messing' is defined as: 'Company of persons eating together'. The Shorter Oxford says that it was 'Originally each group of four persons (sitting together and helped from the same dishes) into which the company at a banquet was commonly divided. Now only in the Inns of Court, a party of four benchers or four students. Hence, a company of persons who regularly take their meals together' and, from 1536 'In the Army and Navy: each of the several parties into which a regiment or ship's company is divided.'

The 'common room' referred to will, when it concerns that used by the dons, be the senior common room of a college.

WALKING THROUGH WINE

by Nigel Buxton

It all began as a personal, private pleasure and only much later acquired professional significance. The wine certainly preceded the walking, though just when and where I drank my first glass I cannot for the life of me say.

Girls, I suspect, largely deserve the credit. Wining was traditionally indispensible to dining, and taking girls out to dinner was a pleasure for which a taste was acquired long before anything so inexpensive and innocent (and boring, one would have said in one's salad days) as walking had exerted any appeal.

Girls inspired the walking, too. Or, rather, a particular girl. Hopelessly in love at the age of thirty with someone whose true affections were otherwise and irrevocably committed, imprisoned Monday to Friday by work in London, I began escaping at the weekends to the South Downs of my native Sussex, finding solace — sanity, even — in the rhythm of long days that left one physically tired and philosophically maybe a touch sturdier.

Then there was Hilaire Belloc, whose essays and verse I read avidly. Sussex man that he was, too, or became, his prose and poetry in praise and celebration of the Downs and walking and wine were heady enough for anyone of like predelictions, and little short of intoxicating for a young man in the condition that I was then. Kipling, in fact, wrote at least as memorably about the Downs, but Belloc was better on wine:

> 'Wine, privilege of the completely free;
> Wine the recorder; wine the sagely strong;
> Wine, bright avenger of sly-dealing
> wrong . . .'

Up there on the Sussex chalk, with a breeze off the Channel, and the sun, and the sound of larks and the scent of the turf, how one fancied oneself on the long byways of France, with all that one needed in a pack on one's back, buying one's wine when opportunity offered, as Belloc had on his way to Rome:

> 'Choosing the middle price, at fourpence a quart, I said, "Pray give me a hap'orth in a mug." It was delicious — full of all those things wine merchants talk of, bouquet and body, and flavour — so I bought a quart of it, corked it up very tight, put it in my sack, and held it in store against the wineless places . . . .'

A more purposeful association of wine and walking was, in a manner of speaking, only a step or two away. From chalk to chalk. From the South Downs to the Côte des Blancs of Champagne. Not in summer, but in

Château Lafite, Pauillac, with the pepperpot tower surmounted by the five arrows bound together, emblems of the five brothers of the Rothschild dynasty who, separately, might be broken but, united, could always endure and triumph.

November when the tracks and lanes about Vinay and Mancy and Grauves ran café au lait, and at lunchtime I crouched in the edge of a wood whose ivy, growing thickly over a fallen tree, made a sort of arbour. Not to spend the night grandly at Moët et Chandon's Château de Saran, or expensively at the Hôtel Royal Champagne at Champillon, as I was to do in years to come, but in the very modest little Hôtel St Nicholas (closed these several years) in Avize, where the only shower was in the kitchen and there were rabbit and pigeon for supper and later, at the bar, the local vignerons in their *bleus de travail* were as generous with their offers of *un petit coup* as with their advice as to where I ought to go and what I ought to see. Since then, I have never drunk a blanc de blancs without thinking of that winter and Avize.

Other walks in France's wine-making areas followed. Not, at this time, with any notion of a systematic association of wine and walking in mind, but because more and more I derived great personal satisfaction — physical, emotional, intellectual — from it. Also because, judging by one's correspondence, there was evidently an especially eager readership for accounts of walking abroad in general and in France in particular, and because, if an element of the exotic was to be a sine qua non of the foreign walking experience, then from several key points of view walking in French 'wine country' offered considerable advantages over walking anywhere else.

Identification and accessibility were the first of such benefits. Good walking country, which for most of us means terrain that is appealing but not physically too difficult or demanding, is by no means always easy to identify, especially when it is abroad.

The vineyards of France, one knew, were for the most part in some of the most beautiful parts of the whole beautiful land: Alsace, the Jura, the Loire, Burgundy, the Rhône Valley, Provence.... Vineyards, one theorized, *have* to be in places that are neither wildly remote nor in any respect hostile, nor especially hard to get to. Yet wine country, one was surely entitled to conjecture, was far from necessarily being dull; the best grapes, after all, were said to be grown on the hillsides, were they not? In sum, then, wine country meant thousands of square miles of accessible, topographically varied terrain, with roads if one required them, but almost certainly an infinity of traffic-free byways and paths when one did not.

'Manageability' might cover a third, not insignificant virtue of wine

Mont Sainte Victoire, in Provence

country seen from the walker's point of view. With rare exceptions (possibly the meticulously signposted paths of Switzerland and Germany, for example) all serious walking calls for serious map-reading; but the consequences of taking the wrong track among the vineyards are likely to be much less solemn than on mountain or moor or deep forest path. That one *can* lose one's way as easily in wine country as anywhere else (*more* easily, it might be argued, when there is usually a multiplicity of possibilities on ground and map) I can bear fervent witness to. But whereas an error even in the Highlands of Scotland might easily be fatal, an error in wine country is seldom worse than wretchedly inconvenient, though last year, in the Corbières, that wild, beautiful *appellation* of the resurgent Midi, briefly lost but caught in the

mother and father of all summer thunderstorms, I thought my last moment might have come.

Landscape on the River Lot

Then there were what our Californian friends might call the 'logistics'. In the very nature of it, good walking country — rural, open in large measure, unurbanized — tends to be ill-equipped with the wherewithal for board and lodging. Camping may be all very well, but paradoxically can be as limiting as it may be liberating. Wine country, on the other hand, by and large has villages and towns, which is to say inns, hotels, cafés, restaurants, far from always five star to be sure, but usually better than tolerable and not infrequently rather grand.

Then there was the wine itself. The more intimately I became acquainted with the countryside where the grapes were grown, and — by chance at first — the people who grew them, the more I was invited to see inside the *pressoirs* and *caves* where the arts and techniques of vinification were performed, and talked with the men (and women, by heavens!) who practised them; the more I swirled and eyed and nosed and chewed and gurgled this or that product of their labours, the more acute became my awareness of my ignorance of the subject in which I had supposed myself to be tolerably well educated, but the deeper and richer also became the pleasure I derived from it.

A sense of place, an awareness of the *terroir*, says Hugh Johnson, is the key to the understanding of the wines of France, even more than those of any other country. A sense of place. An awareness of the *terroir*. . . . Here, I saw (and once seen, it all appeared so self-evident), were the sources of my infinitely increased enjoyment. '*Le vin, c'est le terroir*,' says Émile Peynaud. But of course! As a man is the product of his environment, so must an honestly made wine embody the essential character of the soil in which the grapes are grown. Sceptics might scoff at the professional wine taster's identification of blackcurrants — say — or violets in the 'nose' of a wine, but — mutatis mutandis — the soil that produces grapes is capable also of producing other fruit or flowers. Who yet fully understands the synthesis of bouquet? Walking in Languedoc, one has delighted in the broom — the *genêt* — and the wild thyme, has detected them, or thought one did, in a Minervois. Naming truffles as the predominating element in the 'nose' of a certain Côtes de Provence, I have thereupon been taken to where, on that particular estate, the 'black nuggets' are found under oaks bordering the Syrah and the Grenache.

And at least as significant as the 'place' (the land itself, the climate, the rural environment) were the people. More so with the lesser wines than the greater ones. More so with a Minervois — say — than a Margaux; more with a Côtes du Rhône than with a Corton-Charlemagne; more with a Pinot Noir of Menetou Salon than with a Vosne Romanée or a Nuits Saint Georges.

For although one's occasional delight in the great wines of the world suffers no erosion, the lesser ones are much more the stuff of one's everyday experience. And it is in the cellars of lesser-known (indeed, often almost unknown) estates, in the unpretentious, frequently unprepossessing cellars of comparatively modest, out of the way *domaines* that the most impressive, most exciting experiments are going on and the more significant advances being made.

'*Le vin, c'est le terroir*.' Without doubt, but it is equally (some would say more) the man, or the woman who makes it, who chooses to grow this grape as opposed to that, who decides to start picking today or tomorrow, who vinifies 'classically', or in obedience to some innovative theory; those whose own personal taste determines just how much of one wine or another goes into the assemblage. Individual style can be almost as decisive in the making of wine as in the writing of prose.

But if my forthcoming book *Walks in Wine Country* (to be published in the near future by John Murray) achieves nothing else, I hope it will at least convey something of the rewards that await the lover of wine who is willing to forsake the car and take to the paths through or beside or in sight of the vines. A Gigondas, to me, is no longer an agreeable red wine from somewhere in the Rhône Valley, but a village where, on a hot summer day, I drank deliciously cold water at a spring and had a picnic among the box and juniper high up among the Dentelles de Mirailles. A Minervois is dog roses and cistus and broom and nightingales beside the Canal du Midi under a blue sky. The lovely vin de pays of Domaine Trevallon is the walk from Les Baux over the limestone hills of Les Alpilles and back again, racing the dark.

Good wine is always a delight. It is even better when the name on the bottles becomes hawthorn in bloom on the hills of Sancerre; the blessing of a little shade on a hot summer's day high up on the terraces of Condrieu; the joy of a hot bath, a glass of Champagne, and a prospect of dinner 'Chez Boyer' in Rheims to follow seventeen winter miles on the Côte des Blancs.

Above
Patrick Grubb conducting the pre-sale tasting at the annual
Nederburg auction. In a gigantic marquee, pourers acting with
guardsman-like precision pour the samples for the attending
growers, wine-makers and wine-minded socialites. Later, when
some will have enjoyed the gargantuan buffet in the gardens,
while goddess-like girls parade in fashions especially designed
for the occasion, the auction itself takes place in another
marquee.

Overleaf above

The Presentation of Baby Dionysos

This superb mosaic is from the House of Aion, Nea Paphos in
Cyprus which was discovered in 1983 by the Polish Mission and
so far has only been partly excavated. The dining-room is
'carpeted' with scenes from the life of Dionysos in which,
according to the book by D Michaelides (*Cyprus Mosaics*,
published by the Department of Antiquities) 'Dionysos plays the
rôle of the newly born supreme god, appearing as the universal
saviour'. This, it is pointed out, comes from the Late Roman
period, in about the fourth century AD, when 'the sudden rise of
Christianity started becoming a threat to paganism'.

The mosaic shows Hermes holding the baby Dionysos and
about to hand him over to old Tropheus, behind whom are three
nymphs waiting to bath the infant. The event is taking place on
Mount Nysa, a personification of the mountain being seated
under a tree on the left. Between Nysa and the nymphs stands
Anatrophe (Upbringing) and also present are Ambrosia and
Nectar, who are there to stress the godly nature of the baby and,
on the right, there is Theogonia (Birth of Gods), who, like the
baby, has a nimbus.

In the other mosaics in the series, as in the well-known
'Discovery of Wine' mosaic in the nearby 'House of Theseus',
the emphasis is on the properties of wine which, liberating and
life-enhancing, can endow drinkers with some of the attributes
of the God Dionysos. Cyprus, famous for its wine since
antiquity, has many works of art commemorating the use and
the wonders of wine — Mark Antony gave this 'Island of
Aphrodite' to Cleopatra at least partly because of the wine made
there.

WINE FOR FUN

by Pamela Vandyke Price

If there should ever be a guild or association of those who try to teach wine, the motto would be inevitable: 'How long?', 'How soon?', and 'When?' — for the one question that certainly will be asked in a session of this kind is when the wine is likely to be at its peak. Questions such as: what does the speaker think of supermarket wines, what is the 'best' claret, can there be an explanation of vintage and non-vintage, or appellation contrôlée, or how wine is made 'from leaves' (the latter due to a misunderstanding about Muscadet *sur lie* given by a producer) or even 'How do I get into the wine trade?' are all possible hazards. But the 'How long?' recurs — and is perhaps indicative of the fascination that wine exerts on tasters, which has altered the consumer attitude to the blood of the grape within the past thirty years.

As recently as the late 1950s wine was seldom 'taught' or studied seriously. The somewhat two-dimensional dons in the Cambridge novels of C P Snow may have dominated the corridors of power, but they never seem to have argued back at their 'mentor' when he was presiding over the 'discussion' of a bottle. Students of the wine trade got time off from work to go and listen to lecturers drawn from the higher echelons of the trade — and sometimes indulged in maliciously querying statements made by somebody known (via the trade press gossip columns for those who could interpret same) to be at odds with the speaker. 'Sir — may I read something out of a book?' presaged a tricky quickie. Talks were given at a few tastings and occasionally to meetings of The International Wine & Food Society, but these tended to be semi-promotional, a shipper drawing attention to a new vintage, a merchant to previously unfamiliar wines and, sometimes, comments were made on wines at a 'wine dinner'. There might be some picturesque anecdote, seldom were there any hard facts or technicalities. Wine, as a leisure pursuit, was somewhat esoteric.

Serious study sessions, 'tutored tastings', conducted visits to vineyards and wine weekends began, I think, to proliferate for several reasons; they are certainly now accepted as unquestioningly as underwater swimming, car maintenance and, indeed, every type of 'do it yourself' activity — because both women and men do now have to 'do' wine themselves, either via the supermarket, the wine club or such inde-pendent and specialist merchants as fortunately still exist. In the late 1960s and from then on there were more outlets for wine, there were more wines, more books on wine, more tastings and a spurt of teaching sessions.

For a number of years I have been trying to teach wine and, also, attending the sessions addressed by others so as to learn. Though there is no substitute for having to address an audience. A world-famous musician was once asked his opinion of a well-known piece and replied that he didn't really know it. 'But it was in your recital last week!' 'Ah yes,' said the virtuoso, 'but I haven't

Opposite below
Part of the great mosaic from the western portico of the House of Dionysos, Nea Paphos, in Cyprus, where the god of wine offers a bunch of grapes to the nymph Akme (personifying culmination — hence 'the acme of perfection'). A learned comment by D Michaelides in his book (see p 143) suggests that this is symbolic of the beneficial effect of wine when sensibly drunk — but the irreverant may think that Akme appears somewhat overcome and may be enduring the first hangover!

taught it yet.' My appearance among the members involved in the wine trade at the Christie's wine courses has taught me more than all those years sitting among the students at Vintners' Hall. (And, as I have never been in the wine trade, I can be outspoken about the most eminent 'personalities' and the most costly bottles, if I wish.)

A teaching session is intimidating. (If anyone denies this, then they are probably boring — even people who read the news suffer from 'mike fright' and I admit to knowing something of the feelings of the person who enters a cage of leopards, with a chair in one hand and a whip in the other — never taking his eyes off the animals!) Some settings are taxing in themselves: in aircraft, on board ship, in highspeed trains. I attended one in a 'hide' overlooking a crocodile-infested river, when we spat over the wall fifty feet down to the banks. I also gave a Champagne lecture in the bush, with a sunset flaming behind me and a francolin running about just out of reach. During one after-dinner talk I gave in a London club a cat was hunting a mouse to and fro under the tables .... Luckily the diners were looking at me — *didn't* I try to keep their attention — and not at pussy, but I think the kill was made outside a door adroitly opened by one of the watchful waiters. No one seemed to have noticed.

Every audience is different. Colleagues agree that, for those who arrive after a day's work and who may get hungry as time passes, it is essential to offer entertainment as well as instruction. (At a mere lecture they can have a drink on the way and then go to sleep in the back row.) To cope with a 'performance' — for one is in front of them for a couple of hours or more — the odd story or joke is helpful; if I don't get a chuckle within the first five minutes I know I'm having an off night — and to be on form is why I don't go out to tastings or luncheons on that day. As one surveys the audience, people can often be recognized as belonging to several expected groups. Even years ago at the Academy of Wine, which used to be run in Hedges & Butler's seventeenth-century cellars for a mere dozen people at a time, this division into categories was apparent. There are those who intend to get their money's worth by becoming or seeming to become tipsy, they are shy of spitting; those who have concocted a question to show how knowledgeable they already are; those who try to monopolize the speaker; and those who assume an air of tolerant boredom that can sometimes infect a whole row, like vinegar spilled in a cellar. Sometimes there is definite antagonism: years ago I gave several wine talks in what, in the daytime, were classrooms, accommodation being planned for the infant size, not for the sort of large lady with a bird or glittering pin in her hat who usually wedged herself into a place in the front row and would surge upwards, sometimes carrying desk and chair with her, to demand whether I didn't see myself making the younger generation into drunkards?

There are the whisperers. Should one adopt brusque tactics and ask that we may all hear the obviously fascinating comments? The only thing to do is drop one's voice and hope that the other people will 'Ssh-ssh!' the offenders. Once I had before me a man who fed everything I said into his computer; that wasn't too distracting, although as, by his frequent questions, he hadn't always understood what I'd been saying, I am doubtful about the result. It was not quite as unnerving as when a tape recorder is put in front of the speaker and, at intervals, there will be a rush to change the cassette. I suppose the day will come when someone plugs a Walkman to their ear and, while hearkening unto the instruction of some other colleague talking on wine asks me whether I agree with what they are saying at the same time.

Just as I know I shall always learn more from any group I'm addressing than they will from me, so I am recurrently amazed at people themselves. One woman attending an evening series would munch up all the biscuits put out to accompany the tastings and, when she had finished the plateful intended for everyone at the table, would up and away, before a sample of wine had even been poured! Did she think she was in some refreshment room and was longing for a cup of tea, I have since wondered? Though one never knows. One colleague confided that he was puzzled by the regular appearance of an attractive girl who, when he was about twenty minutes into his subject, would leave the room. The organizer tactfully inquired, after a few of these brief appearances, whether she was dying for a cigarette or simply loathed the speaker? Not at all. Her husband, who had paid for the course, would leave her at the door, then, after a prudent interval, she'd depart for an appointment with another gentleman. And, somewhere in the provinces, there was a man who, every three or four weeks, would don evening dress and depart for a 'wine evening' of a famous dining society. It was only when somebody who *was* a member of aforesaid society moved into the neighbourhood and made it known that there was no local branch, that the self-styled gastronome had to evolve another regular and respectable-sounding rendezvous.

As one who has suffered from various sorts of speakers who may be world authorities on wine but are no Demosthenes as regards oratory — the 'Well — er — um' and 'Y'know' interpolators — I am tough about keeping the audience's attention by making them work too. (They will — they must — get tired even of my voice!) Many of my writings owe much to the contributions of the Christie's and other listeners: bits of information gleaned from someone's grandfather, the family butler, a club secretary, a friend who kept a pub or someone who's done a stint in a cellar, here or abroad — many's the gorgeous phrase or creative notion as to 'what with what' they've shared with me. (Though, to date, no one has solved the matter of why big bottles are called after Old Testament kings, or why a teaspoon handle, stuck in the neck of a bottle of anything fizzy, will, at need, keep the bubbles rising for hours or even days.)

There have been heart-warming episodes that compensate for the terror beforehand. At a wine weekend at The Castle, Taunton, one woman said enthusiastically, 'I didn't want to come with my husband — I didn't think I'd know enough — but I've *enjoyed* it!' There was the elegant woman who attended a detailed Bordeaux tasting, but never made any comment. Afterwards, she told me that her husband had originally signed up for the course, but had died, so she'd come instead — and, even in that time of bereavement, she paid us the compliment of saying she had been interested. As wine was the first interest in life that revived for me when I had had a similar loss I prize this memory.

Although husbands and wives do often attend wine sessions together, it can sometimes be a good idea if they come separately: one can suggest tactful ways of weaning a too-conservative husband from an unadventurous wine routine, or be practical about selecting dishes suited to wines that the wife likes. Years ago I remember luring an ambitious hostess away from her plan to serve marrons glacés with a great Sauternes. There have been other occasions when the revelation of what a fine not-so-dry wine can be like has made the would-be with-it host alter his views about preprandial refreshers. People need to feel quite free to express likes and dislikes — after the talk is concluded if they are hesitant, though few feel inhibited if the speaker encourages enthusiastic participation. Once I did have to disagree with the student who asked if I didn't find the 'deposit' in a wine didn't 'make it somehow fuller in body if swallowed'. . . . I said I don't like bits in my mouth. But it is a point of view.

One type of teaching-teach-in that can be less than satisfactory, unfortunately, can be the one given by a visiting grower or shipper; there are notable exceptions, such as those given by my friend Miguel Torres Jnr, whose vast experience of the world's wines makes it possible for him to appraise wines of other countries and other producers, without doing more than let his own outstanding wines speak for themselves. Some of my California friends, and Don Xiraldo from Inniskillen in Canada, have similar perspectives on wines other than their own and, if a tactless question does risk them voicing an opinion about something made by a competitor, they are adroit at being diplomatic without abrogating their own opinions. But occasionally an organizer will announce with pride that Monsieur/Herr/Señor/Signor/Senhor X — or even Joe Soap from the New World — is to tutor a range of his wines. This can consist of an encomium of all of them, sometimes read out, the speaker not even glancing at the audience (and if people can't occasionally see your eyes, they will think they can't hear your voice) with so much praise even for the lesser successes that people become bored and, certainly, unwilling to risk asking questions.

It's reasonable that a wine-maker should regard his wines as his children, but not even the most devoted parent can or should bombard what may be a discriminating group of wine-lovers with nothing but praise. One of the most memorable 'tutored tastings' I have ever attended was conducted by Baron Eric de Rothschild who admitted that he, personally, *liked* some vintages of

One of the rooms in the glorious museum at Château Mouton-Rothschild, where works of art related to wine are admirably displayed, largely due to the inspiration of the late Baronne Pauline, second wife of the late Baron Philippe.

Steven Spurrier, founder of l'Académie du Vin in Paris in 1972, which now has branches in New York, Toronto, Montreal, Melbourne and Zürich, is also organizer of the Christie's Wine Course in South Kensington, London. Here he is taking one of the sessions. The course was nominated for the Marqués de Cáceres Award in 1989.

Château Lafite more than others, although he also paid handsome tribute to all those of the estate who had surmounted various known problems by the way they cultivated the vines and made the wine.

In looking back, I can see now that many of those monoliths of my early days when I was trying to learn about wine were, by today's standards, insufficiently informed, opinionated, sometimes downright dreary. There were also those who, albeit with an eccentric approach to the subject, did prick my interest into further study. Ronald Avery, Freddie Hennessy, Reggie Cobb and John Smithes, Wyndham Fletcher, Otto Loeb, and, always, my supreme tutor, Allan Sichel, all forced me to go on trying to know more — though none of them were ideal speakers at all. Here, I have to declare that my years at a dramatic school that trained some very big stars have stood me in good stead, because knowledge, in these days of so many ways whereby information is promulgated, is simply not enough — it must be presented acceptably, adapted to many different occasions and 'sold' to the listeners.

If I'm allowed to do a type of 'cross-talk' session with a friend — it must be someone you know well and like as well as respect — I think this can be a two-way delight: there is no one single way to taste, nor one absolute in wine, as Michael Broadbent has pointed out. With John Avery I've several times been able to do a 'twosome': 'You're looking at this wine from the point of view of a merchant!' 'You, Pamela, don't seem to see what it will be like in five years' time!' This encourages the audience to continue in furious discussions later. Or, with Steven Spurrier, who presides at Christie's: 'I'd say this wine will be good for another five years — perhaps get even better —' 'Oh I think it's delicious now.' 'Goodness Steven, you've lived so long in France that you've caught their habit of infanticide — we should never have let that country go!'

Opinions from those who have taught around the world show how taxing it is to address audiences who may vary from town to town in a far-flung country and, certainly, within other wine regions. Steven Spurrier, always quick to spot a potentially 'difficult' member of an audience, is diplomatic, never correctly pronouncing a wine name that has been rendered in tortuous form (would you be able to interpret 'Muscadet leeay'?) and very tactful with anyone who asserts their 'knowledge' because they've 'been there' — astonishing how, for some people, this seems to endow a wine with a superior quality. He tells me that, in Australia, audiences are very technically minded indeed, those in North America tend to be extremely 'vintage conscious', while Canadians are greedy for information of all sorts. Clive Coates, reporting on all-day sessions in the US, says it's sometimes necessary to slow down the pace one might adopt in the UK — people in North America may have to adjust to an unfamiliar voice and tone and, too, sometimes are expected by speakers from abroad to confront or understand wines that are quite unfamiliar – because US sessions tend to concentrate on the classic, well-known European wines. The huge, jovial Bill Baker (once described as a 'little man' by writer Robert Parker, who has obviously never met him) stresses that it's important to adjust the matter of a talk to the audience — both to what they want to hear and can assimilate. A group from the catering trade, say, may not all have English as their first language.

It's tempting to do a comparative tasting of styles of delivery and content from my outsider's point of view: Michael Broadbent is quietly authoritative, definite, speaking with controlled passion and sometimes slyly witty; David Molyneux-Berry of Sotheby's is often more leisurely and academic, ostensibly cool — until some fine and complex wine sparks unexpected eloquence. He has found, in teaching in different regions of South Africa, that there is an enormous variation between, say, Durban and Johannesburg — and even more at the Cape. He stresses that ideally audiences should be seated facing the speaker — if disposed around tables, they can begin to chat (although Liz Berry of La Vigneronne in London finds that her 'regulars' prefer the suggestion of informality by being seated in this way). What David thinks of particular importance is for the speaker to pitch the talk slightly above what may be the capacity to understand and previous knowledge of the audience as a whole — the speaker can always come down slightly, if it is realized that not everything is being understood. But it is destructive of confidence and, certainly, of appeal ever to 'talk down'. Patrick Grubb is a gentle speaker — though he can control huge audiences and charm them into appreciation and laughter.

But there are many more able teachers of wine. And it must not be forgotten that the success of a session depends to a considerable extent on the organization and the sense of the 'pourers': if they start to chat to those attending or, worse, run out of wine because of giving more than the approved measure, then chaos can result. It isn't easy, either, when people insist on coming up to talk beforehand, explaining how they just love Liebfraumilch or how they are going to get one's book out of the library. This is a twitch-making time, like occasions during a dinner at which one is going to hold forth afterwards, and neighbours insist on asking questions — while the speaker wonders whether it's possible to comment on the unsuitable glasses used or to say that at least one of the wines should never have been poured at all! On such occasions one doesn't want to eat much and certainly dare not drink regardless — sometimes I've watched people getting very merry down the tables and have prayed silently that they won't start barracking the talk. It is reported that His Royal Highness Prince Charles will, on the occasions when he attends a dinner after which he is then going to speak, ask practically for a plate of scrambled eggs and a half pint of lager. But can the mere commoner? Often, indeed, such fare would be far more acceptable than the versions of would-be haute cuisine that may have tumbled into the basse cuisine range via the caterer. Once I do remember being asked to speak at my dear friend John Tovey's luxurious restaurant, The Miller Howe, at Windermere and despairing — 'How *can* I talk between all the courses?' The ultimate compliment was paid. 'Would you like to have staff supper — afterwards?' So I sipped and spoke and had a comforting 'nosh' later.

Whereas a mixed audience of lay people can be a possible worry — some wanting to interrupt a lot, some too shy to participate — a group of wine trade persons is really frightening to an outsider such as myself, especially as I don't carry technicalities in my head and, when I've written about a particular wine, I 'wipe' it and have to look up what I wrote about it if questioned. Once I faced a group of growers, makers, technical specialists and other experienced teachers at Stellenbosch: what could I possibly 'teach' them? So, choosing the ground on which to fight, I told them that, being a wordsmith, I feel it is my task to interpret taste reactions for the ordinary layman. A wine was shown at which I asked the authorities why it said 'woolly mittens' to me (evocative of the time when, pram-borne, I would suck my thumb) and not 'old socks'? Once the eminent men and women started sorting out a lay vocabulary, we were all enjoying ourselves — and I learned a great deal.

The female speaker risks overhearing comments when she's behind a door in the 'Ladies': 'Never heard of this woman', 'My husband says women can't taste wine, they smell of so many other things'. I have been tempted to burst forth and tackle the speakers, though to date I've only slipped in a malicious comment when I have later got on my feet to address them.

There are, fortunately, times when an audience, by their warmth and response, however frivolous, however argumentative, spur one on to do better than usual. Most astonishing and rewarding of all there are the times when, maybe after a talk or sometimes at a tasting, somebody will come up and say 'You taught me X years ago — I've always wanted to tell you how it started me off —'. A great pathologist once wrote that if you don't teach, you don't secure for yourself the only immortality worth having in this world. Of course the pupil should go past — or try to get past — the master. But it's wonderful to be the person who started somebody on a career or lifelong hobby. They will never forget you — any more than I ever forget my several teachers.

Standing up to teach wine is like going to a rendezvous with a potential lover — for unless you are willing to love your audience, you cannot make them love wine. You are always apprehensive, you shouldn't take your eyes off them — like the man in the leopard's cage. But it is always instructive and, more often than not, a lot of fun.

HIGHLIGHTS FROM COMPARATIVE WINE PRICE CHART

The following charts have been extracted from the 1989 edition of Christie's complete Price Index of Vintage Wines which records prices of over 6000 wines sold over the past season at auction.

Key to symbols and abbreviations
The prices in the index are lowest to highest obtained at Christie's during the last full calendar year of sales, or the highest recorded in a previous year. Unless indicated otherwise, prices are expressed in *£s per dozen standard-sized bottles, duty-paid* (the conventional London 'hammer' auction price).

The following abbreviations are used:

h	per 2 dozen half-bottles
m	per 6 magnums
dm	per 3 double-magnums
B	per bottle
BE	Belgium bottles
IMP	per imperiale
M	per magnum
TREG	per tregnum (3 bottle bottle)
UK	bottled by a wine merchant in the United Kingdom
‡	price subject to duty and VAT, ie stock sold in bond London or ex cellars Bordeaux

LONDON AUCTION SALE PRICES 1978–1988

Château Cheval-Blanc

Vintage	Calendar Year – lowest-highest price in £s per dozen bottles (duty-paid)										
	1978	1979	1980	1981	1982	1983	1984	1985	1986	1987	1988
1945	840m	500	520–680	780		1200–1640	1750	1720–1880			
1947	380	860–1300	600–860	880–1100	1240–1840	1950–2400		2600–3400	2500–2800	1750–260B	1000UK
1959	210–310	360	255–320	370		720	660–900		880		720–820
1961	290–540	475–560	500–600	520–680	720–860	1000–1400	1450–1500	1550–1850	1400–2000	1800–2000	2600
1962	170–200	195–260	180–200	195–260	240–360	300–460	310–340	380–450	300–400	370–440	
1964	130–185	145–255	165–230	180–290	270–310	320–440	380–540	440–520	420–480	390–600	240–600
1966	170–250	210–270	200–230	250–330	290–420	500–725	680–740	660–840	560–720	620–780m	620–750
1970	155–170	180–250	175–270	175–300	270–360	380–525	420–330	720–760	440–600	480–560	
1971	115–130	140–160	135–165	165–195	230–270	300–380	320–360	230–425	330–360	520dm	440
1975							410–520	540–600	440–500	450–480	440–460
1976							240–330	300–340‡	300–330		420–440
1978							300–360	300–420	350–400‡	330–370	330–520
1982								560–620	460–560	390–520	400–560

Year	United Kingdom index of consumer goods and services										
	1978	1979	1980	1981	1982	1983	1984	1985	1986	1987	1988
Average	197.1	223.5	263.7	295.0	320.4	335.1	351.8	373.2	385.9	402.0	421.7

Château Haut-Brion

Vintage	Calendar Year – lowest-highest price in £s per dozen bottles (duty-paid)										
	1978	1979	1980	1981	1982	1983	1984	1985	1986	1987	1988
1945	680m	650–800	700–780		920	1400–1900	225B–620M	174B–460B	155B–208B	190B–500M	2500
1959	250–420	325–460	300–340	340–460	520–560	700–860	1100–1150	940–1700		800–1050	780–1300
1961	390–560	460–600	420–620	540–680	660–1050	1050–1600	1440–135B	1550–3200	1150–1750	1750–1800	1800–1900
1962	170–200	185–220	180–210		280–360	400–440	420–500	440–540	388–440	540	
1964	135–160	155–250	135–185	185–240	240–280	280–350	380–440	390–680	420–600	440	420–500
1966	165–210	210–260	200–260	240–350	330–440	470–760	580–760	560–980	560–780	600–700	580–780
1970	120–170	175–210	160–200	195–270	270–350	380–600	560–640	480–700	500–640	500–560	460–540
1971	105m	130–145	115–125	125–140	195–200	250–260	280–340	300–400	330–370	340	320–390
1975							400–520	480–620	390–500	380–440	370–380
1976							230–300	260–500	280–350	320–380	320–460
1978							280–360	320–480	320–390	310–400	340–350
1982								600	420–450	360–420	340–380

Year	United Kingdom index of consumer goods and services										
	1978	1979	1980	1981	1982	1983	1984	1985	1986	1987	1988
Average	197.1	223.5	263.7	295.0	320.4	335.1	351.8	373.2	385.9	402.0	421.7

152

LONDON AUCTION SALE PRICES 1978–1988

Château Lafite

Vintage	Calendar Year – lowest-highest price in £s per dozen bottles (duty-paid)										
	1978	1979	1980	1981	1982	1983	1984	1985	1986	1987	1988
1945	900–1900	1080–1800	1000–1150	1160–1680	1600–1880	2200–2500		3100–4800	1800–2700	2700	2800–230B
1959	420–560	500–660	440–550	480–760	760–860	1000–1100	1480–1700	1850–2100	1600–1950	1600–2100	1400–1700
1961	480–660	680–900	600–800	840–1100	1100–1500	1400–2300	2400–2600	1050–2500	1500–2200	1840–2100	1750–1800
1962	210–320	250–330	220–290	260–340	330–420	420–500	440–570	520–640	460–540	480–500	420–560
1964	145–190	200–220	185–220	190–250	270–350	350–370	420–480	350–660	310–390	420	400
1966	190–330	380–500	320–480	380–500	520–620	920–1150	940–1100	720–1150	700–880	700–850	650–720
1970	185–250	220–280	230–330	240–360	460–520	640–740	740–960		600–840	600–720	540–780
1971	120–130	160–170	140–170	155–175	210–260	250–360	310–350	360–500	360–500	310–440	390–420
1975							600–700	640–800	520–720	520–640	480–650
1976							300–400	390–480	350–460	460–540	540–600
1978							420–520	300–700	420–580	420–480	390–560
1982								520–700	500–600	440–560	420–560
United Kingdom index of consumer goods and services											
Year	1978	1979	1980	1981	1982	1983	1984	1985	1986	1987	1988
Average	197.1	223.5	263.7	295.0	320.4	335.1	351.8	373.2	385.9	402.0	421.7

Château Latour

Vintage	Calendar Year – lowest-highest price in £s per dozen bottles (duty-paid)										
	1978	1979	1980	1981	1982	1983	1984	1985	1986	1987	1988
1945	800–990	780–1175	720–1000	1000–1050	1300–120B	2200–2900	260B–280B	3300–5800	1750–3100	180B–210B	250B–310B
1959	250–330	360–520	350–480	350	580–620	660–1100	1150–1300	960–1600	1000–1300	1100–1400	1100–1300
1961	460–520	520–660	540–580	640–864	840–1300	1150–1850	2000–2500	1800–2500	1750–2000	1850–2300	1900–2400
1962	180–210	230–310	210–270	240–330	320–420	400–540m	520–560	520–640	500–600	500–600	460–520
1964	140–190	175–230	180–210	190–250	260–330	340–540	520–580	420–620	480–540	420–560	460–580
1966	165–220	220–330	200–270	260–360	370–400	480–760	740–1000	660–920	680–820	660–850	650–820
1970	140–200	180–300	210–310	230–330	310–440	390–720	580–620	600–820	520–720	560–720	540–820
1971	120–160	145–190	155–160	140–200	200–220	250–320	340–390	360–420	340–350	330–420	340–380
1975							440–620	480–700	420–560	440–560	420–540
1976							280–300	300–390	310–360	360–390	360–540
1978							370–460	460–580	380–480	390–510	400–560
1982								540	480–570	460–580	440–620
United Kingdom index of consumer goods and services											
Year	1978	1979	1980	1981	1982	1983	1984	1985	1986	1987	1988
Average	197.1	223.5	263.7	295.0	320.4	335.1	351.8	373.2	385.9	402.0	421.7

Château Margaux

Vintage	Calendar Year – lowest-highest price in £s per dozen bottles (duty-paid)										
	1978	1979	1980	1981	1982	1983	1984	1985	1986	1987	1988
1945	520–810	700–980	700–860		1050–1240	1450–1800	153B–173B	1800–3000	120B–210B	80B–230B	140B
1959	270–330	300–420	300–360	350–480	360–600	620–900	920–980	720–1250	720–920	750–850	700–850
1961	390–920	500–680	460–560	580–720	760–1100	1120–1850	1600–2000	1720–2000	1850–1900	1550–1700	1700–1850
1962	150–210	200–230	175–220	210–240	250–310	330–440	440–540	360–500	370–480	380–460	400–420
1964	110–165	145–195	165–185	190–240	210–250	220–380	360–400	250–400	270–370	250–420	320–350
1966	155–220	210–280	210–260	280–340	340–440	520–760m	700–760	600–860	640–740	540–650	550–760
1970	120–180	180–260	180–250	200–280	270–420	360–640	480–560	470–700	460–580	460–580	420–540
1971	110–210	125–160	125–170	155–175	190–210	240–300	300–330	350–440	330–410	320–380	320–380
1975							380–480	460–580	350–420	360–420	360–440
1976							220–320	350–460	280–350	310–420	
1978							350–430	520–680	420–500	400–500	420–540
1982								560–660	420–540	380–460	400–480
United Kingdom index of consumer goods and services											
Year	1978	1979	1980	1981	1982	1983	1984	1985	1986	1987	1988
Average	197.1	223.5	263.7	295.0	320.4	335.1	351.8	373.2	385.9	402.0	421.7

LONDON AUCTION SALE PRICES 1978–1988

Château Mouton-Rothschild

Vintage	Calendar Year – lowest-highest price in £s per dozen bottles (duty-paid)										
	1978	1979	1980	1981	1982	1983	1984	1985	1986	1987	1988
1945	1300–1600	1000–1650	1040–1350	1840	1300–2300	3000–7200	360B–200B	320B–460B	310B–420B	370B–500B	385B–550B
1959	310–460	360–540	420–520	440–640	600–920	920–1500m	1500–1600	1450–2000	1640–2000	1600–1800	2100–175B
1961	500–700	600–725	620–720	500–1100	1000–1250	1147–2000	1750–2200	1850–3000	1950–2200	2100–2300	1900–2500
1962	210–300	270–360	280	280–340	340–400	420–600	580–700	620–720	600–660	55B–62B	620
1964	170–175		175–200	210–240	220–300	300–420	370–480	420–620	380–440	390–460	500
1966	175–290	250–400	260–330	310–360	380–520	560–850	820–900	760–1000	700–900	780–850	720–980
1970	155–210	200–310	210–330	240–330	310–440	400–720	580–640		500–650	520–660	520–750
1971	135–185	155–170	150–180	150–195	200–250	240–270	280–380	350–440	360–440	420–520	450–520
1975							480–520	380–620	420–620	460–520	480–550
1976							260–360	330–420	330–400	370–480	420–460
1978							440–500	440–700	370–480	390–520	390–520
1982								620–720	420–660	500–650	480–750
United Kingdom index of consumer goods and services											
Year	1978	1979	1980	1981	1982	1983	1984	1985	1986	1987	1988
Average	197.1	223.5	263.7	295.0	320.4	335.1	351.8	373.2	385.9	402.0	421.7

Château Pétrus

Vintage	Calendar Year – lowest-highest price in £s per dozen bottles (duty-paid)										
	1978	1979	1980	1981	1982	1983	1984	1985	1986	1987	1988
1945		920 UK	1160		340B	490B–720B	400B–720B	8800	490B–660B	560B	550B
1959	440						220B–270B	500M	980BE–1600BE		2100
1961		1560		1980m	2100–253B	185B–1450M	400B–490B	9500	1200M–620B	620B–700B	1350M–2300M
1962	340	440	460–580	620	700–920	57B	1900–100B	1550–1900	1680–1700		
1964	330–380	370–620	440–480	520–620	620–820	760–1380m	1750–1900	1750–2060	1650–1840	1600	1850–2350
1966	400–600	560–720	500–680	660	740–900	1250–2200	2000–165B	1700–2400	1900–2300	1900–2600	220B
1970	270–340	340–420	440–540	520–900	760–1150	1080–2100	1750–1850	1650–2200		1700–1800	1600–1950
1971	220–240	185–380	280	400–500	580–820	740–1210	1800–	1800–2100	1600–2200		2200
1975							1300–1500	2100–2300	1600–1900	1600–1650	1350–1400
1976							620–1100	760–840	800–900	720–920	850–1050
1978							640–1000	760–1100	980–1550	1050–1250	1100–1250
1982								2100	1600–2100	1650–1900	1800–2350
United Kingdom index of consumer goods and services											
Year	1978	1979	1980	1981	1982	1983	1984	1985	1986	1987	1988
Average	197.1	223.5	263.7	295.0	320.4	335.1	351.8	373.2	385.9	402.0	421.7

Château d'Yquem

Vintage	Calendar Year – lowest-highest price in £s per dozen bottles (duty-paid)										
	1978	1979	1980	1981	1982	1983	1984	1985	1986	1987	1988
1945	52B–105B	52B–100B	1400	90B–170B	105B–160B	90B–200B	165B–220B	195B–320B	195B–320B	260B–350B	270B–400B
1959	380–400	340–420		42B–54B	45B–72B	1050–125B	2290–3000	90B–200B	60B–135B	125B–350B	135B–180B
1961	300–420	370–430	480	420–600	580–105M	785–900		60B–95B	840–105B	130B	1150–260B
1962	290–420	320–440	528	370–600	390–600	58B–70B	820–1000	700–860	1000		1000–1350
1967	185–240	250–260		420–580	520–780	660–1450h	820–880	1050–2800	1350–2100h	1700,165B	160B–250B
1970	205		250	250–260		320–400	480	520–700‡	580	800,75B	780–880
1971				235	360–370	400–480		580‡–720	680	840	850–950
1975							420–480	580,45B	720h,48B	700–750	
1976							480h	42B–66B	600–620	680–800	700–1050
1983										680IMP,820IMP	820–1050
United Kingdom index of consumer goods and services											
Year	1978	1979	1980	1981	1982	1983	1984	1985	1986	1987	1988
Average	197.1	223.5	263.7	295.0	320.4	335.1	351.8	373.2	385.9	402.0	421.7

PORT
LONDON AUCTION SALE PRICES 1978–1988

Cockburn

Vintage	Calendar Year – lowest-highest price in £s per dozen bottles (duty-paid)										
	1978	1979	1980	1981	1982	1983	1984	1985	1986	1987	1988
1927	260–300	250–370	350	350	400–420	540–720	66–107B	890–1150	980	1040–1360	
1935	250–260	210–340	210–230	248–270	300–330	725	48B–70B	850–950	900–1500	1000	660–1040
1947	135–155	160–190	230–240	240–260	290	340–440	350	480	420		
1950	82–100	86–94		115–152	120–130	128–195	200–250	180–210	240		180–220
1955	125–155	130–200	135–180	168–185	150–220	260–360	330–370	370–460	330–420	360–450	330–420
1960	66–92	80–100	78–100	98–120	110–120	135–195	175–220	175–230	180–260	180–240	195
1963	62–80	76–96	82–92	105–115	105–135	135–195	210–270	310–360	310–370	290–420	300–320
1967	45–52	52–64	60–84	68–92	76–90	74–115	100–165	125–190	135–180	125–155	125–170
1970	54–58	54–62	60–74	60–84	60–68	80–115	105–145	140–185	165–220	160–200	170–210
1975			50–60	54–66	50–52	60–84	84–86	60–125	100–130	105–115	115–130
1977											

	United Kingdom index of consumer goods and services										
Year	1978	1979	1980	1981	1982	1983	1984	1985	1986	1987	1988
Average	197.1	223.5	263.7	295.0	320.4	335.1	351.8	373.2	385.9	402.0	421.7

Croft

Vintage	Calendar Year – lowest-highest price in £s per dozen bottles (duty-paid)										
	1978	1979	1980	1981	1982	1983	1984	1985	1986	1987	1988
1927	180	310	260				103B		1040–1150		72–100B
1935	240	245–270	250–368	280		850		850	920–960		75B
1945	190–250	220–300	230–280	230–270	300–370	520–720		920–1150	880–1100	1050	1300
1950	92–96	100	84–98	152	115	180	230	200	185–190		
1955	135–150	125–145	135–160	165	180–240	270–320	300–360	300–420	350–500	400–440	330–400
1960	70–80	82–100	80–110	100–115	105–135	145–220	170–230	180–280	185–210	190–220	170–230
1963	66–86	78–98	105	110–130	115–155	145–210	210–280	310–480	310–440	310–360	280–320
1966	50–62	58–76	70–76	74–82	85–105	110–155	180–190	145–220	150–230	195–230	195–250
1970	46–50	56–66	60–68	62–74	60–72	78–110m	100–140	150–240	155–195	165–185	175–195
1975		65	50–60	50–62	48–65	65–70	78–82	78–88	105–120	110–120	110–140
1977									130–195	165–190	155–200

	United Kingdom index of consumer goods and services										
Year	1978	1979	1980	1981	1982	1983	1984	1985	1986	1987	1988
Average	197.1	223.5	263.7	295.0	320.4	335.1	351.8	373.2	385.9	402.0	421.7

Dow

Vintage	Calendar Year – lowest-highest price in £s per dozen bottles (duty-paid)										
	1978	1979	1980	1981	1982	1983	1984	1985	1986	1987	1988
1927	260–300	240	370		390	560	65B	62–80B	62B	95B	40B
1934		195–240	210–220		300	55B					720–850
1945	216–225	240–340	310	270–280	290	760		750–1000	820–920	960–1050	900
1947	125–135	125–145	145	185–210		420–560	500	420–620			510
1955	110–150	135–180	135–150	158	190	290–310	420	350–480	420–460	440–480	360–460
1960	68–76	82–100	78–100	60–120	110–125	135–175	220	155–250	180–230	200–250	200–250
1963	74–88	70–105	84–110	96–125	115–130	145–200		320–360	320–400	320–400	320–360
1966	48–56	62–70	62–92	74–90	90–105	115–160	190	175–230	185–250	230–240	210–270
1970	38–66	58–72	58–70	58–70	60–78	78–120	130	105–220	155–200	170–220	180–210
1975		52–66		52	50	72–78	60	72–145	95–110	115–140	120–140
1977							160–210	160–210	155–200	165–210	170–220

	United Kingdom index of consumer goods and services										
Year	1978	1979	1980	1981	1982	1983	1984	1985	1986	1987	1988
Average	197.1	223.5	263.7	295.0	320.4	335.1	351.8	373.2	385.9	402.0	421.7

LONDON AUCTION SALE PRICES 1978–1988

Fonseca

Vintage	Calendar Year – lowest-highest price in £s per dozen bottles (duty-paid)										
	1978	1979	1980	1981	1982	1983	1984	1985	1986	1987	1988
1927	250–270	340–350	280–320			50B	80B	80–93B	82B	90B	88B
1934	190–250	180–290	208	230–300		460–875	840	75B	90B	60–80B	60–80B
1945	310	250–320	250–310					1050–1100			
1948	165–230	185–230	185–195	230–260	270–280	500–105M	640	650	440–500		
1955	120–150	135–160	145–160	170–190	200–240	324–360	420	370–480	460	420	480–540
1960	68–80	92–94	90–98	96–115	110–120	150–200	200	185–230	210	210–250	200–240
1963	72–84	78–105	96–105	94–125	115–130	145–240	230–260	340–540	310–420	320–480	350–420
1966	48–64	62–76	68–98	80–86	82–120	125–180	170–185	185–270	180–250	210–260	220–250
1970	52–54	56–62	60–68	60–76	60–85	76–105	95–135	155–250	180–230	175–220	190–210
1975		50–55	50–64	50–80	48–76	66–76	76–80	95–140	110–130	120–160	135–145
1977							120–140	190–220	170–210	170–230	185–270
United Kingdom index of consumer goods and services											
Year	1978	1979	1980	1981	1982	1983	1984	1985	1986	1987	1988
Average	197.1	223.5	263.7	295.0	320.4	335.1	351.8	373.2	385.9	402.0	421.7

Graham

Vintage	Calendar Year – lowest-highest price in £s per dozen bottles (duty-paid)										
	1978	1979	1980	1981	1982	1983	1984	1985	1986	1987	1988
1927	250	280–300	300–310	300–350	440			120–135B	950		
1935	210–220	240–280	270		350–440			70B	82–85B		
1945	230–280	230–300	230–280	280	380	540–1150	1000–95B	810–1350	980–1200	1100–1250	980–1100
1948	165–230	195–270	185–230	260	280–350	340–625	820	660	620–840	720–750	850
1955	130–180	135–180	145–185	160–185	195–250	260–380	410–460	420–520	420–700	460–560	480–700
1960	74–82	82–100	84–96	110–115	96–130	140–190	185–190	175–230	190–260	220–250	210–240
1963	78–88	78–105	82–110	100–125	115–165	140–220	240	300–380	310–380	350–400	350–420
1966	54–66	64–76	72–86	78–100	84–120	110–180	160–170	195–280	200–260	220–270	220–280
1970	39–60	54–70	60–86	60–78	66–84	76–125	110–140	185–230	165–220	175–220	185–230
1975		50–60	62	52–82	47–70	74–96	88	95–135	110–150	110–150	120–160
1977							125–145	175–220	160–230	170–250	170–230
United Kingdom index of consumer goods and services											
Year	1978	1979	1980	1981	1982	1983	1984	1985	1986	1987	1988
Average	197.1	223.5	263.7	295.0	320.4	335.1	351.8	373.2	385.9	402.0	421.7

Quinta do Noval

Vintage	Calendar Year – lowest-highest price in £s per dozen bottles (duty-paid)										
	1978	1979	1980	1981	1982	1983	1984	1985	1986	1987	1988
1927	300		400–460	324–348	420		88B				
1931	300–500	408–600	540–680	55–87	123B–133B	140B–300B		135–350B	180–260B	206B	360B
1945	230–400	260		260	310	620	850	740	600	80B	780
1947	94–180	150	288	180–185		30B		500			
1955	125–140	120–145	140–145		180–210	240–320	340–390	370–460	360–390	340–390	350–360
1960	64–76	80–94	82–98	96–120	105–120	130–175	175–220	175–250	145–190	210	180–195
1963	70–76	86–98	84–96	105–130	110–130	140–195	210	300–340	290–340	290–320	280–300
1966	49–54	62–72	66–78	76–88	80–115	90–150	160–195	165–220	165–210	175–230	190–230
1970	45–54	58–70	56–72	58–72	54–86	78–92	100–125	145–220	150–190	155–185	160–200
1975		48–52	52	48–66		74–96	70–82	115	95–110	105–135	110–140
1977	Not declared by Noval										
United Kingdom index of consumer goods and services											
Year	1978	1979	1980	1981	1982	1983	1984	1985	1986	1987	1988
Average	197.1	223.5	263.7	295.0	320.4	335.1	351.8	373.2	385.9	402.0	421.7

LONDON AUCTION SALE PRICES 1978–1988

Sandeman

Vintage	Calendar Year – lowest-highest price in £s per dozen bottles (duty-paid)										
	1978	1979	1980	1981	1982	1983	1984	1985	1986	1987	1988
1927	240	370	370–384	360	230–260	620–660	440–800		68B	90–100B	155B
1935	190–215	230	220		370	48B	57–80B	88–125B	77–100B	80B	120B
1945	205	210–230		260		350–820	780	860	700		68B–80B
1947		160		210	165		30B				
1955	135	115–140	135–145	150	110–120	310	330–340	290–380	135TREG		330
1960	64–72	76–98	80–96	95–105	100–140	135–170	200–220	110–220	165–200	195–220	180–210
1963	62–72	78–88	80–90	84–96	94	130–190	250–260	250–320	280–330	290–310	280–390
1966	48–54	54–60	54–68	80–82	58–68	110–125	135–155	180–200	170–220	190–230	190–230
1970	40–48	52–56	52–60	54–66	41–45	90–96	100–115	135–170	135–160	185	160–200
1975						65	78–80	105	105	105–110	
1977							110–125	155	125–175	165–185	160–170
United Kingdom index of consumer goods and services											
Year	1978	1979	1980	1981	1982	1983	1984	1985	1986	1987	1988
Average	197.1	223.5	263.7	295.0	320.4	335.1	351.8	373.2	385.9	402.0	421.7

Taylor

Vintage	Calendar Year – lowest-highest price in £s per dozen bottles (duty-paid)										
	1978	1979	1980	1981	1982	1983	1984	1985	1986	1987	1988
1927	310–370	330–440	400–492	350–480	420–520	960–90B	105B	105–173B	100–130B		87B–155B
1935	260–360	270–380	270–420	350–460	360–620	720–755	80B	103B–135B	90B–111B	100B–110B	120B–140B
1945	220–310	280–380	290–490	324	480	640–1550	1300	1200–1750	1200–1650	1500–1750	1250–1800
1948	170–245	210–340	220–250	250–300	280–460	440–700	860	740–900	680–750	610–720	62B–80B
1955	145–175	170–220	170–220	180–230	240–300	280–620	520–680	540–680	520–660	540–750	480–700
1960	68–92	96–120	98–120	155–140	120–150	150–220	260–240	210–310	220–280	230–290	250–280
1963	78–100	94–145	96–150	120–155	135–160	190–310	300–330	360–520	340–440	370–520	380–520
1966	66–70	74–90	80–94	82–115	95–135	120–175	185–230	185–290	190–250	220–270	240–300
1970	62–64	68–88	66–90	76–92		86–140	190	180–220	170–220	190–230	195–270
1975		70	86	58–72	60–84	70–90	110	120–150	110–135	125–170	135–165
1977							90–110	200–290	210–290	200–350	240–290
United Kingdom index of consumer goods and services											
Year	1978	1979	1980	1981	1982	1983	1984	1985	1986	1987	1988
Average	197.1	223.5	263.7	295.0	320.4	335.1	351.8	373.2	385.9	402.0	421.7

Warre

Vintage	Calendar Year – lowest-highest price in £s per dozen bottles (duty-paid)										
	1978	1979	1980	1981	1982	1983	1984	1985	1986	1987	1988
1927	22B	250–300	360	276	456	440–61B			63B		
1934		180–300	185			37B			48B		40B
1945	210	200–260	240–300		386	420	740–815	820–880	850–1100	900	
1947	135–150	155	210		240–260	30B	340–520		540–600		
1955	115–140	135–150	135–150	160–175	180–210	220–360	340–390	500	320–440	390–440	380–450
1960	70–110	82–96	84–115	100–130	110–145	140–210	210–220	170–240	180–250	190–260	190–240
1963	62–94	78–110	84–100	105–125	110–140	125–230m	260–280	300–390	280–390	320–400	300–400
1966	56–62	64–82	72–88	74–82	86–105	120–165	195	185–240	180–220	200–250	210–250
1970	50–56	58–70	60–74	58–76	60–84	76–100	130–140	145–210	160–210	160–195	165–220
1975		58	64	48–70	48–64	48–62	115	100–140	95–130	110–140	115–140
1977							98–115	145–200	155–190	160–190	170–220
United Kingdom index of consumer goods and services											
Year	1978	1979	1980	1981	1982	1983	1984	1985	1986	1987	1988
Average	197.1	223.5	263.7	295.0	320.4	335.1	351.8	373.2	385.9	402.0	421.7

Notes on the Contributors

Judith Banister has specialized in silver and applied arts since 1946 and is the author of several books on silver, as well as contributing to other compilations, editing various trade publications and preparing many catalogues for exhibitions. Among her honours is being a Liveryman of the Goldsmiths' Company. For many years she was the Curator of the James Walker private museum of gold and silver in London, she has been adviser to the Museum of Arts in California and to the catalogue of silver prepared at Williamstown in the United States.

Alan Bell is an MA of both Cambridge and Oxford universities and currently works for the Bodleian Library in charge of Rhodes House, Oxford. He contributes articles to *The Spectator*, the *Literary Review* and a diversity of publications and is the biographer of Sidney Smith.

Nigel Buxton began his travels in uniform during five years in the Royal Artillery (when he also learned to fly) and he worked for the Shell Petroleum Company before going to Oxford to read modern history at Worcester College. While still an undergraduate, he wrote features for the weekly *Spectator* magazine, then, travelling extensively and building a reputation as a freelance, he was appointed travel editor of the *Sunday Telegraph* at its inception in 1961, to which he now contributes the 'Man Abroad' column. He is married, with three teenage children, and lives with his wife in London.

Clive Coates, a Master of Wine, was one of the leading wine buyers in the UK for twenty years. In 1984 he 'retired' from the trade so as to launch his own independent fine wine magazine *The Vine*, available now world wide on subscription. He contributes regularly to *Decanter*, *Wine* magazine and many of the leading wine periodicals, both for the wine trade and the consumer. *Claret*, first published in 1982, is shortly to appear in a revised and enlarged edition and a book on the wines of France will also appear in the near future. He lives in London, with his wife, who is a singer.

Robert Cumming read law at Cambridge, qualified as a barrister, then returned to read Art History. After working at the Tate Gallery in London, he joined Christie's in 1978 to set up 'Christie's Education', who run two year-long programmes for graduates and mature students. Several of his many books have won awards in the UK, in Holland and Italy. He was a member of the Arts Council Exhibitions Sub-committee and, in addition to presenting television programmes and lecturing in Britain and abroad, has organized exhibitions for the Arts Council and is on the Council of the Friends of the Tate Gallery. Recently he was appointed Chairman of The Contemporary Arts Society. His wife, who worked for Christie's modern pictures department, is an authority on gardens and garden design. They live in Buckinghamshire and have a small but growing collection of contemporary British painting and sculpture.

Christopher Fielden has been in the wine trade for more than thirty years, including a period when he was sales director of a leading Burgundy house and lived in France. He has a monthly column in *Decanter* and contributes to a number of other magazines in Britain, the United States and Europe. He has had seven books on wine and related subjects published, gives frequent lectures and conducts visits to vineyards all over the world for a variety of organizations, as well as taking part in many of the local activities in the Wiltshire village where he now lives with his wife and children.

Peter Hallgarten joined his family's firm in 1958, after studying chemistry in Zurich, London and Chicago. After specializing in German wines, he became an authority on the wines of the Rhône and, today, also has serious interests in Burgundy. He has written books and articles on German and Rhône wines, also on liqueurs. The latter subject, started as a hobby, has resulted in his creating twenty different varieties, for export world wide. Known on the international wine scene since 1974, Peter has been honoured by the French Government who have awarded him the rank of Chevalier in the Mérite Agricole. He lives in London with his wife Elaine, herself an established author of books and articles on food and cookery; they have three children, although none have followed in father's vinous footsteps.

Margaret Howard, a well-known broadcaster, works mainly for the BBC in London where she is presenter of her selection of broadcasting in 'Pick of the Week'. Through the BBC's World Service her voice is known internationally via the programme 'Letterbox' and a series of phone-ins to many famous people, including the Prime Minister, the Right Honourable Margaret Thatcher (whose first experience of this type of programme it was), the Archbishop of Canterbury, and many celebrities as well as many popular personalities. In 1984 she was made the Sony Female Radio 'Personality of the Year' and in 1987 was admitted to the Sony Roll of Honour in recognition of 'an outstanding contribution to broadcasting'. She has travelled widely — including once spending a year at an American university — and, when at home in London, regularly rides her own horse in the Home Counties.

Sally Kevill-Davies has written for a wide range of publications, contributing regularly to *Wine Press* and *Antique Collecting*, also the British *Times* (in their *Saturday Review* section) and the magazine *The World of Interiors*. She has catalogued porcelain at Sotheby's, written *The Price Guide to Eighteenth-Century Pottery*, more recently, a book *Jelly Moulds*, and is currently writing on *The Antiques of Childcare*. Her lectures deal with ceramics and the history of various aspects of domestic life. She lives in East Anglia, with her clergyman husband and three children.

Patrick Matthews has had a long career in both publishing and photography, has been the editor of Christie's Wine Publications since 1979 and produced the three previous editions of the *Wine Companion*. Currently he is helping Michael Broadbent with a revision of *The Great Vintage Wine Book* and is also preparing a book of his own. He is chairman of both the wine and journal committees of The International Wine & Food Society, makes regular visits to French vineyards with his daughter, a wine broker based in Paris. He and his wife divide their time between London and Sussex when in England.

Nicholas Rootes is the son of Lord Rootes, whose well-stocked wine cellars inspired him from an early age. He specializes in writing about the history of drink and drinking, his book *The Drinker's Companion* illustrating the drinking habits of our ancestors, showing the many artefacts invented for the pursuit of these pleasures. A contributor to *Decanter*, *Punch*, *The Egon Ronay Guide* and *The Independent* newspaper, he also writes regularly for *The Antique Collector*. He has just finished compiling an anthology of drinking quotations and anecdotes and is currently researching prefatory to writing a world history of alcohol from its earliest uses by man to its diversity and consumption in today's society. He lives in London.

Auberon Waugh has published fifteen books, his diaries, plus *The Entertain-*

ing Book with his wife Teresa, herself a novelist, and has been a regular contributor to numerous British newspapers and magazines. The collection *Waugh on Wine* is an assembly of his wine writings from many sources. Now he writes on politics and current affairs for *The Sunday Telegraph* and *The Spectator* and on books for *The Independent*. He edits *The Literary Review*, the monthly that covers books published in Britain, and also runs 'The Spectator Wine Club', as well as writing occasional features for a variety of publications. He has four grown-up children and divides his time between London and his country house in Somerset.

David Wolfe, born in a poor vintage, was, in his early days, about as schooled in epicurianism as a submariner is in mountaineering. After having his own eating place — 'the long thin restaurant with the short fat proprietor' — he became a part-time wine merchant, then, later, a consultant on both wine and food to a wide range of clients. He is the restaurant correspondent for *Decanter*, writes on wine for *London Portrait* and other periodicals in Britain and abroad, was the Glenfiddich Restaurant writer of 1985 and, recently, in London's Chinatown, was acclaimed by a waiter as a 'very good eatah'. He travels widely but his home is in London.

*A*CKNOWLEDGEMENTS

The Publisher and Editor would like to thank the following for their help: the staff of the wine department of Christie's, London; the staff of Christie's Education, London; Australia House and the various offices of the Australian states, London; the New Zealand High Commission, London; South Africa House, London, especially the librarian; the Wines from Germany Information Office; Food & Wine from France in London and SOPEXA in France; The International Wine & Food Society; Wines from Spain; the Cyprus Trade & Tourist Office, London; Martini & Rossi; the KWV, Edward Cavendish and Nederburg Pty; the Master of the Vintners' Company, the former master and the staff at Vintners' Hall in the City; the Goldsmiths' Company; Sir Ewen Fergusson and the staff of the British Embassy, Paris; Michael Druitt Wines; Justerini & Brooks; *The Antique Collector* magazine; the United States Embassy, London; International Distillers & Vintners; the Australian Wine & Brandy Corporation in Adelaide; Peter Devereux; Steven Spurrier.

The Publisher, Editor and Patrick Matthews would like to thank Wm Heinemann Ltd for permission to quote from *A Fashion of Life* by Harry Yoxall.

PICTURE CREDITS

Black and white

Judith Banister 33, 80, 82; Nic Barlow Photography 6, 149; C Basterfield 13, 16; Brown Brothers, Australia 51, 52; Michael Busselle 128; Château Mouton Rothschild 138, 148; Christie's 7 (left, right), 8, 21, 56, 81, 84, 85, 90, 91, 93, 96, 100, 104, 114, 116, 121 (above, below), 135; Deutsches Weininstitut 109, 110, 112; E T Archive 40; Mary Evans Picture Library 41; William Heinemann Ltd 17; International Distillers & Vintners (UK) Ltd 124; Landscape Only 139, 140; The Mansell Collection 24, 26 (above, below), 31, 35, 43/4, 48, 133; Patrick Matthews 22; Museum of Fine Arts, Boston 37; Museum of London 75, 78; Peter Newark's Historical Pictures 121, 122; Sammlung Oskar Reinhart 68; Scottish National Portrait Gallery 46.

Colour

Australia House, London 12; Barber Institute of Fine Arts 89 (below); Michael Busselle 62/3, 64, 107, 108, 125; Christie's 9 (above); Cyprus Museum 144 (above, below); E T Archive 9 (below); The Mansell Collection 126 (below); Martini & Rossi 61, 126 (above right); Museum of Fine Arts, Boston 90 (above); National Gallery of Victoria, Australia 126 (above left); Society of Dilettante Charitable Trust 89 (above); South Africa House, London 10/11; Stellenbosch Farmers' Winery 143.